Dark Age

Jeffrey T. Heyer

2024, TWB Press
www.twbpress.com

Dark Age
Copyright © 2024 by Jeffrey T. Heyer

This is a work of fiction. Names, characters, places, and incidences are either a product of the author's imagination or are used fictitiously. Any resemblance to any actual person, living or dead, events, or locales is entirely coincidental.

Edited by Terry Wright

Cover Art by Terry Wright

ISBN: 978-1-959768-74-6

Dedication

To my wonderful wife, without whom the world would be a darker place.

Chapter 1:

The Tynghed of Castrum Tenebrarum

Ravens rose, raucous, cawing harsh warnings as the great battlemented hulk of the fortress Castrum Tenebrarum hunched dark and long against the glowing evening sky. A lone horseman, Rhys of Caer Waroc, coughed trail dust as he cleared the edge of the forest. He cast nervous eyes all around him to be sure no raider or outlaw or starving man with a stone lurked between the relatively safe obscurity of his forest path and the stronghold ahead. Turning his weary, aging war-horse straight across the broad grassy field, he coaxed it toward the old Roman high-road's stones that led beneath the silhouetted fortress.

Eyes narrowed against the bright sky, Rhys scanned the tall walls ahead and snorted. After so long and rough a ride, if not for horse and steel, men who would have welcomed Rhys a year before, would now pull him down and kill him for whatever they could strip from his corpse. This was, at last, the fortress he sought, and its very size made his heart sink like a stone. This was no half-burnt log palisade that could be rebuilt easily. Somehow the invaders had breached its great stone walls. Rhys blinked up at the battlements looming ever higher while his mount solidly plodded up the steepening hillside toward them. Four hundred years of Roman resources had poured into these fortifications before the empire had abandoned Britain to its fate.

Grimly, the young rider slapped trail dust from his stained and scarred leather armor. Even from here he could see a great jagged rent in the thick outer wall. Rhys tried to blink away the images that burst unbidden into his mind's eye, him riding alone through abandoned cities and burnt farms, gagging at the reek of charred flesh, glimpsing ragged children fleeing into the woods at the sight of a horseman.

Are these blackened walls the image of Britain's future?

Other great relics of an imperial culture had been torn down stone-by-stone by jealous barbarians. Since the great Emperor Arthur had fallen three generations before, no one in the isle could pull together resources enough to feed and guard all the skilled craftsmen it would take to re-erect such walls. There were no more Arthurs in the world. And it might take him weeks just to scout the ruin.

Choking on the dust, Rhys knit his brows fiercely. He had to believe that his mission could help hold back the swiftly falling night. Clutching that belief like a shield, he rode into the great stronghold's lengthening shadow.

Squinting up against reddening light, Rhys turned his tired mount's hanging head toward the char-blackened remains of a now horizontal tower stretching through the fatal gap in the outer wall. A jagged-edged cylindrical section of turret, open at both ends, spanned the great defensive ditch dug outside the base of the wall. Clearly, when the huge wooden beams that held together the base of the tower had burnt through, the tower collapsed, shattering the wall. The bard's face grew taut. How had the crude Saxon invaders set such a blaze inside a defended fortress?

Rhys guided his weary charger into the open-ended stone cylinder and through it, over the defensive ditch, listening to the hoof-falls echo. His bard's imagination was no gift to him as he heard the defenders' screams in his mind's ear, pictured the flames that had felled this tower, dying down quickly, suffocated by the tumbled stone. The howling Saxon onslaught, rough men clad in furs and hides for the most part, only their chieftains in chainmail, must have poured in the way he now rode. Caught in the rear, the cornered garrison would have died as swiftly as the flames.

The old war-horse plodded out the ragged far end of the fallen tower and into the fortress interior, wading in long shadows inked by the low scarlet sun. All around Rhys lay charred timbers, stone stairs leading to empty sky, blackened corners of vanquished buildings.

Until a new sun rose, it would be impossible to make out how many men it would require to re-secure the ruined castrum. There was nothing for him to do but to clear a campsite while he could still see.

For his horse, Rhys found an alcove with ample but no longer complete shelter. After dismounting, Rhys unslung his shield from his back and leaned it against a wall, his two spears beside it. Laying saddle and bridle by them, Rhys pulled a curry brush from his saddle pack and gave his companion a good rub-down.

This set Rhys to coughing again. Every movement stirred ash and irritated his lungs. Years of unpleasant experience assured him that soon he would have trouble

Jeffrey T. Heyer

breathing, yet there was nowhere else to go.

Finished with the curry-brush, Rhys pulled his small harp from the leather case strapped to the saddle. The reddened sun having disappeared in the west, he sat where he was, watching the last light die, fingers wandering through lonely chords, the notes clean and clear in the quiet evening.

Rocks clattered somewhere in the ruin. Claws scrabbled over stone.

Rhys rose at once, looking about, alertly. A chill ran up his spine, certain he was not alone. He set the harp carefully aside and patted Morvran's flank to keep him still. After slinging his shield over his back by its strap, he selected a spear and picked his way quietly through the debris, booted feet feeling their way through the rubble while he probed the spear haft through darker spots.

The full moon caught three thick archways ahead. At the very edge of the blackness beneath the central arch, something white swayed in the dead-still air like a banner in a light breeze. Rhys cautiously worked his way toward it.

The shape ghosted out into the pool of moonlight before the arch, a woman in a white gown. Two more, dressed alike, followed. They must have been stepping carefully. To Rhys' eyes, they seemed to flow over the wreckage-strewn ground.

Morvran whickered quietly, demanding reassurance. The women wafted toward the sound. No armed men followed.

Rhys stepped out into the moonlight before them, and the women stopped. They gazed through the dimness in silence.

Dark Age

The one in the lead was small. Black hair fell below her shoulders, and she stared intently. "Well met, warrior," she said in a voice that was young, high, and perhaps a little lost.

The second woman drifted close behind the first. This one was tall and thin, her cheekbones shadowed, her hair less stark, probably brown by daylight. "Are you alone?" Her voice was deeper, more assured.

"Are you?" Rhys responded.

The third woman tarried a little behind the others, turning her blond head to look past Rhys, scanning the pale splashes of moonlight for other strangers. Hands inside her long trailing sleeves, she gripped a concealed knife, he assumed.

The first woman sighed. "Someone has come at last."

"What are you doing in this place of death?" Rhys asked.

"Seeking life," the taller woman said, her tone musical.

In such sinister circumstances Rhys wondered how it could be that the way she moved and spoke appealed to him.

"Only one horse," the blond whispered to her companions.

"You are alone, then," the black-haired woman said.

Rhys could not tell whether she spoke with relief or disappointment. Perhaps she could not tell either.

"Why are you here?" Rhys asked, vague suspicions prickling the back of his scalp.

"This is our place," the black-haired waif said.

"And the Saxons just let you go after they sacked the

fortress?"

"Only the women survived."

"Uncommonly chivalrous for Saxons."

"They never found us," the tall woman explained. "We fled into a hidden vault, part of an escape tunnel into the forest. None of the men made it to the tunnel."

"And you never showed yourselves to the townsfolk when they came to bury the dead?"

"We have—" the waif-voiced woman began, but her taller companion cut her off.

"We have...a custom of the castrum none can refuse. It is our law, our toll, our ritual. All who come here must bleed."

Rhys frowned. "Do you think the three of you can get a knife past my spear?"

"We don't want to harm you," the black-haired woman said in thin, quiet, plaintive dismay.

"Warrior..." the tall woman said, "we beg you, in love and courtesy, to come with us this night. We will lodge you better than in these ruins."

A wolf howled in the forest nearby, a beautiful, wild, lonely sound. Other wolves began to answer the first from deeper in the surrounding woods, soon joining their voices together in a well-tuned chorus.

They might be mourners for the castrum's dead, Rhys thought. "This would make a lonely bed, but I have a horse."

"The armory's intact," the tall woman said. "It will make a safe stable. Melora will see to him."

The blond lifted her chin in assent.

"Come with us," the plaintive raven-haired woman

said. "See the reason for our custom. I believe you will freely grant what we require."

"Go with them, warrior," Melora said, her blond hair bleached even paler by the moonlight. "Since they beg it of you. I will take good care of your steed."

Rhys nodded.

The waif-woman disappeared into the darkness beneath the central arch.

The tall woman placed a hand lightly on Rhys' arm. "You cannot enter unless one of us guides you."

"Who then leads me?"

"I am Gwenllian the Tall."

Rhys let the woman pull him into the shadow. Once beneath the arch, he was blind, but the women knew the way by feel and led him around obstacles and through a narrow passage into increasingly dank-smelling earth. As the unseen path beneath their feet leveled out, Rhys saw indirect but steady light from candles burning around some corner far ahead. By that light, the small party wound their way past subterranean pillars carved by time and not men.

Rounding a curve, Rhys stepped into direct candlelight spilling from an open vault. Supplies of all kinds stood heaped against uneven walls, and still there was room enough in the cave to house a dozen men.

At the far end of the vault, on a great heap of fragrant brush was spread a sleek samite sheet layered with rich furs. Among them a woman sprawled.

Tall Gwenllian breathed in Rhys' ear. "Our mistress suffers a strange affliction."

The reclining lady's skin was moon-pale even in the ample candlelight. She languished in a white chemise that clung to a form so perfect in its proportions that the sight actually took Rhys' breath away. He felt a fool for being so moved by a few subtle differences between one female form and another. He also noticed that the lady's raven-colored hair had been arranged with great artistry on her silk pillow. The startling beauty of her face was accentuated by delicate painting, and her bed was artistically framed with expensive tapestries, each a tangled labyrinth of Celtic knotwork in gold and silver thread. They formed a most appealing nook amid the rough outcroppings of the natural chamber.

"This is Ellylyw," Gwenllian breathed against his ear. "Lady of Castrum Tenebrarum."

Rhys felt a deep chord thrum in his breast. The magnificent lady looked so unguarded in her sleep that, even knowing her image had been artfully prepared to manipulate his emotions, he desperately wanted to protect her from the lurking dangers of this place of death.

Gwenllian watched him carefully. "Before the raiders came, the Lady Ellylyw began to ail. No physician nor wise woman understood the malady. The chieftain of this fortress, Madoc Broad Shoulders, released a quarter of the troops in his pay that he might send them overseas for foreign healers...all to no avail."

Rhys tore his gaze from the wan face of Ellylyw to stare aghast at Gwenllian. "Had the man no concept of this fort's importance? Was he living in a dream?"

Ignoring the question, Gwenllian indicated the black-haired waif. "Nefyn, here, found a wise man in the forest."

Nefyn lifted a copper basin.

Gwenllian added, "The hermit told us that if we fill

this basin with blood, Ellylyw will live, and if we find a virgin of the right bloodline, Lady Ellylyw might be cured. This is the tynghed of Castrum Tenebrarum, the fated adventure, the required ritual of all who come here. Will you not willingly submit?"

Rhys looked down on the sleeping woman, feeling his spirit drawn half out of his body by the otherworldliness of the encounter. "What you ask is strange...and not easy to give."

"Wake her. Question the lady herself."

Feeling painfully awkward, Rhys reached toward the softly sleeping Ellylyw.

Gwenllian's gentle touch stopped him. "Give her the kiss of greeting." She smiled. "She needs life to rouse her."

Rhys stared at Ellylyw. "Am I in a dream?"

"We do nothing here without the hermit's authority."

Rhys tried to shake off the sense of unreality. He sat on the fragrant mattress beside the unconscious woman, planted a hand on either side of her head, and leaned down. He kissed her soft lips. Her breath was scented, but there was something odd beneath the sweetness...something disturbing.

The lady stirred, brushed a hand against his, and made some half-smothered sound.

"Did you speak?" he asked.

She murmured. "Which are you?"

"Rhys of Caer Waroc."

Ellylyw's eyes opened, dark and surprised.

Rhys stood, embarrassed.

"Don't back away," the lady pleaded. "I need warmth and strength."

Self-consciously, he sat by her again.

She wrapped delicate fingers about his wrist and clung with the tenacity of a drowning woman.

"How do you feel?" he asked, inwardly cursing his humiliating awkwardness.

"Paper thin," she whispered. "Then heavy as lead. No strength, no appetite, endless thirst. I dream and never seem to wake. I have so little life in me. Don't leave. I'm alone. He's gone."

"Madoc, your husband?"

"My husband? Is he here?" She looked about, confused.

"Don't you know what happened to the fortress?" Rhys asked.

Her eyes looked into the distance. Within them Rhys saw an aching need so deep and vast it seemed to mirror his own. He glanced toward Gwenllian and Nefyn.

They waited, tense, as if expecting him to yield. Rhys remembered the first woman he had fallen for. She had been like this...everyone fell in love with her. Rhys gazed into Ellylyw's enormous dark eyes. Was there anything more beautiful left in crumbling Britain? Who was he to say their ritual was madness?

Forcing himself to think, Rhys turned away. "I must scout the defenses for Brathach, Consularis of Eboracum. Have you tried this...this treatment before?"

"It's horrible." Ellylyw's fingers were tight but cool about his wrist. "Most medicines are worse than the sickness, but this lets me hang on a little longer."

Rhys looked at the copper basin and made a quick calculation as to how much blood it would take to fill it. He had seen enough bloodshed to know he would probably survive. He looked at Gwenllian standing nearby, sharp candlelight glinting from a razor in her hand.

The blond woman, Melora, stepped in from the passage. "Your steed is safe. We have better fare here than I found in your saddlebags. We offer you wine and meat and bread to restore your strength, after. You will sleep in a good bed, with someone to keep you warm, after."

Ellylyw sighed. "I just want to be me again."

With an inward pang, Rhys realized the lady's fingers were not really gripping him with desperate strength. They had stiffened in place. He had felt the same thing happen to his own hands when he could pull in too little air for too long. Carefully, he disengaged her slender fingers.

"Let me serve you." Melora set out food-stuffs on a crude table. Hungry ever since his fourteenth year, Rhys sat as he was bidden. "You have a lot of food down here. The town I passed below is hungry."

"They can come any time...and pay the toll."

Rhys raised a wine goblet, then stopped, seeing a distorted figure reflected in the red liquid. The bard turned to look behind him and saw a tall, broad-shouldered figure looming half stooped out of the low opening of a second dark tunnel. Swathed in a dark blue cloak that must have muffled the clinking of his thick chainmail tunic, the armored figure straightened while stepping fully into the vault. Candlelight caught a bestial face: heavy-browed, hollow-eyed, broad-snout. Rhys blinked away his startlement, realizing he was staring at the faceplate of a helmet given an inhumanly threatening beast-like visage by some clever craftsman.

Stepping from what Rhys presumed was the escape tunnel that led to the forest, the tall figure strode heavily across the chamber, chainmail ringing distinctly now, disturbing the sudden silence. The warrior held a war-axe at his side with casual, lethal ease.

Only a chieftain could afford such armor. This man, whoever he was, would have trained with blade-masters far beyond the expertise Rhys' undernourished purse had once hired.

Reaching the table, the chieftain leaned his broad, iron-studded gauntlets, axe and all, over the back of a tall wooden chair in an attitude of weariness, yet he managed to make the move distinctly threatening. Rhys noticed the goblet still in his own hand and extended it slowly in salute toward the metal-clad man. "Greetings, chieftain. I am Rhys of Caer Waroc, surveying the damage for the governor of this territory."

The steel-faced figure raised its left gauntlet in signal, and scraping sounds came from the dark tunnel behind him. Six men-at-arms in heavy leather sewn over with thick steel rings, filed warily in from the darkness to encircle the vault.

Rhys sat very still. The scars on the soldiers' armor and on the faces under their battered helmets were fresh, their dirty cloaks were rent, their drawn weapons notched. Two soldiers had broad streaks of soot across their clothing.

Rhys swallowed hard. "I take it you are men of this fortress."

The armored chieftain regarded him. "We are all that remain." His hollow voice issued from the mouth-hole in the faceplate. "When the tower fell, we cut our way out."

"You have been absent for some time." Rhys cautiously pushed his chair back from the table in the event that he might be forced to move quickly.

"I nearly died," the dry voice replied. "These loyal men got me to the Green Chapel. It took the hermit awhile to knit me together."

Rhys rose respectfully.

The chieftain leaned his axe against an outcrop of rock and unstrapped his helmet. While pulling it free, he allowed Rhys to study his face. The features were strong, somber, the cheeks clean-shaven and the chin bearded, making the long face seem even longer. Suffering had etched dark circles under the man's eyes and carved deep runnels down his cheeks, though the white in his hair was still confined to the temples. Careful stitches held together a line of puckered flesh that ran from his hairline down before his left ear to somewhere below his collar. "I am Madoc, commander of Castrum Tenebrarum."

"You must be hungry." Rhys respectfully gestured toward the seat he had just vacated.

Madoc waved at him to sit back down. "We ate woodland fare. Enjoy what you can, while you can, Rhys of Caer Waroc. Forgive me."

"Of course." It hardly seemed politic to ask exactly what Madoc wanted him to forgive.

The chieftain turned away and moved to the bed where Ellylyw was sitting, arms outstretched. Madoc embraced her tightly. The lady made soft sounds.

Rhys saw Madoc swallow hard and knew the man could not speak without risking his composure. Uncomfortable witnessing such a moment, the bard took

Madoc's advice and ate while he could. The soldiers set their sword-points against the earthen floor and leaned on their hilts, staring at the walls.

Madoc kissed his wife long and passionately, then she pressed her cheek against his, and they sat quietly, wrapped in each other's arms.

Rhys wondered whether the chieftain had returned in order to prevent the tynghed of Castrum Tenebrarum, or to enforce it.

The three waiting women came forward and presented themselves to their chief.

Madoc rose and gave each an embrace and a formal kiss of welcome. His relief that they had survived was tempered by the unspoken awareness that so many others had not. His gaze ran quickly over the bard's old-fashioned leather armor. "You are Brathach's man, then?" His voice was tinged with disbelief.

"I undertook this mission for him."

Madoc digested the implications of that. He kept them to himself.

Warnings sounded silently in Rhys' mind. The battered chieftain before him did not appear relieved that his overlord might soon be sending troops to repair and re-garrison the fortress. Perhaps Madoc believed that Consularis Brathach would never allow the strange custom of the castrum to continue.

Madoc said, "I take it you have bled for a cause before now."

"I've fought when I had to. But it is vital that I complete my task."

"Of course." Madoc shrugged slightly. "In the

morning my men will escort you on a thorough survey of the wreckage."

"I am honored, but one guide will suffice. You will want to post guards. The Saxons might return at any time."

"There is nothing left for them to take...so far as they know. And we hurt them bad. They will lick their wounds for some time. It is better the men stay together. The dead trapped in the rubble attract wolves."

Madoc turned away in dismissal, demonstrating that an impoverished free lance, Brathach's emissary or no, held little status here. The proud chieftain gestured to one of his men. "Stand guard at the escape tunnel." Another he sent to the passage from the ruined fortress, then he tasked the rest to pull an old pavilion from among the stacked supplies and pitch it around Ellylyw's bed.

Gwenllian and Nefyn shook out bedrolls for the men.

The mustiness of the old pavilion made Rhys sneeze as he sat alone at the table, staring into his wine. The smooth-faced blond came to sit across from him. Rhys smiled at her, keeping his black mood to himself.

Melora asked, "Do you have a woman back home, Rhys of Caer Waroc?" Her tone was friendly.

Surprised, Rhys replied, "Only friends."

"I'm not surprised." Her tone sharpened abruptly. "Brathach must have despised you to send you here. You'll never make it back with your precious report."

He peered closely at her. "Why say such a thing?"

"Look at you. Your banged-up harp, your third-hand armor. You're a nobody. You're not half the man of any soldier here."

"I have my own skills—"

Jeffrey T. Heyer

"You don't. You can't change any of this. Ellylyw despises you, you know. The men do, too. Look at them."

"Is this what passes for civilized converse here?" Rhys drank his wine and blotted her from his mind, but her words stung him deeply.

She was not willing to be ignored. "When you stirred up the ash in the ruins, you were wheezing. I know what that means. I used to listen to Ellylyw's physicians."

"It's not a disease," he explained with the annoyance that comes of constant repetition. "You can't catch it from me. Dust and ash and certain plants bring it on."

"But nothing will cure it. The weak die to make way for the strong."

He put down the flagon and looked her in the eyes. "I've seen a wolf that lost both forelegs in a trap. She still caught small prey to feed her cubs. There are more kinds of strength than you know."

"And you don't have any of them." Melora tossed her blond tresses. "I've seen you look at Lady Ellylyw. You'll never touch a woman like that."

"What makes you think I would want to?"

"I know what you think."

"If you did, you wouldn't be sitting this close to me. Go whisper with your friends."

"Nefyn's going to hell for touching the hermit."

Exasperated, Rhys scoffed. "It's good that God has you to decide these things for Him."

"The abbot down in the town says she is damned."

"And God works for the abbot?"

Her brows drew tight. "You're going to hell, too."

"It'll make a nice change from listening to you." He

~16~

drank his wine.

Melora looked shocked. "That's insulting." She stood and flounced back to Nefyn and Gwenllian.

A rough-featured soldier let his comrades finish with the pavilion and took Melora's place. One of the other men called quietly after him. "Callas."

The rugged Callas ignored his sergeant-at-arms and stood by the table, grinning down at Rhys. "Ellylyw's too much for you, mate." He whispered as if to not offend the ears of his chieftain. "You'd melt like a candle in her fire."

Rhys looked up at him, not liking anything he saw. "You have no idea of my passions."

Callas sniggered. "You're no one's man. A free lance. And never seen real combat. The Consularis didn't want to risk his own men this close to the Saxons. When you don't make it back, he'll just send someone else expendable."

Rhys fixed Callas with appraising eyes. "How did you survive the attack?"

The grin left Callas's face, death in his eyes. "Ask Madoc."

The soldier turned and stalked to one of the bedrolls where he sat to watch Rhys with hard, hateful scorn.

Rhys suppressed a shudder of frustrated rage. All his life he had been forced to put up with such attacks from anyone better situated than himself.

Now ebony-tressed Nefyn approached.

Rhys drained his flagon, wishing he could leave these lost souls to their doom.

Nefyn sat and gazed at him, her young face openly disturbed. "You've heard how the custom came to be, and yet you will do as you deem fit?"

Jeffrey T. Heyer

"I am doing exactly that." Rhys poured more wine.

"Warrior, you see that our lady is ill. Why don't you help her?"

He kept it simple. "I never said I wouldn't. But I don't know that I could truly help."

"You're not of a pure bloodline, so you can't cure her." Nefyn's upper lip twitched. "But you are a virgin, so you could help her."

Rhys stared at her, feeling suddenly face-slapped.

"Oh, I can tell," she said with no malice in her voice or look. "And what's out there for someone like you? I know what it's like to wander. For the longest time, I didn't belong anywhere until Lady Ellylyw took me in. Look at yourself—"

"Why does everyone in this place think I can see myself?" Rhys sighed.

"What do you have? A battered war-horse on his last legs, one plain sword, and a harp older than you. You look foreign, too...not pure Briton. What else are you? Saxon?"

He felt reluctant to expose his background to hostile scrutiny, but he was proud of his heritage. "My father was a Goth in the Roman judiciary—"

"A Goth?"

"He was a good man."

"But not a warrior."

"He expanded the system of law that holds us together. Not easy while Picts and Scots and Saxons drive wedges through a country dissolving into factions."

"It *is* all falling apart," Nefyn cried in dismay, "and law won't hold it together. Only blood. You aren't accepted anywhere, but here your blood has value. Never mind

Callas and Melora. I know you've trained hard. You must have made many sacrifices, risked your life, and what's more frightening, risked being maimed in a fight and still having to get by somehow. But your family is undistinguished, because people care about war, not law. And no matter how hard you try, like Ellylyw, your condition keeps robbing you of your strength and letting in the darkness. I've seen you look at her. She reminds you of someone, doesn't she?"

"Not really."

Nefyn turned down her lips in disbelief. "Someone you fell in love with, but who didn't love you back? I know what that's like, too." She glanced toward Madoc. "Don't you want to give yourself to something? Make a difference, finally?"

Rhys pulled a little leather bag from his belt and sprinkled powdered herbs into his wine to help him breathe the musty air. Following Nefyn's too-wide-eyed stare, he found his own eyes caught again by Madoc's wife. With a pang, Rhys realized he had fallen for the lady with no idea who she really was. Nor had he any illusion that he could compete with Madoc Broad Shoulders. And with that hopeless realization, the darkness he had so long held at bay wrapped itself around him in deadly earnest.

What could be easier, asked a tired voice in his head, *than to accept that all your short life has been but a preparation for this one moment of grand sacrifice for so glorious a woman?*

Rhys coughed pavilion dust from his aching lungs. What indeed? He could barely keep breath in his body, as it was. Struck by an uncanny notion, he remembered a bit of the Song of Dindranu, sister of Peredur, who sought the Grail. When Emperor Arthur had still held the British factions together with the fierce fire of his singular inspiration, the Lady Dindranu, heir to a sacred and royal bloodline, had allowed herself to be bled in order to cure an unnamed lady in a mysterious fortress. The unnamed lady lived on. Dindranu died and was considered a martyr.

That had been three generations ago. He asked Nefyn, "How long has this been going on?"

Nefyn's face went blank.

"Was Lady Ellylyw here before Madoc took charge of Castrum Tenebrarum?"

Nefyn shook her head as if having no idea and seeing no relevance in the question.

Was this a chance to achieve a form of immortality in a song folks would sing for a thousand years? Would there be anybody left to sing the Son of Dindranu after another fifty years of invasion, famine and pestilence?

And yet...

He leaned toward Nefyn. "This mission is my chance. Maybe you don't appreciate how vital it is. The last famine hit the Saxons, too. They have to raid us to eat. No matter how much it cost them to crack Madoc's defenses, sooner or later, the barbarians will pour down the highway outside and straight into the heart of Britain...unless we stop them right here. Every day counts. If I fill that basin with blood, I'll be disabled for at least a week. I might die."

"If you return with an impressive report, do you think the Consularis might find you a place in his retinue?"

Rhys coughed, tasting the heavy reek of old canvas. He took a gulp of the now bitter drink. "He might." He stared into her eyes and she stared back. He wondered if she could actually see what he really felt...how thoroughly, how desperately, he was adrift. How before he had met Consularis Brathach, he had ridden aimlessly, seeking a sign, a path that might bear his feet more than a dozen steps in any direction.

Nefyn's eyes had grown so wide it seemed her soul was in danger of falling out of them. "If you will not heal her, tell me what I should do."

"What does your friend the hermit say?"

"To follow your heart. What does your heart say?"

Rhys restrained himself from gazing again at Ellylyw. He looked down into the wine then took a gulp of the herb-bitter drink. "That this bloodletting custom of yours is a shameful act."

Nefyn turned to look through the open flaps of the now fully erected tent. Within it, Ellylyw whispered with Madoc. Watching them closely, the young woman heaved a sigh. "If you will not, then I must do it."

Rhys stared, horrified.

"It's been too long." Nefyn sounded desperate for his understanding. "I can't keep watching him watch her wither and fade."

Rhys couldn't shake the idea from his head. "Nefyn, you're a small woman and very young. If you fill that basin, you will not survive."

"If I die to heal her, I will leave behind a name, and my family will win honor. Would you fight Madoc to save my life? Or Ellylyw's? You couldn't win, and Britain needs every sword-arm she can get."

"You can't mean this."

"Don't you see? The whole world is out of joint...like a wheel slipping from its axle. Some terrible wrong has been committed, and restitution must be made."

"Even if that's why the empire's crumbling, you didn't commit the crime. How can your blood make things right?"

"Jesus' blood redeemed the world. Maybe we're so far off course, the world needs another redeemer. I'm no Christ, I know, but maybe I can save a little piece of the dying light...at least the life of one noble woman."

Rhys groped for words to penetrate her mad zeal. "What good would it do to save one woman at the cost of another?"

"She's a lady. And her lord..." Her voice broke for a moment. "He has six men and a burned-out hold." Tremulously, she forced a smile. "Every woman's fate is to bleed for love."

Grasping at straws, Rhys protested. "I saw you drop your eyes when Gwenllian said you brought the hermit here. You've slept with the hermit, haven't you."

It was Nefyn's turn to blink in surprise. She moaned softly. "I should have bled last night when I was still a virgin. I tried to run away from...from here, to lose myself in the holy man and hide from Fate. Now I must do what I can."

Exasperated, struggling to keep his voice down, Rhys demanded, "Are you determined to die?"

"The abbot in the town below us teaches good Christians to thirst for martyrdom. This is my chance."

Rhys leaned back. "This is a young girl's fantasy. An escape. A waste. I barely know you, but I'm asking you:

don't throw away your life. Even...even for Ellylyw."

Nefyn raised her voice, her face toward Madoc in the pavilion. "Be happy, chieftain. I will give myself that your wife may live."

Madoc stared at her through eyes like holes in the world, wells sunk into the darkness below all being. Ellylyw's face twisted in grief, and she pressed her contorted features against Madoc's stern side. The chieftain looked as if he had been struck by an iron fist. His face aged ten years in an instant, but he beckoned the other waiting women.

"This is not right." Rhys leaped to his feet. In an instant, Callas and another soldier gripped his arms. Two more pressed their sword-points against his leather-clad chest. Callas looked detached, the other soldiers wary, ready to fight with Rhys, but cut to the quick. Nefyn's sacrifice was not the same thing as bleeding strangers.

"I hope I will acquit myself well." Nefyn stood unsteadily.

Gwenllian hurried forward and poured her some wine. Nefyn drank deeply. When she started to lower her flagon, Gwenllian forced it up again, compelling her to drain it.

Madoc rose and walked toward Nefyn, back straight as a lance, proud face haunted. He laid gnarled, powerful hands on Nefyn's black crown in silent blessing. She trembled a little under his touch, and for a searing instant, Rhys feared she would cry. Then her fellow waiting women kissed Nefyn and embraced her in sorrowful, honorable farewell.

"Don't do this," Rhys shouted. The sword points gouged his breastplate, stinging his chest.

Melora knelt by Ellylyw's bed, holding up the copper basin eagerly, glad of any bloodshed not her own.

Madoc took Nefyn's left arm and Gwenllian her right and they marched her before the weeping Ellylyw. Nefyn leaned down, kissed her lady gently, then knelt beside her bed and bared her arm. Madoc knelt on the other side of the basin from her, one hand supporting Nefyn under her shoulder, the other holding her arm tenderly, firmly over the basin. Nefyn gazed steadfastly into her chieftain's eyes, as if her own eyes gave him some precious energy, even as his stare sustained her with some of his vital power.

Gwenllian produced the razor, and Ellylyw placed her trembling hands on Nefyn's head, whispering soothing praises. Gwenllian made a quick, clean incision. Nefyn swallowed a tiny cry. Her blood poured out and began to pool in the metal basin.

Rhys discovered that a living man can experience an eternity of damnation as he stood there helpless in the soldiers' grips, no breath of sound in all the vault but the steady pulse of blood splashing against copper.

Eyes vague, head swimming, Nefyn said, "For God's sake, pray for my soul, for I am at my end." She sagged against the bed in a faint.

Madoc held the girl's arm steady, and Ellylyw stroked Nefyn's hair, and everyone in the quiet room watched the basin fill, spurt by weakening spurt.

At last, Melora raised a small surgeon's pot, dipped out a paste and pressed it over the wound, sealing the artery, then bound it with a strip of fresh linen. Madoc carefully lowered Nefyn's bloodless palm to her side, then massaged her neck and face until her wild eyes opened. Her voice, high-pitched as a little girl's, Nefyn said, "I want Caydwr to kiss me again and give me my last blessing."

Ellylyw hid her face, and the other women looked at each other.

Madoc lied softly, "They are fetching your hermit."

"My Lord Madoc, don't let my body be buried in this cursed country. Put me in a boat on the river and let me go to sea. Chance will carry me. Perhaps to the sacred, central isle where I may partake of the Grail..."

Madoc nodded, forced out a choked reply. "I will set you in the boat myself."

"Rhys," Nefyn called weakly.

The soldiers held him fast. "I am here, Nefyn."

"Take courage from me to give of yourself, if Ellylyw ails again." Nefyn melted limply in her chieftain's hands. She murmured in the voice of a sleepy child, "Savior..."

Rhys felt her pass. The soldiers, familiar with the comings and goings of death, let Rhys sink into his chair and moved silently away, each rapt in his own thoughts.

Two men laid Nefyn's limp body on her bedroll. She seemed now as little as a doll. The other waiting women arranged Nefyn's gown and her hair, then returned to their exhausted mistress, closing the flaps of the pavilion behind them. Candlelight shone through the fabric, and Rhys watched the women's bobbing shadows. Gwenllian supported Ellylyw's back while Melora held the basin and helped Ellylyw gulp and sputter down as much of its warm contents as she could. The women tidied up the spills and left the pavilion for their own linen nests.

The grizzled sergeant-at-arms divested Madoc of his armor, and the chieftain slipped into the pavilion. Rhys watched the wavering shadow-husband strip off his tunic and leggings while looking down at his wife. Shadow Ellylyw raised rippling arms and received him. The candles began to gutter out, but there was no escaping the sounds of their fevered, desperate pawing at stolen life.

The soldiers lay unarmored on their bedrolls or stood their posts at the exits. Ignored, inconsequential, Rhys lifted the wine pitcher. It, too, was empty.

Stumbling to the bedroll the women had laid out for him, Rhys lay, armored as he was, and stared at the shadows still dancing over the uneven ceiling. The world burned down around him, one candle at a time, as he lay under the ground surrounded by Madoc's last, lost men, clinging to a mad commander who could leave his nation open to the fury of the barbarians to fulfill this blood sacrifice for all-consuming love. There, on unyielding stone Rhys lay, living in the tomb of the girl they had all helped to destroy.

Maybe the zealots are right. This is the Aetas Tenebrarum, the Age of Darkness.

The last flame smothered. Yet the darkness Rhys had fought for so long could not wholly claim him. Though he wheezed and struggled for breath in the fust-foul air, Rhys felt his jaw clench, his hand lock tight about the pommel of his sword. Body and mind seemed to ripple, lack of air turning him fluid and formless, but in his heart he felt clear, concentrated. Doomed or not, at last he had purpose.

Rhys swore to himself, there in the dark, that he would never rest until the custom of Castrum Tenebrarum was thrown down in the dust like the fortress walls.

Chapter 2:

The Half-Forged Sword

Flint struck steel and Rhys woke with a jolt. The rough walls of the cave seemed to leap into his sight in the wavering candlelight. Rhys rolled from his pallet, stiff from a night cramped in armor.

The flaps were open on the pavilion. Inside, the two waiting women tenderly helped Ellylyw drink what remained in the copper basin.

Turning, Rhys was struck by the sight of Nefyn's wan corpse on the cave floor nearby. Rhys' body ignored his commands and began to shake. He bit back against an uprush of horror, grief and rage. He aimed hooded eyes at the commander of the ruined fortress beneath which he stood.

Madoc Broad Shoulders was already dressed and toeing his sergeant-at-arms awake. The chieftain's face was a stern and noble mask of tragedy, yet it was hard for Rhys not to hate the man for allowing Nefyn's sacrifice. Rhys quietly watched the stocky sergeant, a man named Morcant, rise and slip the heavy chainmail tunic over his chieftain's head. Madoc adjusted his sword-belt and scabbard while Morcant strapped plate mail tailored to the commander's form over his shins and forearms.

Then Morcant moved off to kick the rest of his men

out of whatever surcease they had found and back into the trap that was Castrum Tenebrarum.

Rhys dipped his hands into a bucket of well water and began the morning's ablutions, wrestling his black thoughts down, alert for anything that might aid him in his new self-avowed mission.

Marius, a short, dark, and thick-armed guard in old legionary armor, was posted at the mouth of the escape tunnel, watching Rhys. Abruptly, he spun toward the dark portal as if he had heard something. Rhys and the other men all drew their weapons. Tall Madoc wrapped his shield arm protectively about his lady, gleaming sword upraised.

A shaggy, long-bearded Briton stepped from the tunnel. He was tall and strongly built. His rough fur tunic and cloak, and the shapeless leather boots strapped about his legs convinced Rhys the man must have been a hermit. The woodman's strong brows knit over his thick nose, and his fingers plucked at the end of his long black beard. To Rhys' surprise, not only did Madoc and his men relax as soon as they saw the hermit, but the very temperature of the chamber palpably rose as the wood-dweller's abundant energy overflowed into everything around him.

The hermit's quick eyes caught the stranger, a peculiar revitalizing shock striking Rhys upon meeting the shaggy man's gaze. Hermits, of course, generally tended to dislike company, but this man strode energetically to the bard, seized his forearm and shook it with strength worthy of a blacksmith. "Caydwr." He introduced himself in a resonant rumble.

"Rhys of Caer Waroc, sent by Consularis Brathach." Rhys smiled. Then he frowned. Resisting the hermit's palpable charm, Rhys toed the copper basin so that it rang. "Was this your idea?"

Caydwr's shining eyes looked through him. "Where is Nefyn?"

All but Rhys dropped their eyes. The bard pointed to the pale corpse. Caydwr cocked his head to one side and regarded the body with pursed lips. "She chose this."

Rhys' face twisted. "She was encouraged to martyr herself...for nothing."

"Let us see." Caydwr bustled past the fuming bard toward Ellylyw. "How are you, my little lady?"

Madoc stood in the way, the runnels worn in his aristocratic face catching the dark and holding it, but the hermit's natural force was too much for the chieftain. Madoc gave way before him.

"Caydwr," Ellylyw chirped, happy as a child.

Rhys was sure he heard the other women sigh.

Caydwr kissed Ellylyw's lips lustily like a lover, then patted her head as if she were indeed his child, peered into her eyes like a conjurer and pressed a hand against her heart like a physician. Madoc hovered uncomfortably, saying nothing. A little color came back into Ellylyw's sculpted cheeks, and her movements seemed more animated. However unorthodox, Caydwr was obviously good for her.

Scowling, Rhys watched the sharp-tongued blonde, Melora, grow weak at the knees and sit on the ground near the table. Dreamily, she sipped from the flagon of wine she had watered down for breakfast.

Caydwr rose, stepped to the seated Melora and reached out.

The young woman's slim hand drifted up into his.

He patted it, then stretched out his other hand, and realizing what he wanted, Melora, cheeks flushed, handed him the wine flagon.

Caydwr pulled herbs from his pouch and crumbled them into the wine, then held the flagon to Ellylyw's lips. "You are better, Elly-Elly. You know it. You should say it."

"I am better, Caydwr, especially when you talk to me. Tell me about your Green Chapel. I always like that."

"Oh, it's beautiful. Great oaks make bigger arches than ever Romans built, and the gold of the sun on shivering green leaves is richer than dyes from Persia. Flowers shock you with hue and float you with scent, and birds sing choruses your friend the bard, there, could never master. I have a bear for a priest and a fox for a preceptor, and when you are well enough to travel, I will carry you there on my shoulders to ease your horse. But you are hiding something from me...I feel it."

"Caydwr." She sounded disturbed.

"No truth is ever hidden completely," he said. "I see signs in your halo. A withered rose. A closed eye. A black horse shies and screams."

Ellylyw looked hurt. "I would never lie."

Caydwr caressed her hand. "Someone has hidden your truth, even from you." He peered into her troubled face. "Tell me who has done this. Do not think, just speak what wishes to be spoken."

"Husband," she blurted out, then lifted a hand halfway to her mouth as if to catch the word and take it back.

Madoc frowned.

Jeffrey T. Heyer

His men exchanged looks.

Caydwr pursed his thick lips, making his moustache bristle. "Your husband could not bury a part of your memory. Who stands behind your husband?"

She shrugged and shook her head in confusion. "The black horse." Ellylyw gasped, then clamped her lips shut as if she had broken some vow of silence.

"All is well," Caydwr rumbled. "You have not betrayed him...whoever he is." The hermit turned to her husband. "She is not accusing you. The truth is not *in* these words, but *behind* them. Perhaps your enemy is a spirit...something that dwells neither in heaven nor earth but in between. I must prepare myself to dream."

"Gwenllian," Madoc said swiftly. "Fetch bedding for Caydwr."

"I cannot sleep in a hole like a badger." The woodman scowled. "There must be stars above and air that moves, and I must be where the dead died. Melora, help me make a nest in the ruins. You're not afraid of wolves, are you?"

Melora's eyebrows tilted up in the middle. She hastily adjusted a few strands of her hair and danced over to Caydwr, seizing his hand happily in both of hers. They laughed together, skipping like children into the passage that led to the ruined fortress above.

Rhys saw Madoc staring at him, weighing his reactions. "This is a holy man, chieftain?"

Madoc's eyes narrowed slightly. "Caydwr was a monk in better times. Hermits arc common enough these days."

"Not like him." The bard's gaze shifted to the forest tunnel. "I take it that he has been coming through this

Jeffrey T. Heyer

tunnel to tend to your lady since before the battle. Tell me, chieftain, how did the Saxons get inside your walls?"

Madoc looked off into space for a while, then: "We were spread pretty thin." He turned ferocious eyes on Rhys. "Let me see your blade."

Reluctantly, Rhys drew his weapon, proffering its pommel to the chieftain.

Madoc hefted it, made a few practice sweeps, then tapped its point on the stone floor. "Decent balance. Good steel." He tossed it to Rhys. "But your smith should have worked it longer. Mine was folded and hammered down and reheated and folded again and again to strengthen the steel. Yours is but half-forged." Madoc stabbed Rhys with a hawkish glare. "I need the hermit. Ellylyw needs him. I will give her what she needs."

Rhys read death in those eyes. "If I don't bring the intelligence the Consularis needs..." he spoke slowly, "Brathach will send a bigger party."

"When he can," Madoc said.

Rhys nodded. "When he can."

***

Rhys stepped through the concealed tunnel entrance into early morning sunshine, sweet and golden. Madoc's retainers fanned out, forming a circle around the bard. A raven shot upward from a black and broken wall and cawed jarringly. The square-jawed Lovan, the soldier nearest to Rhys, grimaced.

Rhys frowned. "The way here was thick with them."

"Ravens love this place," Lovan grumbled. "They've fed well here."

Gwenllian stepped out behind them, brown hair stirring in the breeze. Beside her, Melora squinted into the bright light.

Rhys asked, "Melora, will you show me to my horse? I should see to him first."

The soldiers tensed.

Before Rhys could ask whether they feared he would flee, Gwenllian spoke up. "Oh, I'll do that. You go ahead, Melora."

With a scowl, Melora flung her chin to the sky and marched off.

Gwenllian led Rhys, the soldiers maintaining their circle about him as he moved, to the sooty but otherwise intact former storeroom, its timbers saved from the conflagration by some vagary of the fire. She entered with Rhys. Marius and the stocky sergeant-at-arms Morcant followed.

Rhys saw that his four-footed comrade-in-arms had been well cared for. Spotting the bridle draped over a large trunk, he lifted it.

The two soldiers' hands slapped around the pommels of their sheathed swords.

Gwenllian touched Rhys' hand, stopping him. "Let me curry him and care for the tack. I'll even exercise him."

Rhys frowned at the soldiers.

The woman smiled at him, drawing his gaze back to her. "I miss Renwena, my white-maned mare. I really would love to put your old charger through his paces." She stepped closer and whispered, "At least, with all Madoc's men out here with you, Melora collecting herbs for Caydwr, and me on horseback again, at last, Madoc can finally be alone with his wife."

"Thank you." Reluctantly, Rhys followed the soldiers back out into the courtyard. Immediately he set about examining the damaged defense-works, the circle of men moving to remain always about him. The sense of being enclosed even in the open was a powerful distraction, as was the question that rang in Rhys' mind: *Will anyone ever hear my report?*

Nevertheless, he made careful mental notes as he proceeded. A row of ballistas, Roman-style artillery pieces, looked as if they might easily be made ready again to sling boulders over the walls, but he found little else of import until he came to the sally port.

A low, narrow, heavy-timbered gate, the port was just wide enough to allow one man at a time to pass along a short tunnel through the thick outer wall. It was designed to enable the garrison to slip a small force outside the walls by dead of night in order to spring a surprise sally against a besieger's flanks. If the ambushers were chased back to the port, their pursuers would find that the low lintel and shin-high block at the threshold forced them to enter the fortress slowly and at a stooped and awkward angle, making it impossible for them to defend themselves. Four guards at the courtyard end fighting in shifts could hold the passage against a thousand men.

What bothered Rhys was that the sally port hung open.

Following his gaze, the soldiers shifted about uncomfortably.

Abruptly, Rhys stooped through the open gate. Along the floor of the passage Rhys noted scattered fragments of brush and splotches of tar. At the far end, the outside gate was set five feet above the ground. It had been cleverly camouflaged by the builder to blend with the stone of the wall, but a chunk of timber and rock-imitating paint had been chipped away about one edge. A bent lance-head lay in the trampled grass outside, and fragments of an unusually thick lance haft lay nearby. Curiously, the wooden haft was painted black, and the ruined blade was black steel.

The soldiers busily scanned the countryside for the enemy and did not notice these details. Rhys thought, *The Saxons have no cavalry. They do not wield lances. I thought only Scots used black steel for use in the dark. But no Scot would be so far south. And they do not use cavalry either.*

Retracing his path up the uneven stone wall, Rhys ducked inside the sally port and made his way along the tunnel. Stepping over the awkwardly high threshold, he ducked into the courtyard again. The bard knelt and examined the gate on the courtyard side. It, too, showed deep gouges along the edge of the gate as well as its frame. He knelt and examined a clutter of broken Saxon weapons and fragments of British shields littering the ground about him. Turning his head, he was slightly shocked to find himself eye-to-eye with a wary crow poised atop a hitching post. The big bird cocked its head this way and that, considering the bard uneasily but with tremendous deliberation.

"Something to tell me, brother?" Rhys asked.

A stone whipped past to crack the black skull and fling the body from its perch amid a scatter of feathers and droplets of blood.

Rhys turned furiously on the square-jawed soldier who had flung it. "What do you think you're doing?"

Lovan cocked his head, looking at Rhys with one contemptuous eye. "Brother to black devils, are you?"

"Bird, not devil."

"They eat the dead."

"And you like your meat alive? Did it never occur to you that if ravens seek the dead, you might observe them and find your former comrades unburied in the wreckage?"

"We'll never find them all. This place is cursed."

"Then have the decency," Rhys shouted, "not to spill more blood in it." He realized that he was far more furious than he had reason to be.

"You're not a knight to give me orders," Lovan yelled back at him, with more than a hint of threat in his voice and manner.

"Lovan," Morcant snapped.

Lovan turned to his sergeant. "You think I shouldn't kill crows because the spirits of the dead live on in them?"

"Just leave them be, can't you?" The sergeant-at-arms was irritated and disgusted.

"I want an answer," Lovan hollered. "Are you Christian or are you pagan? Do you believe crows are spirits of the dead?"

"*I* believe..." Rhys said, "that our priority here is to scout the wreckage for the Consularis, and I don't want stones whizzing by my ears while I'm doing it. And there are things to be learned from the behavior of birds." He then set off angrily along the wall.

Lovan pushed close to block his path, so close that

Rhys smelled the man's ring-studded leather armor, unwashed since the battle, sharply redolent of fear and life-saving exertion. "*You* believe?" Lovan growled. "Then believe this. We may have been spread thin on the walls, but our chieftain had this fortress battened down tight. Take a look around, Brathach's man. The Saxons got in. Carrying fire. Did the souls of their dead carry it in their wing feathers? Hah! Someone let in the raiders. Someone brought the wrath of God down upon us. Someone who knew which cave in the forest snakes into the vault where Ellylyw lies."

Rhys broke in. "Possibly—"

"Caydwr is no good Christian," Lovan galloped on. "He's a crow-lover like you and Morcant, here, brother to beasts, not the servants of God."

"Madoc says—"

"Madoc is my commander, not the voice of God. Ask the abbot down in the town about Caydwr. How many sermons has the holy prelate preached against the misguided fools who go into the forest at night to find the hermit...get him to heal them...to find their lost cows...to make love philters for them or pretend to tell them their fortunes? Madoc is just as blind—"

"Enough," Morcant barked. Several men backed him up this time with their own protests, even taciturn Callas.

Lovan persisted. "I've followed Madoc Broad Shoulders through hell, so I have the right to say it. Madoc turns a blind eye because he won't rely on God to decide when his lady will die. If the hermit cares more for soulless animals than good Christians, why wouldn't he sell us out to the Saxons? He's more than half pagan already."

The other soldiers began urging their sergeant to shut up Lovan, but Morcant just shook his war-weary head.

"There are other kinds of Christians than you," Rhys put in before turning away, sick of the discussion.

"No." Lovan blocked his path again. "If you don't follow the priests, you don't follow God. You're not Christian just because you say you are."

Morcant tried one more time. "Trusting the Church is not the same as trusting God."

"It is."

Marius snorted. "Then God changes his mind a lot."

"Blasphemy now?" Lovan cried.

"My people..." Marius pressed, "were endowing churches when yours were still offering milk to the fairies. How many times has one Bishop of Rome changed the policies of his predecessors? How many comrades have you lost when one lord of the church raids the diocese of another over whether to use two fingers or three in a blessing?"

Lovan's eyes widened. "Heresy has to be dealt with."

"Stupidity, too," Marius said. "But you're right, Madoc is blind to some things...he keeps you for a retainer."

Lovan had his sword half drawn when Callas leapt on his back and pinioned his arms. That surprised the lot of them.

"Since when do you care..." Marius asked of Callas, "if Romans fight Arians over who's a heretic?"

"You can all damn each other to hell," Callas shouted. "But keep your swords sheathed 'til you see a damned Saxon. Roman, Arian, Manichean or Orthodox, you can all count, can't you? There's six of us plus Madoc. That's all. And two thousand Saxon raiders within three days ride. Brathach won't be sending more men 'til he's had his precious report, and if this scrawny bard doesn't get back with it..."

Lovan stopped struggling and Callas pushed him away in disgust.

"Ahh..." Lovan spat. He shrugged his armor back into place. "It's the hermit I hate, not any of you." Lovan's eyes skipped over Morcant when he said this.

Rhys pushed on and rounded a partially collapsed barracks before the tension could dredge up any more half-submerged conflicts.

Before them stood a Roman bathhouse, its walls intact, though the roof lay in fragments about the floor. Stepping inside, the party saw Caydwr and Melora standing naked, washing each other from one of many buckets scattered about a well.

Lovan gave an outraged cry, waving at the hermit. "That one's no soldier. We can do without him debauching our women."

Unsheathing, the furious soldier dashed awkwardly over the broken ceiling tiles that shifted unpredictably under his booted feet.

Morcant started after his man, but Callas caught the sergeant's arm. "Let the hothead solve one problem for us."

Seething, Rhys whipped out his own sword and sprinted after Lovan.

The wetly gleaming Melora ducked with a cry to cower behind the well while Caydwr waited patiently. Most hermits were rail thin from meager meals of watercress and roots, but Rhys noted as he ran forward that, though lean-muscled, Caydwr was well filled out. The hermit even smiled a little, unconcerned that he was naked and confronting an enraged professional swordsman in full armor.

Yelling, sword raised, Lovan clattered up to the hermit, sweeping his blade down hard and fast, but somehow Caydwr was already inside the swing, blocking his arm, planting a broad hand in Lovan's face and heaving him backward. His footing lost on the scattering tile fragments, Lovan stumbled, flailing.

Rhys planted himself before the hermit, facing the soldier. "Stop it, Lovan. Brathach needs the truth, not your hates or fears."

The man-at-arms regained his footing and hefted his sword. "You side with this pagan bastard?" he raged hoarsely.

The other soldiers spread out behind Lovan, finding safe vantage points from which to watch.

Rhys yelled, "Maybe I don't understand him—"

"Hah!"

"But the hermit's alliance with beast and bird yields better fruit than all your hatred."

Lovan's eyes sparkled with zeal. "The next world is what counts...this one is dung."

"It's a work of art," the bard declared, passionately. "Would you spit on your creator's masterpiece?"

"I spit in the devil's eye." Lovan swept his sword in a bright arc over his head. "And on any that defend him. The hermit's a monster. He preys on women. He's damned that girl, and you, too, for helping him. Look at the naked bastard. Is that how a Christian acts? He's an animal."

Caydwr chuckled. "Of course."

Lovan turned red, and spittle flew from his lips. "You heard it."

"You see nothing that God did not make," Caydwr pointed out calmly.

"Did he not give you shame, as well?"

"Oh, man made that."

"Nor fear of God's wrath?"

"God's wrath I felt before I became a hermit...when I was like you, Lovan. God will kill me one day, because He kills us all. It is His way. I trust Him to choose the moment. You think you want the next world so much...the path to it is not through blindness or lack of experience. God built the world for you to get through. Even this place of darkness will aid you once you find its secret."

Lovan lunged, thrust his blade at the hermit's heart, but Rhys slapped it aside with his own sword. The soldier fumed at them both. "Then you serve death and hell."

Caydwr grinned. "I am brother to both, as to life and open sky. What are all your holy words of forgiveness if you do nothing to forgive? Only when you experience everything can you leave all sin behind."

Rhys parried another frenzied thrust.

"You heard him," Lovan raved. "He openly advocates sin. He thinks the fall of Castrum Tenebrarum was a good thing. I'll carve the blood-thirsty bastard—"

"You won't," Rhys declared, catching Lovan's blade in a circular disengage, sweeping it to the side.

Lovan responded with a flurry of strikes and thrusts, pressing Rhys hard, backing him away from the hermit and the woman. The fighter's nimble feet stirred up the ash that lay everywhere, stinging both men's eyes, choking Rhys.

Already Rhys was panting, his heart hammering at his chest, in terror that he might die in so senseless a fashion, leaving his mission unfulfilled, his nation in peril, his life a meaningless waste...

Lovan put his back into a cut toward Rhys' thigh. Rhys parried, but the force of the blow drove Rhys' own blade back against his leg. He would have a long thin bruise there tomorrow, but the leather armor saved his skin.

Rhys was only just holding the man off, and each breath grew harder to draw as his breathing passage swelled shut. Eyes watering in the sight-burning flying ash, the bard spun in a circle to add impetus to his blow, fighting silent and hard, while Lovan roared, flailed and swore.

Not yet fully recovered from the recent battle against the Saxons, Lovan tired abruptly, withdrew several paces, swept his blade through empty air in a showy set of practice cuts and parries to belie the reason for his retreat.

"Do you think you can take me, Rhys of Caer Waroc?" Lovan blustered, his throat dry.

The bard made no showy moves of his own, simply holding his blade in the ready position before him, preserving his strength, panting bitter air while he still could. "Maybe I can't take you. Maybe you'll explain to Chief Madoc that you killed the man that was to get help from Brathach...and then you killed the hermit Madoc hopes will cure his wife. Will you kill the naked woman, too? Then race around the ruins slaying ravens...maybe burn the forest?"

"You're such a fool." Lovan sheathed and turned away. Steam misted from under his armored collar as he crunched tiles while heading toward the shade of the bathhouse wall. There he leaned against the stones and rested without being too obvious about it.

Rhys sheathed, too, then turned to the hermit.

Caydwr nodded pleasantly, then sniffed at his underarms. Satisfied that he was clean enough, he helped Melora rise from behind the well and make her way to her clothing. She made a face at Rhys while blushing furiously.

"Lovan's right about one thing." Rhys wheezed, amused. "I've never known a Christian like you, hermit."

Caydwr laughed, helping Melora lace up her gown. "That's why I left the abbey for a hermitage. But truth is truth. Someone will always discover it, no matter who kills whom. Bury the truth a hundred times, it will always come back and bite you in the neck."

"So..." Rhys gasped, "you take a little truth from the Pagans and a little from the Christians?"

Caydwr shook his shaggy head while shrugging into his rough-edged fur tunic, now that scarlet-faced Melora was dressed. "The Pagans take a piece from God, the Church takes another piece. I see what I see."

Rhys watched him sit on the edge of a dry bath and tie his boots about his shins. The bard was torn between what had become his admiration for the hermit's oneness with nature, and the deep unease he felt about some of the man's actions. Could this be the traitor who had opened the sally port to torch-bearing Saxons? Brows knit, Rhys asked, "So you think the purpose of being human...is to become as human as you can?"

Jeffrey T. Heyer

Tugging his boot-laces, Caydwr grunted. "Good words. You should believe them."

"I think I do."

The hermit wrapped his belt about his waist and tied it. Then he reached out and tapped Rhys on the forehead. "Not up there." He tapped Rhys' heart. "In there."

Rhys frowned. "I feel passionate about this. It's what fuels all my songs, all my poems...all my quests."

Caydwr absorbed this, then sat a moment, eyes unfocussed. He poked Rhys' armored solar plexus. "Believe it there."

Rhys eyed him, misease mounting. "Did you tell these people to fill that basin with blood?"

Caydwr rose and walked over to Melora. Clearly wishing herself anywhere but here, shrunken into herself with embarrassment, still the girl could not help but loosen at his touch and flow into his hands like butter. He leaned down, kissed her lips softly, then gave her backside an affectionate slap, sending her off without a word.

"It's all to do with blood, somehow," Caydwr said in answer to Rhys' query. "Ellylyw's lineage, perhaps. Deep, powerful underground streams. I do not see it all yet. You spent the night in Castrum Tenebrarum. What did you dream?"

Startled, Rhys reluctantly condescended to review a bad night's visions. "I dreamt the events of my life were moves on a board game. I played gwyddbwyll against an opponent who blocked my every move, picked off my pieces, turned my strategies against me. Then I looked up...I saw no opponent. Instead, I saw that my gaming table was on a bridge of glass. I heard a terrible shattering behind

Dark Age

me, felt my stomach lurch as I started to fall...and awoke."

Caydwr studied him. "You lost a woman."

"What?"

"It's been a while, but you still miss her. You lost your way."

"Why do you say this to me?"

"Because it is for you to hear. It's not the woman who really matters. It's what she hides behind her."

The bard stared at the hermit, trying hard to make sense of the statement. "I loved her."

"Oh, yes."

"I still love her, in spite of the way we parted."

"That is apparent. Just not the point you need to grasp."

Rhys shook his head. "What I need to understand is what is going on here...what caused the fort to fall...and whether Madoc can still lead an army to guard this highway."

Caydwr shrugged. "It doesn't matter."

"It's vital," Rhys exclaimed, his voice rising an octave. "How can you not grasp this? If the Saxons recover before we do, they'll march straight into the unprotected heart of Britain."

"As God wills."

"As we allow. Don't you understand what those barbarians will do?"

"Kill. Rape. Steal. Burn. Throw down churches, governments. Root out as much of your civilization as they can and use the pieces to start their own."

Rhys stared at him, astonished once more. "Exactly."

"Humanity will never learn. Only individuals can."

~45~

Rhys felt uncomfortably close to infection by as mad a rage as had claimed Lovan. He staved off an outburst. "How can we remain individuals if our way of life is destroyed...if we don't protect what our ancestors sweated blood to build? If we don't spill our own blood to claw our way farther up the ladder?"

Caydwr shrugged casually again. "You can't stop the fall of night with your report. Or your sword. Or your harp. You must understand what is happening, as must I, or I would not be here. But not for your report. For your soul. You should not be a bard."

Rhys reared back like a pricked stallion. "Why do you say that? You've never heard me sing."

"I don't say you aren't good at it," Caydwr replied. "You should be a hermit, like me, and finish your quest for yourself, not waste your time trying to reach people who can't understand what you're saying."

Rhys shook his head again, unable even to imagine the notion. "How could I stand aside and contemplate my soul while my country crumbles? How would I face my ancestors in the next life?"

"I'm hungry," Caydwr announced. "You are woman-haunted, Rhys of Caer Waroc. If you do not focus your whole soul on problems of the soul, your invisible opponent will checkmate you again and again to force you to find him. Only a woman can lead the way. More than that I cannot tell you. I must find food and meditate on my dreams."

Caydwr walked off across the scorched courtyard, leaving Rhys to go back to studying the castrum's breached defenses, surrounded, always, by the ring of Madoc's men.

***

Gwenllian returned on Morvran to lock him again in his safe-house with a bundle of newly reaped provender. Melora brought herbs from the woods, and the two women had just gone down to the vault when the gaunt soldier Kanin, his restless eyes ever on his surroundings and not on the quarrels of his fellows, called, "Wolves!"

The other men leaned over the battlemented wall atop which they were making a slow progress. On the torn grassy slope below, a well-coordinated pack of gray carnivores headed for the gap in the wall.

"Get to the vault," Morcant ordered.

The soldiers scrambled for the stairway, Rhys hurrying after. The wild things must have been hit by the famine, too, the bard thought. The pack would be careless of injury, willing to die for a mouthful of meat.

Rhys stopped outside the tunnel's iron-studded gate. "Caydwr is out there."

The last of the soldiers, Lovan and Morcant, looked back at the bard. Lovan said, "Let them have him," and pushed past into the narrow tunnel.

Morcant muttered, "We can't go after the hermit. The wolves will be inside the curtain wall by now."

Rhys felt his face set. "No more sacrifices, Morcant."

The sergeant grabbed at Rhys' shoulder to tug him into the tunnel, but Rhys jerked free. Morcant's black brows joined above his nose, an effect like storm clouds gathering. "That's not your decision to make, boy. Get in."

From the darkness of the tunnel behind the sergeant, Callas snapped, "There's no time to argue."

"You're with us or you're not, boy," Morcant growled with a trace of regret.

Rhys had decided. "I'm with Caydwr."

Lovan's tattooed arm craned out of the shadows and helped Morcant haul the weighty gate to a crashing close.

Rhys dashed across the courtyard, calling for Caydwr. Wolves, heavy as a small man, crouched low to the ground and encircled the bard. Rhys ran on, sword in hand, shield on arm. As Madoc's men had, the circle of wolves moved with Rhys, flowing effortlessly over the debris.

Yellow eyes bright with hunger, the lead wolf lunged, snapping long fangs, snarling ferociously.

Rhys dodged, swinging his shield. Another wolf lunged with a hideous growl, pulling up just out of reach of the sweeping sword.

Another sprang, then another, each stopping just out of range, each deflecting Rhys from his path, herding him to their leader's chosen ground where taking him would cost the fewest casualties.

"*Caydwr!*" the bard cried.

"Over here," the hermit called, casually.

The wolves backed up, growling at Rhys, but quieting at Caydwr's approach. The gray-backed circle opened, letting the hermit enter. Caydwr placed a friendly hand on Rhys' shoulder and led him across the courtyard.

The wolves protested volubly, but widened their circle and made no more lunges.

Rhys stared at the man in amazement.

"They know me for one of them." Caydwr chuckled, patting his furs. "Oh, I didn't kill my brother for this." He smoothed the pelt affectionately. "He was a friend of mine.

One day I found his body with an arrow through it. He willed me his coat to remember him by. Ah, here's a nice burrow." Caydwr pushed Rhys into a stone corner, all that was left of the great hall. The hermit stood in front of him and smiled at the wolves. They howled in protest, but Caydwr laughed. "It's better this way, friends."

The lead wolf ran off to paw at the ruins in search of corpses; the rest followed suit. A mournful howl or two later, Caydwr and Rhys sat alone in the cool evening air, watching light fade from an orange sky.

Rhys thanked him.

Caydwr enjoyed another good laugh.

"I don't believe you let in the Saxons."

"Ah?" The hermit collected rubbish to make a fire.

"The castrum has a hidden entrance, but someone outside knew how to find it. Before the Saxons arrived, a single man, armed as a knight with black weapons, worked quietly and patiently between the guardsmen's rounds to pry open the sally port, breaking the bolts."

Caydwr turned round eyes upon him. "The figure behind Ellylyw's dreams...the one who hid her memories of him, even from herself."

"If you say so. The knight in black must have closed the sally port behind him or the patrols would have spotted it. But Madoc dismissed a quarter of his forces to spend his treasure importing Gallic physicians. Then the Saxons came. They were numerous, but they had no siege weapons, so Madoc must have massed his remaining forces above the main gate. So long as Madoc held the gate, he knew all the Saxons in the world could never crack these walls. A spotter in the tower could signal Madoc to dispatch men along the parapets and throw down any scaling ladders the invaders might throw against any wall."

Caydwr shrugged, unimpressed with strategy.

"But the marks left by the black knight's weapons ruined the sally port's camouflage, revealing it to the Saxon scouts, and with all the men above the main gate there were no guard patrols to prevent the Saxons from opening the unbolted door. Rather than risk bottle-necking a hundred men in the narrow passage if the defender in the tower spotted them, the Saxon commander sent in a handful of men with tinder and torches to set fire to the tower.

"With his reduced forces, Madoc could only lead a few men from the gate to fight the blaze. When the tower fell and shattered the outer wall, the handful of men with Madoc dropped their buckets and fought their way out the sally port while the main Saxon onslaught poured through the breach and swept the defenders from the walls."

"So..." the hermit said while laying out a hearth circle with loose stones, "you've worked out for your master how the fortress fell. And I now know a black knight brought this darkness on Ellylyw." He pulled three chair legs from his woodpile, made a tripod of them and arranged tinder between and about them. "Yet, I don't know who the knight is or what he did to her. And we are locked out of Madoc's vault."

"Until morning."

"Ah, but then you will be on your way with your report, hoping the Consularis will put an end to the custom of Castrum Tenebrarum."

Rhys looked at him in surprise. "Madoc's guards are all down in the vault. It is my chance to escape, isn't it?"

"What else can you do?"

Rhys thought about it. He knew himself a half-trained bard who might at any time find himself unable to breathe, pitting himself against a chainmailed chieftain, his veterans, and this mysterious black knight...

Caydwr pulled flint and steel from his belt pouch and struck them together, contemplatively. "The black horse I saw in Ellylyw's halo...this knight is its rider. Only finding the knight of the black horse can cure her."

The thought of Ellylyw out of reach in the vault plucked at the young bard's heartstrings. The thought that the hideous custom by which she survived would again be enforced, twisted his guts. Then, too, once he reported back to Eboracum, he would have no say in what transpired.

Rhys watched Caydwr's fire blossom and decided to thrust himself of his own will into the forge and come out a brighter blade or be burnt to slag. "I will find the black knight who unwittingly doomed this fort, and I will free Ellylyw of him."

"And Madoc?"

"Whatever it takes."

"Whatever it takes," the hermit repeated.

The die was cast.

Chapter 3:

The Black Knight's Assault

R hys' leather armor creaked and pinched as he craned over the battlements, peering into the moonlight, surveying the scars the Saxon horde had left on the grassy slope below. Madoc strode to him, lance-haft straight, eyes on the bright moon just rising above the distant forest. One of his men leaned against an embrasure behind him, relaxing as best he could in leather and steel. Madoc's chainmail pinged slightly as he turned toward Rhys, moon-shadow harshening his haggard features and picking out the white at his temples.

"We are all pleased," Madoc said without expression, "that you survived the wolves."

Rhys felt less than overwhelmed by Madoc's warmth. "Your men were quick to sacrifice me...and the hermit."

"They were obliged to secure the escape tunnel, the only part of this ruin we *can* still secure. You know I would never countenance the hermit's death."

Rhys' smile was bleak. "Lucky for both of us, then, that the wolves seem to be his friends. Your hermit has returned to his Green Chapel to meditate."

Madoc gazed out across the torn landscape, brows furrowed.

Rhys watched him. "How is Ellylyw?"

Madoc's aristocratic face grew sterner.

"If I may ask."

The chieftain's gaze flicked over him. "You disapprove of the custom of Castrum Tenebrarum."

"This is not the way to save her."

"You saw," the somber chieftain whispered, his eyes boring into Rhys. "When poor Nefyn filled the basin with her blood, Ellylyw revived."

"Nefyn died."

"But Ellylyw lives. Blood has power. The whole world is ruled by carefully maintained bloodlines."

"Never try to impress a bard with fiction, Madoc. It is my job to memorize the deeds of the great houses. Most were set up by ruthless opportunists. Three quarters of our current crop of aristocrats are prominent because their ancestors sided with the Roman invaders against their own people, which is why half the provinces threw out their chieftains along with the Romans and created their own governments."

"Government of the commons." Madoc spoke in quiet disdain.

"They've done no worse than the chieftains," Rhys pointed out. "Besides, any breeder knows a purebred pays for its specialization. Breed a horse to race and it'll be skittish as a stag."

The Frankish man-at-arms, Clothar, sneered Madoc's broad shoulder. "*Desrees.*"

A faint, cold amusement glinted in the chieftain's pale eyes.

The gibe bit deep, though Rhys tried to conceal the fact. He recognized the word from the songs of Emperor

Arthur's court. Frankish minstrels sang of a knight of the Round Table called Sagramore Desrees, or Sycamore Tree the Perennially Sick. "Certain animals and plants affect my breathing, but there are herbs that help—"

"But do not cure," Madoc cut in, cold as the sharp steel by his side. "Like Ellylyw. The Roman physicians would say your condition is caused by the mixture of your British and Gothic blood. And, *bard,* man of *fictions*, all men of science agree that bleeding is efficacious medicine."

Rhys, a great respecter of science, could find no way around that.

"As for the Consularis," Madoc added, "it remains to be seen what faith he'll put in the report of a rootless free lance."

"*If* you get back with your report," Clothar muttered.

Music wafted up from the forest beyond the rent, grassy slope below. High, clear piping pierced the quiet night. The men peered intently toward the distant tree line.

Moonlight caught two-score gray backs rippling across the open grassland before the woods, apparently in the wake of the unseen piper. The eerie music faded away as the musician moved deeper into the forest, the wolf pack following.

"No one from the town would come this near the castrum," Rhys declared, "for fear of your bloody custom."

The Frank mumbled in disturbed awe, *"Le meneu de loups?"*

The lines worn down Madoc's long face masked his expression in shadows. He stared into the distance.

Clothar turned his heavy brows and pointed beard

toward Rhys, eyes lost in moon-shade. "You trusted the hermit...now he's shepherding the wolves against us."

"Keep watch," Madoc ordered Rhys. Then the chieftain dashed down the stone steps to the courtyard. He sent two men to guard the entrance to the vault and escape tunnel, and a third, Callas, to patrol the courtyard, poking his naked sword into shadows about the ruined buildings. Madoc and his three remaining soldiers, cloaks flowing after them, rushed out through the gap in the castrum's wall.

Rhys watched them recede over the blowing grass, following the eerie music. Higher, sharper than the distant piper's notes, a horse screamed in the night, setting Rhys' scalp prickling. He spun about to stare down into the moonlit courtyard. With a metallic clatter, Callas landed on his face in the rubble. A man-sized blackness flitted past the body into the dark obscurity by the hidden tunnel mouth.

"Madoc," Rhys shouted over the battlements toward the now distant figure. Then turning on his heel, the bard raced for the steps. Leaping down three at a time, seized by nameless dread, Rhys hurtled ever faster toward the sound of terrified cries and the clash of shorn metal.

Careening from the steps, earth flying by under his reckless boots, heart hammering, fear battered Rhys like black wings, fear for Ellylyw and her women down in the vault.

Rhys raced past the prone Callas, glimpsing no pooled blood, just a dent on the back of the motionless figure's helmet. Somewhere in the darkness ahead, a guard screamed, and Rhys plunged into the shadow before the tunnel gate. A blacker shadow swirled ahead, wrenched a long blood-glittering black-steeled sword out from the chest of the gasping Kanin, then rushed soundlessly into the tunnel beyond. Kanin fell across the twitching torso of Lovan.

These were the best of Madoc's former troop, the only ones to cut their way out when the castrum fell. Their swords gleamed shattered on blood-slick ground, Lovan's tattooed and severed arm still clutching his sheared shield.

Breath wrenching in and out of his lungs, Rhys slung his light shield onto his left arm, thrust his slim blade ahead of him. His leather armor felt paper-thin about him. With no idea what he could do against such a foe, Rhys raced on into the torch-lit tunnel, threaded its twisted turns, clattered to a stop in the candle-lit subterranean vault.

A dozen paces ahead, the black-cloaked knight thrust a black gauntlet toward Melora cowering across the chamber. The blonde collapsed, stunned, though struck by nothing Rhys could see. Gwenllian pulled her dagger, backed into the table, her teeth on edge, lifting her blade to strike. The black knight surged smoothly forward, seizing Gwenllian's wrist in one hand and her throat in the other. The woman could make no sound and her hand went limp, dropping the weapon.

Rhys clenched his teeth, threw himself at the cloaked back, sword upraised. The knight sensed him, spun toward him. The glare of his eyes pierced Rhys, and the bard stumbled, tore his gaze away and swung his sword blindly. The black shield swept out, bashing sword and wielder aside to strike the cave wall and crumple at its base.

Rhys blinked at the lights popping before his eyes,

seeing the black knight turn toward Ellylyw. The lady sat in her bed, eyes wide, fur coverings clutched beneath her chin. Rhys tried to force his limbs to move, but they were iron, welded to the floor. His heart screamed but he could make no sound.

The earth rippled silently under him as he watched Ellylyw drop the furs and lift her chin proudly. The black gauntlet touched her hair, ever so gently...

***

And it was suddenly later without Rhys having been aware of any passage of time. The deadly knight was gone. Madoc and Caydwr knelt by Ellylyw who lay still, dead white and shrunken.

Caydwr's voice rumbled, "Her flesh is cold. She's been dead for hours, yet her spirit lingers in the vault."

Madoc grimaced, the scar distorting his expression. "I'll sit with my wife's body..."

***

Then it was later still. Just like that. By fluttering candlelight Gwenllian was applying wet linen to Rhys' forehead. She smiled, seeing him open his eyes. He realized with a start that he was no longer slumped against the base of the wall, but lying on his back on his bedroll. Stars shimmered beyond Gwenllian's candlelit features.

"You've been out for some time," she told him, her voice hoarse. Bruises showed dark on her throat. "Madoc moved us to the armory. Half the roof is gone, but the walls keep out the wolves."

"Madoc is alone with her in the vault?" he croaked.

Gwenllian nodded. "Ellylyw is—"

"Dead. I saw."

The simple words hit him like the fall of Rome, the end of an age. She might as easily have said that dawn had died.

"Who's left?"

She gave him a canteen of sweet well water.

It made him feel more human.

"Callas was unharmed," she told him. "Melora's all right, too. Kanin and Lovan died guarding the tunnel. Madoc and his men got back to find the black knight with Ellylyw. The knight killed the three with Madoc, then swept past him down the tunnel." She tried to blink the faces of the dead men from her sight. "Why do you think the knight didn't kill us?"

Rhys knew why, but it took him a moment to make himself say it. "Wasn't worth the time. He wanted every instant he could get with Ellylyw."

Wind soughed quietly through the ruins.

"I know you're not very experienced," Gwenllian began. "But you must have learned some strange things as a bard. What's happening here?"

Rhys sighed. "Nothing like any legend I ever heard. Our world is coming apart. Maybe all its rules are broken."

"That sounds like something a bard would say."

"I can tell you this much. The black knight loved Ellylyw. Fiercely."

The waiting woman looked at him, askance. "How can you know that?"

"I saw his eyes. He loved her like..." Rhys swallowed. "Like Madoc did."

Gwenllian sat back on her heels, expressionless, regarding him.

Rhys knew she could read the depth of his loss. Bleakness lay on him like frost. He closed his eyes, ashamed of his pointless passion. The waiting woman rose and walked away, little puffs of ash rising with every step.

He had wrapped his hand around so little in this world. And what little he had grasped sifted like ash between his fingers. Ash stung his lungs, lay bitter on his tongue. Rhys rose and followed Gwenllian out through the scorched door into the courtyard.

She was gazing off into the distance. "Don't," she said, before he could speak. "I don't feel that way about you. I've seen your eyes."

He let her move away.

Rubble clattered, deeper in the darkness.

"Draw your dagger," Rhys told her, "and go back inside."

Not wanting his bared blade to catch moonlight, Rhys held his scabbarded sword quiet against his thigh and slipped cautiously from shadow to shadow. A patch of moonlight ahead revealed a burdened figure making its careful way toward the gap in the outer wall. Rhys ducked back, pressed his spine against a pillar.

The figure was Madoc. He was carrying the limp body of Melora.

"Murderer," Rhys whispered, then caught himself. Gwenllian had said that Melora was spared by the black knight, like the two of them. Had she since been bled to death to fill the copper basin? Yet he had never actually seen Madoc compel anyone to bleed for his beloved. Could the chieftain be covering up someone else's crime? But for whom would he sacrifice Melora? For whom would he cover up? Surely for no one but Ellylyw, and she was dead.

Wasn't she?

Pulse suddenly pounding in his temples, Rhys tried to swallow, but his mouth was too dry. His throat felt scorched. Clutching the cool stone to hold himself back, Rhys watched the bowed chieftain make his way out through the shattered wall and forced himself to consider.

To confront the war leader would mean certain and useless death. Rhys headed instead toward the tunnel. Steel glinted ahead: Callas, the last guard. Drawing a deep breath, Rhys stepped out into the moonlight and strode with what he suspected was insane determination toward the tunnel.

Callas stepped from the shadow that masked its mouth, shield on arm, sword in hand, warning quietly, "Turn around, bardling."

"I'm going into the vault."

"You're not." Callas's voice shook and spittle flew. His old arrogance was gone. In its place was something verging on panic.

"What's Madoc hiding?" Rhys demanded.

The battered veteran's eyes opened wider than Rhys would have thought possible. Those glistening orbs convinced Rhys that Callas had seen something...something down in that vault...something that had shaken the old campaigner.

Abuse streamed from the mouth of the wide-eyed soldier, his rough voice cracking, his scarred face shaking with the force of his verbal assault until he ran out of breath.

Rhys seized the moment, shouting, "In the name of the Consularis—"

Callas thrust his sword toward the bard. "By Christ, I'll carve the Goth half of you from the Briton..."

Rhys leapt backward, tugging out his blade.

Callas charged, sweeping two-handed slantwise at Rhys' neck.

Without a shield and afraid to risk his blade in a parry, Rhys dodged, weaved and feigned, annoying the frenetic attacker into wilder and wilder jabs and slashes.

This viciously swinging professional was far more skillful than Rhys, so the bard knew there could be no question of disarming Callas or hurting him just enough to make him quit. Last soldier in this crippled fortress though Callas was, Rhys knew he had to kill the man or be killed by him.

Again, Rhys jumped back. He crouched to one side, ducking into shadow.

Callas swore, furious that he had to keep whirling his heavy blade and could not immediately cut down so weak a foe.

From the darkness, Rhys flung ash and pebbles into Callas's face, then sprang to the man's left, swinging sideways, two-handed, for all he was worth. Rage and ash distracted the veteran fighter just enough for him to misjudge where to position his shield, and Rhys altered his blade's trajectory, managing to cut low behind the shield where his sword-point sheered through steel rings.

The ringmail saved Callas's life, but he bellowed as broken circlets drove into his flesh. Callas spun to face his attacker's new position.

Rhys risked everything, rolling forward under his enemy's shield, thrusting his blade up under the ringmail skirt, punching its point through the man's soft underbelly.

Shrieking horribly, Callas flailed blindly downward at the supine man. Unable to get clear, Rhys swung out his gauntleted left hand. Callas's blow was wild; Rhys was able to slap the flat of the blade aside from his head. Even so, the sharp edge sliced through Rhys' gauntlet, stinging the back of his hand, the sword-point simultaneously clipping a thick chunk of leather from Rhys' shoulder. The impact jolted and pained Rhys, but drew no blood.

Callas pulled himself backward off Rhys' blade, his shield hand clutching uselessly at the spewing gash. He fell to his knees, crying, "You cheated."

Rhys got to his feet. "You have twenty years of battlefield experience on me, size, weight, better armor and a shield. I had a handful of ash."

The bard circled behind the big soldier.

"I'm the better man," the agonized veteran spluttered, flailing his sword ineffectually behind him.

"So you've always said. And yet..." Rhys could not leave Callas to die slowly in agony. The bard forced in a deep breath, swung two-handed down, severing Callas's neck bones. The veteran dropped, knocked out of his senses, life's blood spurting quickly into scorched rubble, dead in moments.

A waste.

There was no telling how long Madoc would be gone. Rhys hated to lose time, but could not know how soon he might have to fight again. Loathing the grisly business, he stripped the body of its ringmail, used the dead man's cloak to rub off the worst of the blood, then pulled off his own crude gear. A few moments later, still fastening the last straps of his upgraded armor, Rhys dashed into the narrow tunnel, scraping rings against the rough walls of the passage in his rush, bursting at last into the candle-lit vault.

One wall of the chamber had been reinforced by the Romans. Iron shackles hung from crossed beams so that prisoners might be stored there with the rest of the castrum's supplies. Suspended by the wrists from those shackles hung Ellylyw.

She raised her head and met his eyes. He felt like someone punched him in the chest. Forcing himself to inhale again, Rhys stepped slowly forward. "Lady?"

"Bard," she said softly.

He plucked a thought from the maelstrom in his mind. "Your disease...it's some new plague...it left you entranced, clinging to life so faint we couldn't see it."

"What is life?" she asked. Her voice was different. Delicate, yet vibrant with restrained energy. "I left this body. I looked down and watched Caydwr try to revive me. I saw Callas drag you out with the dead soldiers. I watched Madoc wrap my empty limbs with his and try to bring me back with the warmth of his own body. I didn't know Madoc could weep. Years ago, he watched his three brothers die in one battle and never shed a tear. He turned to iron and slew Saxons for three months without relent before he returned to Castrum Tenebrarum. For me he wept and wept. And I floated up there and watched. I tried to get away, but something pulled me back into cold flesh, and I opened my eyes and called Madoc's name. I think something broke in him. His heart, perhaps, or his mind."

Rhys shook his head, struggling to absorb this. "He...he bled Melora for you, didn't he."

He looked at the chains, at the little spatters of dried blood on her white gown. He forced himself to swallow hard, surprised to find how achingly grieved he was at seeing her in Madoc's chains. "Oh, Ellylyw, look what he's done to you."

"Nothing is the same, Rhys." She smiled a little sadly.

He realized how much she had regained of the re-energized look he had seen in her after she had drunk from the copper basin and lain with her husband. Yet how different she was, now. Her pallor was more pronounced than ever, yet her lips were ruddy and pliant, rather than dry. There was a curious gleam in her unblinking eyes. Candlelight seemed drawn into them to pool there.

Rhys tore his eyes from hers and leaned close to examine the locking mechanism of the shackles. "I don't know how to release these..." He wheezed.

"Still bound." She sighed.

So close to her that the hackles rose on the back of his neck, Rhys realized that even her scent was different. There was something lacking, some vital quality Rhys could not identify, but its loss was somehow alarming. He suddenly remembered a dream in which his horse had gamboled up to him, frisky and playful like a colt. Rhys had stroked the mount's broad back and felt the ends of the severed spine rubbing together under the skin. The horse was fatally crippled, yet trotted away as if it could live like that.

Rhys swallowed again and laid a hand on Ellylyw's shoulder to reassure her...and to banish the dream from his mind. Though he could feel only the inside of his glove, touching her struck him a deeper pang. The dream of the crippled horse stayed with him. He could feel, though he knew not how, that something indefinable was terribly wrong.

No matter. He must do all he could for her.

She turned toward him and smiled.

Seeing her face so close to his own was another shock. The delicate features, the prominent cheekbones, the stark contrast of raven-black hair and smooth white skin...they tangled every tendril of emotion snaking up from the bard's writhing depths.

"You cannot help me," Ellylyw told him, as if confiding some personal secret.

"I'll find a way to free you," he promised her, trying to keep her beauty from turning his thoughts toward sensual satisfactions that could never be.

"He'll come back," she warned, with no sign of fear. "He'll shatter you."

"Madoc's on his way to the woods. It'll take time for him to hide Melora's body. Have you seen where he keeps the keys?"

"Oh yes." She nodded toward a small crater in the uneven stone floor beside a heavy iron mace. In the base of the crater glinted fragments of a smashed, twisted key.

Rhys looked at Ellylyw. "My God, he never means to let you go."

"Never," she said, mildly amused.

Rhys fought dizziness aroused by the mounting strangeness of the encounter. He rubbed sweat from his brow with the back of his left hand. The slash through his skin stung from the salt, and he felt the smear of blood it left on his face.

"You were hurt for me." Ellylyw spoke solicitously, as if to a child.

Self-conscious, Rhys plucked his kerchief from around his neck and rubbed the blood from his face.

"Please. Let me reward you."

Rhys stepped toward her, as in a dream. Suddenly remembering that this was Madoc's wife, a woman not well, and terribly vulnerable, trapped in this terrible place, he stopped himself a few paces away from her. Rhys concentrated on calming his labored, wheezing breath and normalizing his heartrate, but his head was light, and the world seemed to be tilted off kilter, everything in danger of sliding off to the right.

Ellylyw looked at him as if he had done something tender and dear. "Let me see your poor hand."

Rhys knit his brows, tugged the slit gauntlet from his hand, ignoring the sting. After tucking the glove behind his belt, he held up his hurt hand and shrugged, embarrassed.

"Please," Ellylyw purred, eyes shining, a curious smile playing about her lips. "You have shed blood for me. Callas is in the sky, barely tethered to his cooling clay. In a few days he will pass elsewhere. But he took some blood from you."

"You see it's nothing."

It was still bleeding, but not enough to waste time bandaging until the lady could be brought somehow to whatever might pass for safety in these mad times.

"It's precious," she said. "Come closer."

Rhys wheezed in a breath, stepped closer, lifting the

injured hand close to her eyes, feeling himself blush, intensifying his embarrassment. Ellylyw tilted her raven-tressed head to one side, then the other. Fascinated by her every movement, Rhys thought of a weaving adder he had once watched, facing off against a broken-winged hawk. Realizing the air in his lungs had gone stale, he finally exhaled.

Ellylyw leaned her head forward and kissed the wound. He was startled, aroused, distressed that he had allowed this, afraid he would allow more, delighted that she felt even this much for him, desperate for some expression of deeper affection, all in one bewildering rush.

She let her amazingly soft lips linger. The very tip of her tongue touched the sliced skin so very, very slightly. Fresh blood beaded. Her lips compressed, drew gently at the wound. The stone floor beneath Rhys' feet rippled as reality thinned around him and bubbles of some other world rose through this.

Rhys shook his head slightly as if to negate the experience, or withdraw his consent, or ask her to stop, but she drew gently at the wound, and some energy from outside himself surged up from the base of his spine and out through the top of his skull. Her eyes were fastened on his, and he did not withdraw his hand.

Rhys felt something tie him to this woman more irrevocably than any marriage, and yet he felt the bond had always been there, foreordained, recognized but unadmitted until now. Who was Madoc to stand between them? His host who had broken bread with him in time of famine. A commander vital to Britain's crumbling defense. A man trapped in tragedy. A prison warder. A madman. A torturer

Jeffrey T. Heyer

of women...

Ellylyw's hands strained toward Rhys. She moaned
faintly as the shackles pressed her soft flesh, stopping her
hands just shy of Rhys' face. His citadel of logic was
crumbling. Her slim arms writhed against the restraint. He
clung to the knowledge that he had to get her free before
Madoc returned. Beneath her long white skirts, her legs
rubbed against each other as if longing to wrap around his.
To tarry here was death.

Yet somehow that danger made the moment sweeter,
knowing that he could not only share love with this
exquisite woman, but immolate himself like a moth
marrying a flame.

The mocking voice of Callas came to him, shockingly
loud and rough in his head: *"She's too much for you,
boy...she'd burn you out. Better stick to ugly women who
want to forget for a night."*

The words jolted him, and he gently disengaged his
hand to take a step back. The air seemed to go out of the
room at even that small degree of separation. Her image
swam. Ellylyw looked so far away, though he knew she
was within his grasp.

"Ahhh..." She sighed, chiding gently, "where have
you gone?"

Her lithe movements were far too comfortable. Did
nothing about this ghastly imprisonment disturb her?

"Please..." he began, then forgot what he had meant to
ask.

"You will never leave this vault," she told him, her
grin taut, taunting, possessive, as if he were now a known
quantity, all mystery drawn out of him, reducing him to a

minor retainer at the back of her hall. "You and I will always be here, now."

His fading wits again sharpened by the sting of seeming diminution, Rhys tore his eyes from her sensual splendor to look about the candlelit space. Spotting a heap of tools, he hurried to pick through them.

Ellylyw called after him, "Melora was right about you."

That brought his eyes back to her.

"Melora said you would never complete your mission. Brathach will have to send a better man."

"Why tell me this?" Rhys asked, doing his best to hide from her that she had just struck him a more telling blow than Callas could manage while fighting for his life. Rhys turned back to the tools, plucking out old torturer's weapons and mason's hardware, giving them a look and then tossing them aside.

Ellylyw shook ebony tresses back behind her shoulders, then let her head sag forward and stared at him over her brows. "You killed Callas when he was weak. Melora always said there's not much in you. The world is falling apart, and you're what's left."

A sudden mad fury seized Rhys as if she had pricked an old wound. "Where is Melora now?" he demanded. "Where are you, for that matter, Lady Ellylyw? Where is your powerful chieftain Madoc? *I'm still here.* And how was Callas weakened? He seemed spry enough 'til I took him down."

Ellylyw grinned, raising her chin as high as it could go. She shook her dangling tresses behind her. Her breasts pressed against the tight fabric of her bodice, her delicate fingers rippled the air as she twisted her wrists in the shackles. "Callas had his qualities." She laughed quietly.

"This place is driving you mad," Rhys said in horror, tossing metal implements right and left, searching for anything useful. "You don't love me. That doesn't matter. I am going to get you out of here."

He found two pry bars, swung them hard against the stone floor to test their strength. They rang jarringly in the stone chamber.

"What good are you alone?" Ellylyw asked in an insinuating voice unlike any he had heard from so seemingly gentle a woman. "Don't you want to just surrender? Become part of something? Get off the road and settle in some minor court, singing songs for bored underlings in backwater Britain, far from the Saxon threat? Settle for some unremarkable woman and turn a blind eye to her wandering ways?"

Rhys was trying hard not to listen. He walked up to her, stumbling a bit because the world still felt skewed to one side. He hefted a heavy iron lever in each hand. Her eyes were wide, her grin tight. He was certain she was now as mad as Madoc.

"Do you want to hurt me, Rhys?" she whispered. "To even the score with all womankind for breeding with the bigger, stronger, more aggressive males?"

"Stop sticking pins in me, and let me concentrate."

He got the tip of one lever through the ring on the back of a wrist-iron, and the other through the first link of the short chain; its other end was fastened to the beam. Setting himself carefully, Rhys pressed the levers in opposite directions, teeth gritted, breath laboring, until spots popped in his vision.

"You're not the hero." Ellylyw taunted him. "You know that." Her tone softened abruptly. "Oh, Rhys, you have songs inside you no one else can sing. I wish I could help you bring them out."

He pressed on, forehead dripping, stinging his eyes, harsh taste of ash and salt on his lips. His arms shaking with the strain, he felt as if he had been there for hours. Finally, he relaxed, pulling free the levers and sagging down on the floor, panting and puffing, lungs aching.

Rhys let his head loll back as he leaned against a boulder. He shook his arms to keep them from stiffening, then let every muscle in his body go limp in order to concentrate as much rest as possible into as little time as he could.

"If you loose me," the lady said, her voice again soft and kind. "What could I ever do to repay you?"

"Live." Rhys gasped. "For a start."

He rose, fumbled the levers into their places and strained again, groaning and panting. Arms shaking, he imagined these chains were everything that had ever held him back, every blind prejudice of the folk around him, every weakness in his body and his mind, every humiliation that had ever slapped him in the face, every injury, every foe he had ever faced. Still the iron held, still he wrenched and pressed, powered now by all his fear of what might befall. When that dried, too, Rhys pressed on with all the insane optimism that welled in him whenever his depressions faded, and that kept him singing, fighting, wandering, long after the rejections he had faced swelled beyond his ability to count.

His whole body ached now, and he felt the strength burning out of his core. Afraid that if he stopped to rest again he would collapse, he bent down, his body pressed against her white-clad side, hanging and hauling on the bars with all the impossible love that had never found expression, moaning loudly, racked with shakes in every limb, drenched with sweat.

One of the links gave a little and the lever slipped from it, striking Ellylyw with terrible force at the base of the neck. Rhys tumbled to the floor, the other lever flying from his cramped hand to pinwheel and strike the far wall. Echoes rang through the vault.

"Oh God." The bard half sobbed.

Ellylyw slumped, hanging limp from her trapped wrists, glazed eyes half closed.

Spent, Rhys wrapped his boneless arms about her ankles and lay on the floor gasping like a fish.

Everything he had ever done had been but to bring him to this, the darkest moment in a dark age.

One little slip...

His personality collapsed like the fortress above. He lay like rubble, detritus about her feet, a low, huddled monument to futility. Swirling consciousness dissolved, and his exhausted essence sank to the lowest ebb at the very border of the land of the living. Lying at the bottom of the world, there was nothing left to do but die or let some other force move through his emptied being.

Broken, his unconscious soul chose the latter.

Chapter 4:

Ellylyw Risen

Rhys opened his eyes. He was alive and staring at the foot of Ellylyw's gown pooled on the rough floor beside him. What traitor part of him had chosen to revive? He managed to pull his feet under him. He felt like an old man beaten with a stick. Slowly, he stretched his aching muscles back into alignment within the unaccustomed weight of ringmail. He rubbed dry salt off his face, erasing evaporated tear-tracks, then forced himself to look on Ellylyw.

He saw a dark purple bruise across her collarbone.

Ellylyw raised her head, opened those piercing eyes, and looked into his soul.

His heart missed a beat.

He croaked inarticulately, threw his arms around her, pulled her to her feet, and squeezed the breath out of her while kissing the side of her neck, again and again, his face buried in her flowing hair. Her sleek skin tasted strangely bitter on his tongue.

Arms still locked around her, Rhys lifted his face to gaze in wonder into her eyes. "You are alive. Alive."

He flung off his remaining gauntlet, cupped her miracle of a face in his hands to run his thumbs over her cheekbones, feeling her flesh against his and assuring himself Ellylyw was alive. The more he drank in the sight and scent of her, the more he ran his hands down over the sleek waterfall of samite pouring down from her shoulders, the sweetly pliant flesh beneath the thin material as cold as the iron that bound her, the less Rhys could believe she was really there. How could this small and fragile body have survived that crushing blow...that blow from the pry bar in his hands.

He heard himself confide in a passionate voice he could scarcely believe was his own. "I wanted so much to be the one to free you."

Neither he nor Ellylyw had seemed to be themselves since he had fought his way into the vault. She gazed into his eyes. "I so wanted to be alive for you."

As his hand came to rest on her collarbone, Ellylyw turned her breathtaking face to kiss the wound on his hand with those cool lips. Her eyes closed as if she gave herself entirely to the kiss. His wounded hand and his cramped and exhausted arm tingled strangely, and he found he was losing all ability to think of her as Madoc's wife.

Madoc. The selfish aristocrat, the madman responsible for the fall of Castrum Tenebrarum. The Saxons had been seriously weakened by their losses in battle. They needed time to tend to their wounded and collect their strength. Then, with no fortress to protect the road, the barbarians would pour into the interior, fill their arms with loot, and return to their beach-head ten times stronger, leaving Britain ten times weaker, all so Madoc could cling a little longer to a woman who was never truly his.

"Give yourself," Ellylyw whispered.

Rhys' tongue stuck to the roof of his mouth. The rest

of his body knew what she wanted and pressed tight against her responding pressure. He felt as if the iron links he had tried to break had instead bound him to Ellylyw.

"I can give nothing," she breathed, "do nothing. At least let me see you feel."

Rhys cast off the last shreds of impeding intellect, blinding himself to the madness of the situation in a volcanic rush of love and compassion. Face burning hot with blood, he seized her cheeks, pulled her mouth against his, kissing, laving with his tongue to explore the thrilling texture of her lips, sucking them, overwhelmed by passion and sensation. His hands slid over the thin, silky gown, marveling at every firm curve beneath, trembling at the pure sensuous shock of her.

"Damn you." Madoc's quiet voice came from behind him.

As he turned, light as from an afterimage burst in Rhys' inner eye. The bard felt the unbreakable iron links that had chained him to Ellylyw now thin to soap bubble ephemerality and pop, leaving him adrift. Ellylyw gave a little cry of loss, but whether she mourned for him, for Madoc, or for herself, Rhys could not tell.

The broad-shouldered chieftain stood in the mouth of the forest tunnel, every line in his worn face etched as if by a dagger, his hair and beard disordered, his wide eyes a little wild, dirt on his knees, his cloak, his gloves. His sword-hand twitched twice. Madoc's voice was desolate. "There's no solution but death, is there."

Stalling desperately, Rhys demanded, "What have you done with Melora's body?"

The subject did not interest Madoc. He stared past

Rhys. "Oh, Lady..."

"You killed Melora," Rhys pressed, though slightly less certain.

Madoc's eyes narrowed at what he saw, then sharpened. He swung his shield from behind his back and unsheathed his sword with smooth and practiced ease. Strolling unhurriedly, he angled his approach to back the bard from before the lady. "I will not have it." His voice was toneless, dry.

Aching from his long struggle to break Ellylyw's chains, Rhys knew he could not defeat this master man-killer, so he did not draw. His wits shrieked at him, *It's death! Save yourself!* But he watched, numb, unable to believe the tenuous, bitter-sweet moment with Ellylyw was already stripped from him. Like his short life, it seemed his death would be abrupt. Pointless.

"Death it is, then," Madoc said without passion. He stood now, in front of his wife, setting his back to her as he faced Rhys, feet apart, relaxed, ready. Behind him, the lady's eyes, closed on her own inner pain, opened, then fastened on her husband's powerful back.

"What have you done to Ellylyw?" Rhys demanded, his voice shaking a bit as he prepared himself to spring at Madoc's first movement.

"Apparently nothing," the chieftain replied, eyes hollow. Madoc stood, sword poised before him. He had chosen his ground and meant for Rhys to initiate the fatal combat.

Rhys felt like doing just that, but hesitated. "Will you just hold her down here while the Saxons and the Consularis and all the world flow over you?"

Dark Age

Madoc seemed to consider the idea, then: "What would be the point?" He swept his sword above his head into guard position, parallel with his shoulders. Rhys leapt forward, hands raised, knowing his only hope was to do what Caydwr had done to Lovan; get inside the killing stroke before it could descend.

Ellylyw threw herself against her chains. The warped link snapped. Her freed hand closed on her husband's right shoulder and yanked him back.

Madoc pivoted toward her as Rhys hurtled into him, the chieftain simultaneously sweeping back his left arm, slamming his shield hard into the bard's face.

Cushioning the blow a little with his raised arms, Rhys toppled backward and hit the floor. Not yet healed from the black knight's blow, Rhys lost all feeling, forced to watch from what seemed the back of a tunnel as Ellylyw's freed hand struck Madoc's sword-hand with such energy that to Rhys' numb amazement, the slim, sickly woman knocked the weapon from her husband's grip.

Madoc never paused, sweeping his shield up and sideways, ramming the iron rim against his wife's temple in a brutal, deadly blow, knocking her to the side so that only the remaining shackle kept her upright. Spinning to build momentum, Madoc struck the rim against her other temple, snapping her limp body back against the crossed beams, audibly cracking her skull. Reversing, Madoc spun and struck her full force a third time.

Rhys watched, as from the depths of hell, what he thought must have been the death of Ellylyw.

She slumped, hung by her left wrist from the one unbroken chain, the mussed hair at either temple matted and shiny with blood. Madoc stared breathlessly down at her. Impossibly, her lips trembled.

Abruptly possessed by a cold fury, the chieftain flung aside his shield, seized Ellylyw's long hair and hauled her upright. "Get out! Get out of my wife's body, devil," he cried hoarsely.

Ellylyw gave a cry of pain and dismay, and pity welled up in Madoc with such force it washed away the madman's ability to think her possessed.

With a strangled cry, Madoc pulled his wife into his arms, cradling her, treasuring her. She sagged, limp, able only to look piteously into his eyes, tears welling in her own. The fierce chieftain groaned, sank to his knees, embracing her legs. She sagged over his shoulder, black tresses hiding her face. Madoc moaned wordless, soul-wracked worship.

Rhys could feel his limbs about him again, his wits coming back into focus, and watched for his chance to re-enter the fray and swing the balance of fate in some new direction.

Madoc rose, his wife draped over his shoulder. Reaching under the collar of his tunic, he caught a chain hanging from his neck and pulled out a ring with four bulky keys. Selecting the smallest, he fiddled it about in the manacle's lock. Though he had destroyed the proper key, this one was close enough for the crude mechanism, and the shackle released his wife's wrist.

Carrying her to her make-shift bed of now dry but still fragrant brush, he lowered her onto the furs and moaned. "It's really you, at last, Ellylyw, lady love."

She bit her lip and rolled onto her side. He lay beside

Dutch

her, pressed against her back, wrapping his mail-clad limbs about her delicate form, then dabbing his kerchief at her bloody temple.

Rhys surreptitiously gathered himself to spring.

Madoc kissed the side of her face again and again. Ellylyw turned to face him, put her hands on his shoulders and pressed him back against the bedding. She sat astride him, smiling down with a pale ghost of Ellylyw's old warmth.

"You know how I feel," she said in a lover's voice. Her lips drew back. She lunged down at him, fastened her teeth in his throat, shook her head from side to side like a wolf, tearing open the wound.

Madoc bucked and gurgled, locked his hands about her thin sides and heaved, but she clung to him. Against the wall, Rhys got his hands and knees under him, aghast. Madoc rolled over the clinging woman and onto the floor, struggled upright, his wife's legs still clamped about his waist, her ankles crossed tight behind his back. The powerful chieftain stumbled about the vault, tugging at her, his blood draining in deep gulps down her throat.

He pounded mailed fists hard against her back ribs, but she would not let go. Sinking to his knees, he seized great handfuls of raven hair and yanked back, at last pulling her mouth from his throat. Bright blood pumped from the torn flesh.

She unlocked her ankles, set her feet against the floor and shoved hard, knocking him backward off his knees, slamming his head against the floor. Seizing Madoc's hair in turn, Ellylyw cracked his head hard against the stone. Her husband lost his grip on her tresses. She lunged down

Jeffrey T. Heyer

again, sinking her teeth once more into his throat, uttering little sounds of gleeful satisfaction as she battened on his blood.

Rhys stood, drawing his sword. The sound of blade sliding from sheath pricked up Ellylyw's ears. Madoc sighed out his last breath, limbs lolling limp. The lady looked up, her wide eyes catching Rhys, turning his blood to ice. Then she went back to supping the last of Madoc's ebbing life-force.

Rhys felt the world whirling. He had to do something, couldn't stand here, should kill her, strike off her head with his sword, stop her ghastly feeding. It couldn't be her, couldn't be the woman he had held in his arms a moment before, so passionate, so responsive...so cold, so staring, so unlike the Ellylyw he had known, so changeable and inexplicable and ineradicably hostile.

"What's happened to you?" a forlorn voice cried. With a shock Rhys realized it was his own.

Ellylyw lapped at the wound, raised her delicate, gore-wet face, candlelight spilling from her gleaming orbs as from a yellow-eyed wolf. "I slept. I woke. This is some new sleep." She rose from Madoc's husk, spread her arms, and spoke through bloody lips. "This is what I am, Rhys of Caer Waroc. This is what you love. You can never have any other woman...only me, if I so choose."

Rhys doubted it would do much good, but he picked up Madoc's shield.

Ellylyw tilted her head slightly, a quizzical smile playing about her scarlet lips. She licked more crimson from sharp teeth. "I have already tasted you. You are bound to me, like Madoc and the others."

"Others?" he croaked out. His flesh and bones suddenly felt paper-thin.

Ellylyw smiled, her face bright with the promise of a future only she could see. "Oh yes. Everything Madoc hid in the shadows, I will bring forth. There are shadows in you, too, young Rhys. I want them...out where all can see. The Pagan power is crippled. The Christian sun is too bright, and it breeds shadows wherever it burns. You will help me see that every truth they bury comes back to bite them."

"You are not Ellylyw."

"Part of her. He awakened me."

"The black knight?"

Her lips compressed in a little smile of secret knowledge. "I will waken Madoc. Soon he will be freed of what was, as I am, and locked from what might have been, as you will be."

"What do you want of me?" Rhys could not help but ask.

"You see?" She turned to the side, one sculpted leg, as pale as her silks, showing through a torn seam. "You wish to be mine, already. I need you to sing songs of darkness in which I can live and to help me to avenge all that has been marred. I am a shadow cast by clerics. My secret lover gave me form. Madoc built me a monument to desolation in which to dwell. But I needed you to unleash me on the world. I cannot expect the day-folk forever to bring their bright offerings to this lonely place. There will be no more basins of blood. I need you to whisper in a thousand ears for me. Warn them I am coming. Let them know my wrath shall be implacable, my revenge sweet as sex."

Rhys clung to a bard's best weapon, words. "I've seen loss do strange and terrible things to people—"

"If you could see your own reflection," she broke in, "you would see a fortress thrown down more terribly than Tenebrarum."

"Whatever you have lost, somewhere in you is everything I loved."

She laughed and posed her leg in the torn skirt, balancing it on graceful toe tip. She plucked at her long, hanging sleeves and spread them like moth wings at her sides. Lifting her chin proudly, jutting her breasts, swiveling to show him the narrowness of her waist, she replied, "This is what you worship, blood and all. The light was the mask you preferred. This is reality uncovered."

Fearing her tongue could hurt him worse than could her teeth, he shook his head. "If you want me to say that I love you truly, deeply, passionately, hopelessly, I say it now. If you want me to recognize that knowing you were Madoc's wife and wanting desperately to do the right thing, and respecting him as a powerful chieftain made no difference to my heart, I'll say that, too. I love your beauty, yes, of course. And if you want me to admit that...even seeing you like this, with his blood on your face and those sharp wolf's teeth showing between your lips...that I love the hardness in you, the animal, the thirst, the fury and the pride as much as I loved the gentle kindness...I'll even give you that. You want to revel in your strength. I understand. I'll tell you plainly what you can already see: you have the power to tempt me with everything I fear and reject, as well as everything I long for. But I loved the warm woman who smiled at me. That part was as real as this."

She dropped her pose and swayed toward him, compassion gentle on her pale face. "Poor boy. There is only one way to understand. The hermit was right. You must experience everything."

And maybe that was it. Maybe that was why he had to come to this damned place. Maybe this was the one form of desolation he had not yet experienced, the one degree of loss of self to which he had not yet succumbed. Perhaps if he allowed himself this, like a man fallen into the sea, he could at last touch bottom and push again toward light and air.

"I'm ready to turn my back on all my world," he told her. "But not to go with you. If the light's so bright it burns, still I won't trade it for the dark. One swing of the pendulum is no better than the other."

She pressed her cool flesh against his scarred armor, one slim hand brushing sylph-light up his ringmailed chest to caress the side of his tense face. "Be the one man," she coaxed, "to stay with me of his own will. Not even my dark love can claim that."

Her eyes were huge and he could think of no place but in them that he would rather lose whatever remained of himself. Sadly, he stepped back, raised Madoc's shield, hiding her face from his eyes with its wood and iron.

Springing, hissing, wrenching and flinging the shield from his grasp, she raked claws down his face. Shocked, he looked at her half-hooded eyes, her open mouth, sharp fangs exposed, her tongue moving moistly to utter another inhuman yowl and hiss. The pain in his face was intense and helped him focus his depleted forces.

He allowed himself to buckle at the knees and twist

down toward the floor. As she savored her instant of triumph, Rhys spun, driving his sword into her slim abdomen, throwing all his weight forward, roaring in outrage that he should have to do this hateful thing, forcing her back and back across the room until she lost her footing and fell onto her bed. Brush flying from beneath the covers, he leapt after, planting a foot on either side of her hips and, both hands on the hilts, ramming the blade down and out through her back, to drive through the heaped brush and nail her to the wooden frame beneath the bed.

Ellylyw wailed and curled around the blade, clutching its sharp edges 'til her palms and fingers bled. Tears of pain slid down her cheeks. "I'll love you forever." She wept. "You'll never get away."

Rhys kept his weight on the weapon. "Tell me what I want to know, and I'll release you."

"Please, please..." She turned reproachful eyes on him, tugging at his already over-burdened heart.

He forced himself to demand harshly, "Where is this dark love you spoke of...the one who made you like this?"

She stretched one hand up toward him, the fingers splaying back from the cut palm like a little girl's. "Do it for me. Ride to the Way Amorous...cross to the Dolorous Mount...be each other's fates and help me find mine. If you loved the dark girl *and* the light...no more can I wed one man and not the other. I beg you, release me."

Rhys sprang back from the bed, leaving the weapon jammed in the boards beneath. He dashed to Madoc's sword, snatched it from the floor, and plucked up the fallen chieftain's shield.

Ellylyw wrapped hurt fingers again around the blade

that pinned her and heaved.

Rhys drew his dagger, used it to cut through the thin chain about the dead commander's neck.

Ellylyw screamed as she forced the sword-point up from the imprisoning boards and sat up in bed, her torso convulsing around the transfixing steel while oozing precious blood.

Rhys yanked the keys from the broken chain and ran for the escape tunnel, meaning to lock the gate at its far end behind him. He ducked low, ran into the tunnel, narrow rock walls flashing by. He heard another feminine shriek of pain and rage, then the clatter of a tossed sword striking the floor where he had stood moments before. The tunnel lengthening behind him, he heard Ellylyw's voice cry, "How could you?"

Chapter 5:

The Dolorous Mount

R hys reined in his steed just shy of the forest's edge. From under the arching boughs stepped the shaggy hermit heading toward the ruined fortress.

"There's no one left." Rhys gasped. "We'll find our enemy at the Dolorous Mount."

Wild-maned Caydwr tugged his black beard, surprised. "No one goes there. The abbot has forbidden it on pain of burning."

"Where better for the black knight to hide?"

The hermit shrugged, clapped his broad hand into Rhys', and pulled himself up onto the war-horse's sturdy back to settle behind the bard.

Old Morvran clopped ponderously along the narrow forest path as Rhys told his companion all that had transpired.

"Mm," Caydwr rumbled. "What can a bard in captured ringmail do against this black knight? He cut his way through Madoc's men and fought free of the great chieftain himself."

"I will find a way."

The hermit flicked wild hair from his face and regarded the young bard. "The Dolorous Mount is in my forest, but I do not know the way."

"The route is called the Way Amorous."

"Ah. The old Goddess had a shrine there." The hermit ran the thick knuckles of one hand through his waving mane. "Youths and maidens met within a ring of stones for a mass marriage and bedding. The ancients thought so much good energy released at once made the crops grow better and the animals breed quicker."

"Did it?"

Caydwr shrugged. "The priestesses are long gone from that place. At least, the abbot knows of none, or he would burn them. Some say the wells dried up when the wise women left the Way Amorous. Others say the Lady of the Waters is still there, part and parcel of the place...the underground stream just went deeper."

"If Morvran goes much farther with the two of us..." Rhys patted his stolid mount's neck, "he'll have no strength for the charge."

"I have been thinking. There is a strange black horse that grazes by day in these parts. He shies from me."

"Not even the wolves do that."

"His neigh is distinctive, high and furious. I have heard the same cry near Castrum Tenebrarum at night."

"You think it is the black knight's horse?"

"He'll know the way to his master's hold."

"Guide me to his pasture."

***

The huge black horse plucked delicately at succulent green blades, ears swiveling warily. The hermit had inched as close as he dared. Gently, Caydwr tossed a treasure halfway between himself and the cautious beast: a little green apple. The steed started at the movement, but so rare a treat could not be resisted. The war-horse warned the man with a snort, then plodded to the apple while Caydwr backstepped before him. After quickly crunching down the savory delight, the stallion looked about for more. Caydwr stepped closer to the tree in whose branches Rhys crouched, his shield and cloak removed and his sword strapped across his back. The hermit tossed another of his precious stores, payment from an arborer whom Caydwr had healed.

Apple by apple, the canny woodman drew the skittish steed toward the small pile of fruit beneath the boughs. When at last the black beast reached the prize, Rhys eased his position just enough to let blood back into his cramped feet. Not wanting to cheat the beast, Rhys let him feast until the pile was exhausted. Then Rhys sprang onto the black back, clutched his knees against the broad sides, and wrapped his arms around the powerful neck.

Rearing and screaming, the war-horse lashed the air with iron-shod hooves, then bucked and leapt and sprang about the grassy dell. Rhys clung to him for dear life.

Caydwr hid behind a tree and watched.

Furious, but unable to dislodge the stranger, the stallion raced into the woods, crashing through brush and ducking low-hanging limbs, snorting and squealing and neighing his outrage.

Rhys clung, breathless, praying to Epona the old Goddess of Horses to let him keep his grip. The poverty that had prevented him from buying a saddle until long after he had acquired and tamed his abandoned, half-wild war-horse stood him in good stead. Jostled, banged and heaved one way and another, Rhys kept his grip, and the horse could not dislodge him.

Determined to rid himself of the hated rider, the black knight's mount raced for home, making the journey as rough a ride as his equine wits could manage. Bright-lit foliage slapped Rhys' face. The huge muscles under him bunched as the beast sprang over a ditch and smacked through waving leaves before breaking out of the forest and galloping toward a rushing river. Bouncing between hoof-beats, Rhys caught glimpses through flying mane of a half-finished bridge ahead and something bulky beyond.

The river neared, and Rhys realized the horse had veered from its well-trodden path toward the partial bridge and was now racing straight for the river itself. The current was swift and apt to prove deadly to a man weighed down by ringmail. Rhys gathered his breath as best he could on the jolting way, then flung himself from the horse's back, now crashing and rolling on the brushy bank and sending dirt flying.

The stallion splashed into the water, slowing as he felt the rider gone, then, too deep, his hooves lost footing. The rushing current spun the black mount halfway about while sweeping him downstream. The war-horse neighed high and wild and vengeful, thrashed the cold water with killing strokes, but he could not harm his hated and now distant foe. A force he could not resist whirled him away around a curve and beyond Rhys' sight. A pity. He had no wish for it to drown.

Winded, he puffed and shook dirt from his hair as he rose. Brushing himself off, he scrambled up the steep bank to the bridge. This end of the structure was stout enough for a rider. Rhys clambered onto the weathered boards and started across.

A bouldered mound loomed out of the river at the far end of the bridge, no doubt the Dolorous Mount he sought, but the bridge had never been completed. Perhaps the Romans had left the Isle of Britain before they had finished modernizing the ancient Way Amorous. Midway, the planking and railing ended. Only a bare framework extended beyond to reach the little island.

The framework was no easy climb. Rhys doubted he could make it in heavy armor like Madoc's, or the black knight's. The bard's struggles the night before weighed upon him now, making him ten times heavier than usual, but he stretched his arms from beam to beam and hauled himself over the raging river until he set booted heels on solid ground again.

Sides heaving, Rhys brushed sweat from his brow with one gauntleted hand and looked about. But for a narrow path leading up from the base of the unfinished bridge, the island's lower slopes were impassably overgrown with scrubby blackthorn and brambles. No boatman braving the swift current could fight his way ashore through that. Rhys looked back the way he had come. He hoped Caydwr was following with Morvran and his shield and spears. It would be a slow walk for the aging horse, even unburdened, there was no question of waiting for them.

Rhys wondered if he would be able to make it back over this bridge. He was getting no less tired, and the day was starting to wane.

"No point in worrying about that..." he told himself,

Dark Age

"until I find out whether I'm going to be killed."

He started up the narrow path through the blackthorn. Another unpleasant thought struck him: the stallion, which he hoped would thrash its way to the bank before the river got too broad, could never have crossed that half-bridge. The black knight must climb the bridge in heavy armor, bearing saddle, bridle, lance and shield, to call his horse from grazing in the woods whenever the knight felt like making a midnight raid.

Rhys swallowed, realizing that he had better hope to catch the knight napping.

The narrow path led him past the edge of the blackthorn brambles. In the open space above loomed a ring of monoliths taller than himself. The path passed between two of the standing stones. There within the ancient stone ring, just across a small stretch of grass and little white five-petalled flowers, a short walk ahead reared a stone building. It had the look of a Roman temple or mausoleum, but was cruder, probably built by some pious eccentric a generation after the Roman withdrawal. Situated where it was on the Dolorous Mound, this, Rhys presumed, must be called the Dolorous Chapel.

The quiet of the forest about the river and its island was suddenly shattered, rent by raucous cries. A great flock of black birds rose from behind the Romanesque building, speeding upward *en masse* on swift wings, roiling like a storm cloud in a fast wind. Abruptly, the whole flock dove down at Rhys. It made no sense. Ravens had learned to follow armed bands, since the dead lay unburied wherever armies marched, but carrion crows did not swarm against the living.

Screaming harshly, the black storm flapped about him, buffeting his face with ebony feathers. Claws scraped his forehead. Rhys flung up his arms as plunging shapes pecked at his eyes, scraped talons over his leather and mail, blinding and deafening him with their mad rush. He yelled and waved his arms, expecting them to scatter and disappear, but the ravens wheeled and dove and pecked and clawed, cawing and croaking on all sides.

Arms before his face, Rhys waded through them, feeling his way blindly, tormented by an irrational fear that he might suffocate in such a flurry of black feathers. His toe caught on a rock and he stumbled sideways, but he caught his balance with difficulty. He raised his arms higher and glanced under them to reorient himself toward the building. A beak stabbed through the skin by his left eye and he bellowed, "Enough."

Out flashed the sword he had taken from Madoc's corpse. Rhys swept the blade blindly through the air before him. He felt it strike one of the birds, heard a piercing scream as the bird fell, then the others whirled away together, high above him. The wound by Rhys' eye was small, but the pain was so great he could only catch glimpses of the world around him. He stumbled against something soft and stepped to the side, blinking through illusory flashes of light. He put one hand over the pain-blinded eye and saw with the other a woman sprawled at his feet, black tresses, long black sleeves and sumptuous black skirts spilled over green grass and white flowers, bright blood welling from a sword-wound in her side.

The pain and its accompanying illusion of flashing light seeped through his skull to blind his right eye, and he put his hands over his face, squeezing both eyes shut. Caws and cries growing louder above alerted him. Rhys glanced up just long enough to glimpse the flock soaring down at him again, then turned and ran for the chapel, leaving the woman in black to her own strange fate. Another flurry of black wings disrupted further his damaged sight, claws and beaks pecking and tearing at his hands, trying for his face.

He ran straight into the stone wall of the building, slid along it, half afraid to bat at the tormenting birds for fear he would somehow strike another woman. Then his side was no longer pressed against stone and he was tumbling through an open doorway. The birds wheeled away, unwilling to enter the dark enclosure.

Rhys sank, bruising his knees on a hard floor, massaging with a groan the area around the cut by his left eye. The pain and the blinding after-image flashes died away with the caws of the retreating birds. Rhys looked out through the doorway and saw flattened grass and scattered white petals, but no woman's body. The birds, too, were gone into the clear sky.

Turning his back, Rhys let his eyes adjust to the dimness within. Why should any of this surprise him? Empires were collapsing, Britain's civilization dying, Saxon barbarians massed on the nearby eastern shore. The vital fortress of Castrum Tenebrarum was breached and empty, leaving the high road into Britain's heartlands unguarded. Why should Nature not be as mad as Madoc Broad Shoulders, the chieftain who had dismissed a quarter of the castrum's forces to spend his treasure on physicians for his lady Ellylyw. If that sweet lady could become the thing Rhys had unwittingly loosed from her chains in the vault beneath Castrum Tenebrarum, surely all the old rules of life were broken, and horror alone reigned over this new Age of Darkness.

Where was he, then? He looked about, wondering. If this was a chapel, why was the marble floor bare of pews? If this was a shrine, why were the walls devoid of religious images? To the right, beside the door, stood a simple stone plinth atop which was carved a board for gwyddbwyll, the woodcraft game. Black men and white, intricately carved, stood ready for play on the board. Rhys picked up a black piece, a knight, and looked at it closely. It was armored like a miniature of the deadly assailant he had glimpsed below Castrum Tenebrarum. Rhys set the piece down in a standard opening gambit and moved deeper into the room.

At its far end he saw an unorthodox, oblong altar surrounded by four thick unlit candles in four-foot-tall stands set at head, foot, and either side. Stretched out on the low altar like some kind of offering lay a knight.

Rhys' hand flew to his hilt. There was the same black armor, the thick rectangular plates riveted Sarmatian-style, edge-to-edge over leather, a layer of chainmail beneath.

The black knight's helmet was open. His face shone pale in the dim, indirect light, eyes closed, but not in peace; his features twisted in an expression of suffering. Brown blood dried in a pool on the altar's surface and in seven ghastly rents through the thick armor. One mighty blow had cloven through the sleek helm into the man's crown. Another blow had been powerful enough to sheer away half of the cheek guard that had hung down from the right side of the helm. It hung there no more, and the pallid, clean-shaven jaw beneath had been gashed and broken. A third blow had creased the metal along the knight's left temple. Any one of these strikes should have been immediately disabling and probably fatal. Perhaps the black knight's opponents had hacked him after he fell.

The knight's right arm lay across his torso, hand about his pommel as if he were afraid he might have to rise from this tomb and fight again. His left hand lay beside him, fingers bent at an unnatural angle from a deep gash through the back of the gauntlet. His unknown opponent must have shorn sheer through shield and gauntlet to mangle his hand so. Two steel plates on his torso were twisted where a lance had sped fast enough to punch a wide hole between them and through the chainmail and bone beneath. Another lance wound gaped in his lower abdomen, another through the stomach. The lance had broken off in a third wound, leaving a length caught in his ribs, a little below the heart.

Rhys brushed stinging sweat from the scratches Ellylyw and the ravens had gouged down his face, thinking that if Madoc and his men had given the black knight such deadly wounds, and the knight had still escaped and made his way here to die, then this nameless warrior could not have been human. So, Rhys had worked it out aright: the black knight must have been the one Ellylyw called her dark love, the one who had made her like himself, a creature such as Ellylyw had now become. Bowing his head, Rhys covered his good eye with his hand, hurt even to think of the lady, but he forced himself to reason it through. There was not much reason left in the world, so he thought that he might as well use it while he could.

Forcing in a deep breath, Rhys plucked up the will to look again at the corpse. So, this was the black knight, the one behind all the horror. Certainly, someone must have feared or hated him like the devil to have inflicted so much damage.

But how had the black knight's enemies finally killed him? Rhys had seen for himself that these creatures did not die from mortal wounds. Could it be that, dependent on the blood of the living to maintain their half-alive state, they were vulnerable to the massive blood loss such terrible wounds would cause?

Something caught Rhys' eye. He looked closer at the blood and now saw thin lines of bright scarlet that had trickled from a wound over dry brown smears. The same was true of each of the wounds. The knight on the altar had begun to bleed afresh after lying here. A chill ran up Rhys' spine. Songs described a dead man's wounds weeping blood when his murderer stepped into the room. Here stood Rhys, and the black knight's wounds bled afresh.

"Yet..." The rational part of his struggling mind insisted on saying, "the night I caught the black knight in Ellylyw's vault, he had swept me aside, leaving me stunned and helpless. I never gave him these wounds."

Nevertheless, Rhys felt an uncanny guilt as he looked at the freshly bleeding wounds. It also occurred to him that Madoc and his men, fighting in close quarters in the vault, could hardly have used horsemen's long lances. What he saw made no sense.

Evening was eating the light outside. Rhys pulled flint and steel from his pouch and struck the front candlewick aflame. Its light wavered across the damaged face in the ruined black helm half-turned toward him. The deep lines in the anguished features quivered.

The sword flew from Rhys' scabbard as he leapt forward, both hands sweeping the pommel above his head, swinging with full momentum, throwing all his weight and muscle and fear and rage into one flashing arc, striking the neck before the knight on the altar could rise.

Rhys' sword snapped, and his hands and forearms were struck numb. His whole body was jolted. For a terrible moment, his breath caught in his throat, his mind scrabbled desperately for some grip on the situation, certain that fell magics had maimed him. Then he felt seven kinds of fool. This was no man before him, dead or alive. Rhys' blow had cleft a divot from the supine shape, and in the gap he saw marble...this was an effigy, carved and painted with all the realism of the best Roman sculptors. The wavering of the candlelight had made it seem as if the stone face had moved. And any child who had ever swung a stick full force against a stone wall had felt as pained and stunned as Rhys' arms felt now.

He groaned. It had taken the whole hard-earned fortune of his short life to acquire what Madoc had called his half-forged sword. Now that work-a-day weapon lay useless in the vault below Castrum Tenebrarum, Ellylyw's blood drying on the blade. This weapon of Madoc's could probably have shorn right through his old sword at the first blow, and was worth more than Rhys was likely to earn in a lifetime. But no blade could cut stone. The weapon now short a good hand's-breadth and lacking a point.

Deciding he might as well act like he still had a future, Rhys shook the feeling back into his arms and picked up the severed tip to tuck it behind his belt. He knew he could never afford to reforge such a blade, but perhaps he could make a dagger of the fragment. Sheathing the rest of the sword, he unstrapped the scabbard from his back and belted it to his side.

Casting his eyes about to see what else he might learn from the chamber, Rhys noticed that all the candles were notched so that one might gauge the hours as they burned. Great pools of wax had congealed at each base.

Strange...they must have been lit many times by visitors, but who would come here? No, they must have been left to burn for several days before some wind got in and extinguished them.

Aided by the single wavering light, Rhys examined the altar beneath the effigy more carefully. Walking around it, he spotted on the rear an inscription in a language he had never seen. He walked round to the front again. The candle threw enough light to let him read inscribed below the marble figure in Latin:

YURI OF THE DOLOROUS MOUNT
KNIGHT OF HUNGARY
KNIGHT OF THE LITTER
COMPANION OF THE ROUND TABLE
LORD OF ESTRAKE

Rhys sighed. He had let his overwrought imagination blind him. This was no altar, but a bier. Whatever this Yuri had been, he could not be the black knight Rhys had come here to face.

He sat on the marble floor. His muscles ached, and a heavy depression was settling over him. Worse, the thick dust in the old building was tightening his lungs and filling them with fluid. He could not stay long. But having intruded on this scene of death, and having struck the fallen warrior's image, he had to pay his respects.

Rhys remembered from songs of Emperor Arthur's court what must originally have been the same character as the one named on the bier. Urre of the Mount, as it was usually spelled in Britain, had been an Ostrogoth in the land of the Huns who fought one Alphegus, whom he slew, though himself mortally wounded in the struggle. Alphegus' mother used enchantments to make her way unseen past Urre's squires to the maimed knight's bedside.

There were two versions of what happened next. One claimed that Alphegus' mother ensorcelled the Hungarian so that his wounds would never heal until the best knight in the world pulled the broken lance-tip from the ribs in which it was caught, and probed all seven deadly wounds to remove fragments of wood and steel. The other version maintained that Urre died of his wounds, and that the function of the best knight was to remove the broken weapon from the wound, fasten the steel point to a new lance and avenge the dead knight.

Both traditions agreed that Urre's own mother placed him, either dead or alive, in a horse litter, and then, with an armed entourage, set out in search of the best knight in the world. She sailed to the court of the Emperor Arthur, for surely the one man to unite the embattled British factions and drive back the Saxons and the Pictish raiders, the Irish pirates and the Norse must be the best knight in the world.

Surprisingly, it was not the great Arthur himself who achieved Urre's cure, or any of his famous knights, but a little-known newcomer, a young Breton from Armorica who was called Llancleawc. He had been trained by the

White Lady herself, the great priestess embodying the widely worshipped Lady of the Waters and the greatest healer of her age. This Llancleawc, alone, was able to clear and heal Urre's seven wounds.

With a swiftness considered magical at the time, Urre then recovered and became one of Emperor Arthur's own knights and a constant companion to Llancleawc who had released him from his long suffering. Urre helped his Armorican healer gain a great reputation in the far north of Britain where Llancleawc slew many of Urre's foes and seized their lands and shared their treasures with the Hungarian, making him eventually the Lord of Estrake.

Of course, this Urre would have died, one way or another, decades ago, like Arthur and all his men...and with that inevitable conclusion of his train of thought, Rhys' eyes popped open. When had he shut them?

Rhys glanced out the doorway. Night had fallen. He forced himself to stand, his knees stiff, his feet full of needles. He stamped to aid circulation, which proved remarkably painful and raised more dust. He was struggling for breath, his fingertips tingling, not a good sign. He had been exposed to the dust for too long. The candle swam before his eyes. Fortunately, Caydwr had given him a more potent mixture of the herbal infusion that often helped him.

He started to reach for his pouch when something dark moved at the base of the altar.

Wheezing breaths wracked Rhys' thin frame as he struggled to blink his eyes clear in the dim, wavering light. A hole slid open at the base of the altar, and from it a black-gauntleted hand crept forth, groped upward like a huge spider running up the side of the altar. Before Rhys could gather his wits and strike at the black arm, the steel claws clenched about the candle flame and snuffed it.

Utter dark.

His wheezing breaths were shockingly loud in the dark room. He scrabbled in his belt pouch for his flint. Seizing it in his left hand, he drew his truncated blade with his right and held it in front of him. Frantically he struck the flint at his hilt, hearing stone grating against stone in the darkness ahead. Striking again, and again, at last he set sparks flying and caught a flash of a black figure standing before the opened bier.

Blind again, Rhys swung his blade toward the invisible presence, then struck the flint again on his hilt. Another flash of sparks revealed the black figure to his left, too close. Rhys swung toward its new position, struck sparks in time to see a black arm sweep toward his face.

Darkness and a terrible blow struck him at once. Rhys flew sickeningly, frighteningly disoriented, then all breath was knocked from him as he slammed down crunchingly hard, sliding along what he realized must be the floor, to fetch up hard against the base of the tomb, the snuffed front candle toppling over him, spattering hot wax.

Blind, his side numb where it had struck the floor, the broken sword lost in the darkness, Rhys struggled just to pull breath back into his flattened lungs, panic gnawing at his self control. Metal clinked in short, swift steps toward him, steel claws clenched his arms like the jaws of wolves, and Rhys was heaved up, head swimming from lack of the air through which he flew, unable to tell how far he must fall, then bright light flared in his head, his teeth rattled, and all his bones jarred. Stone grated above him while once again he could do nothing but fight with all his strength to pull in a breath.

At last, one wheezing gasp slipped in, choked immediately out, then Rhys was coughing, his lungs clutching at the insubstantial essence of life. His eyes watered, he hacked his throat dry, then wheezed quietly until the numbness throughout his body split back into separate aches. His head hurt worst, but that hardly mattered.

He bruised knuckles and stubbed fingers against smooth marble on all sides. The knight had shut him in the tomb.

Rhys pushed up against the stone lid, set himself, legs pressed against the sides of the box and getting his back into it. He heaved and struggled himself into a sweat and never budged the lid an inch.

Fighting for breath, his muscles turning to water, his brain slowing, his lungs filled with fluid. There was little enough air in the small space, already stale with exhalations.

Rhys forced himself to stop, focus instead on calming himself, not hard as despair set in. He wanted to weep like a child. Having spent so many years struggling to breathe, he had no desire to die this way. Drowning was a bad enough death, but to drown in his own phlegm...no. No more such thoughts.

He slowed his breathing, shut down his bodily processes as he had learned to do in childhood, slid himself into a light trance, in which the body, barely maintaining itself, required little air.

The mind, reduced to a semi-dream state, images

began to fill the dark: flashes without logic, but not without purpose. All will and rational thought shut down, and the depths of Rhys' being finally flowed up to save him. Rhys was shown himself, standing in the setting sun, his shadow huge against the wall of the Dolorous Chapel. The black knight stepped out of Rhys' shadow, swung out his arm to strike...

Rhys knew the knight as the enemy that always pursued him no matter where he went, the foe Rhys could never see but whose enmity always surrounded him, the enemy Rhys could not kill.

Then scenes from the bardic Elegy of Urre began to unfold before him, or perhaps the Hungarian knight had lain in this crypt so long that his memories had stained the thinning air and seeped now inside Rhys' wide-open, half-suffocated soul.

Rhys saw the dread enchantress, mother of the slain Alphegus, tall and thin, pale, piercing-eyed, saw her grin a wolf's grin, saw her feed on the blood of her son's slayer, the mortally wounded Urre. Rhys knew in his core that it was the witch-woman's bite that ended Urre's life but put some Eastern plague into his blood that caused him to awake by night.

The images bursting into Rhys' mind's eye showed him glimpses of Urre lying dead in his litter by day, of his people moving the litter from place to place. By night he woke to a kind of half-life, but the stump of the lance in his ribs, the fragments in his wounds prevented the damage from healing as Rhys had seen Ellylyw heal what should have been mortal wounds.

So Urre remained trapped in his litter, crippled, unable

by night to rise and live; unable by day to let go and die, endlessly bleeding and replacing his lost blood with that of others, captured by Urre's kin.

Rhys watched knight after knight try the crude battlefield surgery that prevailed at the time, some on the corpse by day, others on the moaning cripple by night. No man could have survived having his wounds torn open so many times. But Urre could not die, and no healer could remove all the fragments that maimed him.

The chieftain Llancleawc stood in lurid torchlight, short, squat, powerful as a boar, glowering, obsessed with plans and obligations he saw as fate. Raised from infancy to reconquer lost lands of the Lady of the Waters, Llancleawc would do anything to achieve the Lady's goals. Told he would be reputed the Best Knight in the World could he but cleanse Urre's wounds, Llancleawc had Urre stripped, his wrists and ankles shackled, stretching the Hungarian out until he hung horizontally in the air, between two blocks, waist high to Llancleawc.

Rhys watched Llancleawc's exceptionally powerful fingers probe about in the screaming Urre's wounds. In a ruthless age, Llancleawc was famous for his ability to disengage his feelings, driven only by the cold fury he had learnt from the priestess who had raised him. The more Urre strained against the shackles, the fiercer Llancleawc dug his nimble, merciless fingers into torn flesh, until the Armorican had plucked the last fragment from the wounds and only the lance-head remained.

The watching physicians and knights shook their heads. None had believed that any man could survive such shock or the attendant blood loss or endure such prolonged groping through his wounds without succumbing swiftly to sepsis. Yet Urre still screamed. Even so, none had found means to remove the lance-head without ripping out Urre's ribcage along with it.

Llancleawc hefted a blacksmith's hammer and heedless of Urre's rolling eyes and agonized howls, struck the exposed stump of the lance a terrible blow, driving the wooden shaft clean through the ribcage, punching the lance head a full foot beyond Urre's back into the open space between the two blocks.

Llancleawc reached below. The now exposed base of the lance head afforded the grip he needed and with rare brutal strength, Llancleawc wrenched the weapon out of the shrieking victim.

Abruptly Rhys' head filled with the image of a later Llancleawc, on horseback, summer sun glinting from his armor, as he frowned down at the corpse on Urre's palanquin, bourn by the Hungarian's people alongside Llancleawc's marching men-at-arms. The war-party's passage was contested by one of the enemies Urre's people had made, by reviving him with the blood of captives on their march to Arthur's court. Llancleawc had set the lance head he had wrenched out of Urre on a new wooden shaft. He spurred his horse into a swift charge, punching the steel point clean through the shield, armor, and chest of the kinsman of one of Urre's victims.

Rhys saw by moonlight the ambitious Armorican resting while Urre rose from his litter and fought as Llancleawc's champion, a mighty shadow warrior. Together, Armorican and Hungarian carved a kingdom for Llancleawc and the domain of Estrake for Urre, seizing lands from Saxon and Pict invaders and from British adherents of Arthur, alike.

Rhys saw the Emperor Arthur himself, a great black bear of a man, confront the stocky Llancleawc in court, accusing the renegade Armorican of fanatical devotion to the Lady of the Waters. In sorrow and in wrath, Arthur impeached his comrade of seizing lands from his allies instead of aiding Arthur against the foreign invaders. The grand convocation of the Round Table found Arthur's supposed friend Llancleawc, hero of the north, guilty of having betrayed their Supreme Commander and the cause of united Britain. The Emperor proclaimed that for the security of the isle, Llancleawc, Urre, and their followers were exiled to the far north where the Armorican might continue to rule the lands he had recovered in the name of his dispossessed Lady of the Waters, but never again set foot in Emperor Arthur's realm.

The vision of a moonless night darkening a wooden palisade grabbed the floating Rhys, and he felt that this was a year later than the last vision. A battered and weeping knight, one arm hanging twisted and useless at his side, was led into the northern hold of Estrake and brought before the high seats of Llancleawc and Urre to tell them that Britain's hope, Arthur the Emperor, had fallen with half his army at Camlann. Worse yet, the combat had been against a rebel nephew, one Medraut, who had led the other half of united Britain's troops, destroying in one stroke both the union and the better part of the island's armies.

Llancleawc's banishment was thus lifted, but for all his faith in fate, he soon found he was no Arthur. Llancleawc and Urre were the terror of the north and kept their lands against all comers as long as Llancleawc lived, but they could not reforge broken Britain. And to Rhys' day, no man had ever healed the country's deadly wounds.

This same ferocious, inhuman warrior, Urre of the Mount, was Rhys' foe. The bard realized that the black knight could not be defeated by courage and combat alone. Only a weapon that could not be drawn from the wound would stop Urre.

Rhys choked, coughed, wheezed, hating the staleness of the dead air he could barely pull into irritated lungs. He, alone, had realized Urre's secrets, and he was dying, useless and alone. His fingers stung as if stuck full of pins and needles, asleep from lack of breath. He dipped them into his pouch, wrapped them clumsily about the stone vial Caydwr had given him. Managing to pry out the cork and convey the vial to his lips, Rhys sucked down more than a days worth of tincture.

He collapsed against his hard bed, hoping the herbs would relax his lungs enough to keep him alive a little longer. Caydwr might yet arrive, hear Rhys' feeble cries from the crypt and break him out. Unable to support more thought than that, Rhys' mind fell back into the space it had found between wake and sleep. This time fragments of his own life flickered fitfully before his mind's eye:

On his seventeenth birthday, abandoning the childhood town in which he had found no place, picking a road at random, hoping that if only he might ride long enough, he could feel there was somewhere he had arrived...

The refined, slick-bearded, toga-draped Brathach, Consularis of Eboracum, with that infuriating trace of smile half-hidden at the corners of his lips, hinting that if Rhys brought him a trenchant enough report as to how the castrum had fallen, the powerful Brathach might find him some minor position and the young bard could finally come in off the endless roads...

The face of the lady Ellylyw, the most beautiful woman Rhys had ever met...

The copper basin filling with blood from the slit artery in Nefyn's arm...

The unstoppable black knight scything through Chieftain Madoc's men, unstoppable as a storm wind, batting Rhys aside with a blow from his shield, not bothering to kill the bard...

Worst of all, Rhys saw again the unkillable, feral thing Ellylyw became, gorging on Madoc's blood, playing with Rhys' battered emotions, tasting blood from the bard's cut hand, writhing at the point of his sword, still not dying...

The images died out like sparks. Realizing he still held the vial emptied of Caydwr's medicine, Rhys tried to release it but could not, his deadening digits locked unresponsively about the smooth cylinder as in premature rigor mortis.

Rhys had made his last move. He surrendered himself to the cosmos, if it might find some better use for what was left of him than to cast it aside.

Consciousness contracted to a vague awareness of the needle-like jabbing that moved gradually up his arms and legs toward his vital center, bringing coldness. It did not matter. For the first time in his life, Rhys felt at peace. Let the cosmos do with him what it would.

Chapter 6:

Urre of the Mount

Something hurt his eyes. Light. Rhys had forgotten what that was.

A wondrous, intangible substance poured down about him, and his lungs filled with it, flushing his system with wonderful air. The tingling began to recede toward his extremities.

Stone grated against stone, light increased, and his vision focused. The lid of the tomb raised and was set aside, and the pale, gaunt, clean-shaven features of Urre peered down at him. The sight of his enemy set Rhys' heart hammering. Now that he could breathe, lightning bolts shot through his limbs, and he felt Caydwr's tincture fill him with a strange energy, not his body's own, a nerve-jangling, mad power to replace the strength air-starvation cost him.

The black knight reached into the coffin and hauled out his still-living victim, heavy ringmail and all.

Rhys felt the marble floor again beneath his tingling feet. His temples throbbed and the candlelit air around the knight seemed to ripple like water. Black specks filled his vision, but none of that mattered. The energy from the tincture cleared his lungs, accelerated all his bodily processes, recovering for him more strength and control than the black knight could imagine; screaming within

Rhys, seeking an outlet in action.

Rhys glared hatred down the dark tunnel of his vision at the hard features before him. The bard focused only on the tight-lipped mouth, avoiding any glimpse into those will-weakening eyes.

Urre of the Dolorous Mount shook Rhys like a rag doll to rouse him. The black knight's sonorous voice intoned, "Come, I need you." The knight kept Rhys upright with one hand, dragging him with inhuman strength out the mausoleum door.

Rhys let his arms hang limp, his feet stumble and catch so that the knight would think him still half-suffocated as Urre of Estrake hauled him across the grassy slope toward the encircling stand of stones, the half-built bridge invisible in the darkness beyond. "Call your steed," that deep voice commanded.

So, Urre's horse had been carried too far downstream to come at his master's beck. *He needs me to provide him the means to reach Castrum Tenebrarum and his lady.*

Ellylyw.

Without thinking and with a speed and precision he had never before mastered, Rhys whipped his dagger from the sheath behind his back and drove it through the monster's eye.

Urre staggered back with a cry of pain and surprise, releasing Rhys, black gauntleted hands clawing at his face.

Rhys ducked close, whipped the black steel sword from his enemy's scabbard, and swung with all his strength at the black armored neck.

Blinded by pain, Urre sensed the blow coming, swept up his plate-armored left arm to block it, but Rhys drove the knight's own blade through thick steel and banded muscle into forearm bone. Wrenching the blade free, Rhys whirled it over his head and cut again and again without pause, driving Urre back, giving him no time to pluck the offending dagger from his ruined eye.

The black knight's left hand now useless, Urre gave ground, step-by-step, ducking, jumping, parrying when he could by sweeping his right arm in against the flat of the flying blade, slapping it aside.

Steel rang in the dark forest hush as Rhys chopped divots from Urre's arm guards. All Rhys' world had contracted to this one need to keep spinning and hacking, to drive the knight back and back, to give no quarter, as Rhys' life had given him no quarter, to cut apart the black armor, plate-by-plate, to get at the thing beneath, as life had stripped everything from Rhys, bit-by-bit, to uncover the power that lay within.

A leather strap gave under the onslaught, and Urre's right shoulder guard slid partway down his arm, further hindering his attempts to parry. Rhys pressed on, relentless, holding nothing back. Each moment might have been his last, for his opponent had countless advantages while Rhys could only hope to prolong the effect of surprise. The moment Rhys lost this one advantage, he would die.

Urre, forced to give ground steadily, sight impaired, racked with pain, one arm useless, showed no sign that he would ever tire, while Rhys felt the hermit's medicine burning rapidly in his system and knew that the fiercer his flame, the quicker it must exhaust its fuel. Rhys cut low at plate-sheathed shins, hammered overhead at the black helm. Urre's armor was starting to break up, but he had lost

Jeffrey T. Heyer

little blood, and Rhys knew the Hungarian had endured seven years of agony to destroy his enemies.

Rhys drove the black knight between the upright stones, leapt after him, only to find that Urre had sidestepped behind a monolith, forcing Rhys to change the direction of his attack and buying the knight time to finally pluck the dagger from his eye. Blood coursing down from the pierced eyelid, Urre parried with the dagger, unable yet to get close enough to make a strike of his own.

Rhys pressed the attack, but he was no longer driving his foe down the steep slope toward the rushing river. Urre backed along the ring of stones until he saw a chance to lunge with the dagger. Rhys dropped to one knee on the Hungarian's blind side, clutching the sword pommel in both hands to catch the full force of Urre's hurtling body on the weapon's point. Sparks flew as the point scraped over steel, catching between two dented plates, and Urre's momentum knocked Rhys backward onto the grass, driving the sword through the chainmail beneath the plates, through the leather tunic and the cloth beneath to pierce Urre's side.

Leaning down toward Rhys, his full weight on the blade thrust two inches into his abdomen, Urre lashed down with the dagger, unable to reach his foe, but pressing him hard against the ground. Rhys threw himself sideways, kicking up both legs, unbalancing Urre so that the heavy knight stumbled sideways to his right. Again on Urre's blind left side, Rhys wrenched free the sword and sprang behind him, getting in a swift hard stroke that tore links from the back of Urre's neck and drove others into the leather and flesh beneath.

Spinning, Urre flung the dagger into the space from

which he thought the blow had come, but Rhys was already dropping onto his back so the dagger flew over him. He kicked out hard, tripping the big warrior. Urre could not catch himself on his ruined left hand and skidded and clanged down the steepening hill, smashing blackthorn scrub, increasingly entangled in the tearing brambles.

Rhys thrust the black sword into the earth, left it standing ready at hand for quick retrieval, clawed up a big stone and flung it down two-handed, catching the rising Urre square in the back with a satisfying clack. Urre fell to his knees, toppling forward again, rolling, twisting, clutching one-handed at cracking barbed branches.

Racing after him over smashed blackthorn, sword again in both hands, Rhys sprang from above, landed point-first, square in the buckle on Urre's left side that fastened his breastplate to his backplate. The buckle shore in half, and the blade drove clean through the Black Knight's abdomen and deep into the earth on the other side. Impetus and impact cost the bard his grip on the pommel, and he fell past into the last of the thorns, his boots splashing river water beyond.

Urre gasped, his right arm pinned under his armored torso, his broken left hand batting uselessly at the sword it could no longer grasp.

Nearly spent, Rhys dizzily pulled himself upright, ripping his ringmail free of the thorns that had kept him from rolling into the spray, glad for once that he was not clad in heavy plate like the knight. The bard cast his eyes about, heaving great, racking breaths, and spotted a small boulder cutting the current and tossing up little spumes of water. Rhys stepped thigh-deep into the cold stream to grab it from its pile. One knee, banged harder in his fall than he had realized, went out from under him. Rounded rocks rolled together under his remaining foot, sending Rhys over sideways, shocked by the cold immersion and tugged outward by the current. The boulder flew from his hands.

Thumping painfully against a great boulder, Rhys flailed, bounced along its side, flung his arms around it and held on, facing back the way he had come.

Urre still lay on his side, pinned to the island, staring after him with his remaining eye.

"I'm tired of darkness," the deep voice rumbled.

Rhys was too stunned to try climbing out yet. He stared back at the transfixed knight, knew Urre must be bleeding terribly.

"Why Ellylyw?" Rhys called out, voice quavering with six kinds of passion. To his surprise, the black knight replied without pause.

"I love her. You love her. Madoc loved her. She was the kind of woman men fall in love with, whether she wills it or no. Why have you come to the Dolorous Mount?"

"I had to see your face."

"Seeking your own reflection?"

"I found you."

"What you seek stands behind me, not within me. And nothing on this island will fit you for Ellylyw. She sent you here to die."

"Death is not the end. And I have work to do." Rhys tried to climb the boulder, found it too smooth, lost his grip and slipped deeper into the water, coming to rest with his mouth just above most of the splashes.

Urre's eye still watched him, motionless.

Dark Age

"Tell me of Arthur." Rhys spat water. Catching his breath, he realized he was parched after the fight and gulped down a little of the river.

Without hesitation, Urre obliged him. "Arthur was the only ruler I ever willingly served. Llancleawc I made my partner, but Arthur inspired the Christians, the Pagans, the Mithrics. He was elected to lead the armies of united Britain twelve campaigns in a row by a grand convocation of the Cornish, Welsh, Logrean, Lothian and half a hundred smaller nations. He made even me feel like I was part of something. When Arthur fell, an age ended. I realized that Llancleawc's betrayal was what weakened Arthur. I left the north forever, had myself interred here. Britain is maimed. A wasteland. The best knight in the world could not heal her seven-times-seventy wounds."

"So, you feed off the chaos?" Rhys tried again to clamber up the boulder, slipped again into the drink, unintentionally swallowing more water, barely holding on against the current. The water lay heavy in his stomach.

"I discovered at last," Urre called after him, "that I could feel a kind of love again. A mad, consuming fire, but the one thing that warms my cold bones. I care for nothing else. Blood is the medium of passion. Without passion, all is ash."

"Yet you infected Ellylyw with your plague."

Urre lay silent. Rhys gulped air, pushed himself as far down in the water as he could get without losing his grip on the boulder, then kicked and bobbed upward, throwing his arms up to embrace the rounded peak of the rock. At last, he got his knees pressed against its sides and let go with one arm to reach up farther, grope out a fingerhold and use it to lever and pry himself up out of the river's pull. Gathering himself together, he leapt like a frog back into the island's thorns.

His ringmail protected his torso, but his leggings, even his boots were pierced; his flesh was pricked, his hands and his face were scratched painfully. Struggling upright, he picked his way carefully toward his foe.

Urre was gone.

The crushed thorns were black with blood in the light of the setting moon. The Hungarian had wrenched himself free of the earth. Rhys followed the flattened plants back up the hill, twice catching a toe in a thorny tangle and going down on his unprotected hands into the biting guardians. But most of the blood along the way was not his.

Dark patches and spatters led back into the circle of stones, then beyond to the mausoleum. Bone weary, aching, scratches stinging, bitter cold, Rhys stopped at the threshold of the Dolorous Chapel and drew the severed tip of Madoc's sword from his belt. Pulling his kerchief from about his neck, Rhys wrapped it around the base of the fragment and settled it as best he could in his right hand. Then he stepped through the dark portal.

No sound came from within. Rhys made his way slowly toward the bier, water squelching in his boots, pattering from his soaked clothing. His foot came down on something painfully rough and hard, his flint. He recovered it and, reaching the sepulcher, used sword-point and flint to spark alight the candle at the bier's foot.

Urre lay in the open sepulcher, his sword, wet with his own blood, again clenched in his one good hand, pommel against his chest. The blood had already dried about his ruined eye, but at Rhys' approach, fresh scarlet seeped from the deep puncture and from his left forearm and from his sides. There was no other sign that Urre of the Mount was not as dead as any other corpse.

Wearily, Rhys looked down at him. "What do we do now? I can't join you in your enslavement to Ellylyw. I don't know how to heal you. How can I make you my ally as once you were Llancleawc's?" The bard tucked the flint into his pouch, and recovered his broken sword from the floor, then moved to the plinth beside the door. Gazing at the gwyddbwyll game board, its men set up for play, he mused aloud, "There stands the king within a ring of hunters. Which do I play, the man trapped in the middle, or the knights trying to bring him down?"

An odd creaking and clinking outside alerted his weary wits, and Rhys stepped to the door. Something hard smacked into him, knocking him back against the plinth, sending gwyddbwyll men flying to clatter loudly across the floor, rolling everywhere.

A knight in white-plate armor dragged a great siege crossbow behind him into the Dolorous Chapel. His broad white-steeled foot crunched down on a rolling gwyddbwyll man, grinding it against the marble.

"What are you doing?" Rhys demanded, outraged, though not entirely sure why. Perhaps in part it was because this white knight had knocked him aside as casually as Urre had done on his last visit to the vault.

The knight turned a featureless faceplate toward him. Unseen eyes peered through the cross-shaped aperture in the steel helm. The white knight continued past Rhys, heaved up the siege weapon and dropped it atop the open crypt, either end of the long bow at the weapon's business end sticking out beyond the marble edges. Up onto the bier the white knight clambered, straddling it, one iron foot on either side. He lifted up the weapon's tail until its projectile, a great steel bolt, was aimed down at the black knight's heart.

Rhys started toward the white knight, and the warrior whisked a dagger from its sheath and flung it in the bard's direction, forcing Rhys to throw himself to the side. The knight loosed the taut bowstring, catapulting the steel quarrel through armor and flesh to chink loudly into the marble bed beneath.

Rhys sank down on the floor, the last of the tincture burned out of his exhausted system.

Hopping lightly down onto his steel-shod feet, the white knight strode toward him.

The ragged bard just stared up at him, too shocked and empty to muster any defense.

The knight undid the catch on his faceplate and flipped it up. A leathery, amiable countenance smiled down at Rhys. The knight extended him a hand. When Rhys took it, the man yanked him to his feet, casually shoved him back against the wall, then stood directly in front of him, making it obvious that he had nowhere to go. Gazing curiously at his find, the knight said conversationally, "You don't look like much and you're scratched to ribbons, but while I was crossing over the river, I saw you fight a good fight against that monster. Why get in my way when I'm finishing him off? Were you after the credit?"

Rhys shook his head. "What are you doing here?"

"The abbot hired me. Made it sound like I was after a

devil or something. So, I brought a little artillery with me."
He hooked a thumb at the body in the casket. "That one
must have had some fell magics under his belt." The knight
unconcernedly crossed himself just to make sure, then
gestured toward the siege engine still lying athwart the
open sepulcher. "That thing's not really made for one man
to lug around. Guess I'll leave it for my squires to pick up
in the morning. They'll have your horse, by now."

The knight pulled a leather flask from his belt, took a
pull, then handed it to Rhys. "Come with me."

The bard took a good swallow of brandy, enjoyed the
burn as it went down. Warmth spread from his belly, gave
him enough strength to wobble after the briskly striding
knight.

Two chainmailed squires waited at the island end of
the unfinished bridge. They looped a rope under Rhys'
shoulders and gave a shout. The rope was part of a pulley
system they had rigged and whoever was at the other end of
the bridge began hauling Rhys swiftly over the framework
he had so laboriously climbed that afternoon. Four
businesslike squires on the completed side of the bridge
helped Rhys out of the rope and reset the system to bring
over their master.

Rhys walked off the bridge to feel solid earth beneath
his feet. There stood old Morvran, reins fastened to a bush
he was desultorily cropping. Rhys' good friend whickered
at him, and the bard rubbed the steed's forehead. "So
Caydwr made it here after all." He patted Morvran's cheek.

The horse snorted contentedly and went back to
lipping the bush for its tastiest leaves.

Looking back toward the bridge, Rhys noticed

Jeffrey T. Heyer

something moving beside it at the river's edge. Climbing carefully down, he found a level space where he could stand safely and from which he could see to the river's surface by the near end of the bridge.

There hunched a stunted oak from which hung Caydwr, one leg caught in its branches. There was a spear through his chest and his head and arms hung in the water, the current tossing them, causing the movement that had caught Rhys' eye. The bard sank down on the grass.

The white knight clinked up behind him. "Had the devil in him, that woodman did." The knight chuckled, sociably. "The abbot said the hermit had once prophesied that he would not die by earth or air, fire or water. On another occasion this same fellow supposedly announced that no blow by any weapon would take his life. Well, the hermit was strong, I'll give him that. Awfully friendly for a Satan worshipper, too, but I suppose the abbot knew his own business. Anyway, this Caydwr fellow shared our supper, while the boys were rigging the ropes. The shaggy headed old wild man even had a second course of the poison the abbot gave me for him. Gave him enough to kill a bear, I did, just to make sure. Your hermit, there, wolfed it all down and asked for more, and never so much as belched afterward."

The knight was warming to his story, well satisfied with his night's work and already honing the anecdote he would glean from the job. "Seeing the poison didn't work, 'Old ways are best ways,' I say, and run my best spear right through him. The hermit just looks up, surprised, drops his flagon and takes himself a walk out onto the bridge. I pull out old Firebrand, here," the knight affectionately slapped the hilt of his sword, "and trot after him, thinking I'll have to take his head. The woodman sees me coming, dodges back, but the flat of my blade smacks the spear shaft in him and topples him off the bridge. His foot catches in that tree, he strikes his head on a rock under the water, and you can see the rest. He died not by mortal weapon, earth, air, fire or water, but by poison, spear, sword, fall, hanging and drowning together. As you might say, by air, water *and* earth."

The white knight led Rhys back up the hill. Having recovered the siege weapon, the squires were setting fire to the oil they had poured over the finished half of the bridge. This amused the knight. "The fire'll spread to the tree and the hermit in it, and then he'll be killed in that element, too."

Rhys blinked numbly at the grinning warrior, then loosed Morvran's reins and swung up into the saddle.

"Don't you want escort?" the knight asked, a little hurt at Rhys' lack of conviviality.

"I'll rest far from here." Rhys turned Morvran's head to the forest.

***

Morvran tapped the ground, impatient to be off, but Rhys kept him just below the wall of the half-burnt fortress while he gazed down at the last living inhabitant of Castrum Tenebrarum.

"You look different," Gwenllian said.

He gestured toward the scratches healing on his face. "This makes such a difference?"

"Well, yes, but I meant you look...darker. More

Jeffrey T. Heyer

confident, maybe."

He looked up at the thick, stinking black smoke rising over the fortress. "Ready to leave?"

"There's nothing left." Gwenllian sighed, following his gaze. "The abbot had all the bodies burned, along with the dead who were seen to walk again in the town below."

"What about Ellylyw?" Rhys hid from her that his heart was in his mouth.

Gwenllian shrugged. "Her body is gone, too. That's all I know."

"You didn't see the abbot's men burn it?"

"I hid. They might have killed me for helping fulfill the custom of the fortress."

"Climb up. I'll take you to Brathach."

She hesitated.

"You can explain your part in this any way you like. I won't contradict you."

She took his hand, about to swing up, then paused. "As long as you understand we're just friends."

He pulled her up behind him, mumbling to himself. "At least there's that."

"If Brathach doesn't give you a place after all—"

"He won't." Rhys was certain.

"Will you become a hermit like your friend Caydwr?"

"No." Rhys flicked the reins and started Morvran on the long journey toward Eboracum. "I'll keep questing for my reflection."

Gwenllian shook her chestnut hair. "How long can you keep that up?"

"All my life. And the next. And the next."

Chapter 7:

The Chapel at the Crossroads

The sun slipped behind dense foliage, and still the man and the woman on the weary war-horse saw no sign that humans had ever set foot in the thick forest. Even the path they rode might have been worn by deer. Dusk deepened and the path opened into a clearing. In its center stood a little dry-stone chapel. The young bard lifted his claw-scarred face to look from the lonely building ahead to the path beyond where it branched in three directions, each obscured by long shadows.

Leather creaked as Rhys raised a hand to wipe the dust from his face. A few last sunbeams glinted dully on the heavy rings sewn over the stained leather as he scanned the terrain for dangers. The building was square and unimaginative, clearly Roman in design, and since the collapse of Arthur's united Britain, there were few chieftains who could afford to erect such an extravagance so far from any defensible city.

No doubt these stones had been set when the Romans still ruled the isle, and only the commons had felt the oppressor's whip. Rhys presumed the builder was some forebear of Madoc Broad Shoulders, the ruins of whose command lay now two days ride behind. There had been a time when a chieftain who loved the hunt would not have feared to erect his tomb this far from his court.

The young woman riding behind Rhys, liking him well enough, though not in *that* way, and nervous at traveling alone with him, had just been complaining that she never met any gentle, compassionate men who would listen to her. Having done just that ever since he had taken her from Tenebrarum, Rhys turned his horse's head toward the chapel. "Perhaps you don't see what fate puts before you. Or you don't grasp what your heart is really set on."

"What do you mean?" She loosened her grip about his ring-mailed waist and leaned the side of her brown-tressed head against his shoulder, not in affection but in weariness. "And why are you leaving the path? You don't mean to spend the night in that chapel?"

"It has walls and a roof."

He reined up in a tall, three-sided lean-to built to shelter four horses at a time while their riders were in the chapel praying. Dismounting before it, the bard tested the wooden walls. Gray and desiccated with age, they felt firm enough, nonetheless. He helped Gwenllian dismount, then set aside his saddle packs and unsaddled his steed.

"There's a brush in the pack," he told his passenger. "Curry Morvran while I scout the chapel. There's no guarantee we are the first travelers to spot it."

Gwenllian took the brush willingly enough, missing her own mount, but protested. "Other travelers? There are no other horses tied up here."

"Brigands go on foot."

"Outlaws? Only a day's ride from the fortress?"

"I take it you never traveled," Rhys remarked dryly. "Human carrion crows are only one of the dangers between here and Eboracum. The famine left starving men everywhere."

"Men?"

Rhys looked at her soberly. "Little bands of men survive a while in wild places."

"I understand that. I'm asking about their women and children."

Rhys set his focus on a quick survey of the remaining rations in his saddle-pack. "I've never seen any."

"What happened to them? When people flee their farms or towns before the Saxon invaders, they must..."

She stopped, gazing aghast at Rhys.

"Don't think about what happened to them. Just work at surviving." He slung his shield across his back by the strap, then flipped free the leather loop that kept his sword snug in its scabbard. He walked to the chapel door.

It was open. The gloom inside was thick, and he proceeded cautiously, though there was little to see. Whatever religious furnishings had once decorated the place had long since been carried off. He saw only a bare chamber with thin slit windows just wide enough to allow an archer to defend the building.

Stepping to three square marble slabs set flat and level with the dirt floor before the altar, he learned from their Latin inscriptions that here the chapel's builder and his two sons had been interred standing upright, still facing the Saxon enemy on the eastern coast.

Beyond the inscribed marble was the only raised structure remaining in the stone room. Rhys thought at first that this altar was topped by the painted carving of a fourth knight, remembering wryly his mistake at the Dolorous

Chapel. But there was something wrong with the graven image...something that disturbed him. Rhys squinted through the dimming light seeping through the arrow slits, took a step forward, and then stopped, realizing with a shock what was wrong.

The figure on the altar was clad in leather tunic and breeches, what a knight would wear *under* his armor. A sculptor would have depicted him fully armed, guarding the isle even in death, like his forebears whose bones still stood within the floor. What lay across the altar before him could only be a corpse.

Glancing quickly once more about the shadowy chapel to assure himself he had not missed any place an enemy might be lurking, Rhys stepped onto the middle marble slab and leaned close to examine the dead man.

With another sharper shock, Rhys recognized the contorted face.

Before him lay the same knight of the white arms whom he had met at the Dolorous Mount, the mercenary who had loosed a ballista bolt through the heart of the black knight, and who had slain Rhys' friend, the hermit of the Green Chapel.

The dead man's face was bruised, and deep tracks from fingernails ran across one cheek and eye. His wrists, too, now lying at his sides, were discolored as if he had been pinioned by them. The rest of his skin was nearly as white as his painted armor, now missing, had once been.

Worst of all, there was a nasty bite mark on either side of his throat. The man had bled to death, the body had not been washed and prepared for burial, but simply laid here, and there was far too little spilled blood. Neither were the bites those of any wolf or bear. The shape of the jaw that had made them was human.

Any other man in Britain would have been perplexed, but with a palpable blow, it struck Rhys exactly what had happened, for Rhys alone knew what unearthly eastern plague Urre of Hungary had brought to Britain. The bard still did not know the name of the cursed affliction, but with a pang, he pictured again the face of Urre's lover the Lady Ellylyw lying lifeless, or so it had seemed. Rhys' breath quickened and his fists clenched as, against his will, he saw again the lady arisen, leaping on her armored husband, shaking her head like a wolf, worrying the wound in the war-chieftain's throat, the slim gentlewoman tearing the life out of Madoc Broad Shoulders, her tongue lapping up the blood that pumped from ripped arteries.

Rhys raised his scarred face, his heart pounding in his throat, trying to dam the flood of images that engulfed him, his thin frame shaking as he relived that horrible night, his stomach sickening, twisting with the realization that this woman he had, despite all intention, come to love, was no longer herself, that only stolen blood kept her half-dead body moving in a parody of life.

Fingering the scars that marked him for life, Rhys fought to still the shakes, remembering well the terrifying energy that gave these revived people, these revenants, so ferocious a strength.

With a groan, Rhys turned away from the corpse, feeling vicariously Ellylyw's pain as he drove his sword clean through her, pinning her to the bedframe beneath, seeing her again writhing about the blade that did not kill her as it would certainly have killed any human or animal.

"Gwenllian," he choked out in a half laugh that subsided into half a sob, "you told me the abbot burned all the bodies at Castrum Tenebrarum...the same abbot who had hired this white knight to nail the originator of the plague to the bed of his marble tomb, then burn the bridge to Urre's river island."

Rhys leaned on the altar's edge, nodding half in dread and half in relief, accepting that having wrenched free the sword that pinned her, Ellylyw must have escaped the shattered castrum before the abbot arrived to burn all those she had infected. The body before him was proof that Ellylyw was somewhere in these same woods, and he alone knew that she existed, what she was, and what she craved.

Exhaling deeply, he forced himself to look again at the knight's body. There was little light left, and there was something about the placement of the mercenary's hands that bothered him. Had he brushed against them after his first examination, moving them?

But before he grasped what had disturbed him, something small and dark sitting beside the dead man's head caught his eyes. The bard picked it up and held it toward the waning light from a narrow embrasure. The thing in his hand was a small carved knight painted black, a gaming piece from a gwyddbwyll board. Soot rubbed from the carving onto Rhys' fingers.

He had held this very object in his hand when he had found Urre's tomb. Gently, Rhys set down the gaming piece, noticing peripherally that the dead man's head seemed now to be facing him whereas before he thought it had been—

"Are you all right?" Gwenllian called from outside.

"It's been a while."

"Don't come in," he shouted. His voice rang from the walls, and his head felt a little light as he realized that Ellylyw, having taken this mercenary's blood in revenge for his destruction of her dark lover Urre, had infected the white knight, too.

He hated to do it, but Rhys faced the corpse yet again. Its motionless hands were now at either side of the ravaged throat, as if feeling the crusted wounds in the corded sinews.

Rhys jumped back, fore-shortened sword flashing from his scabbard. He swept it two-handed over his head. The corpse opened its eyes as the blade slashed down. With an inarticulate cry, Rhys chopped through the thick neck, sword-edge thudding into the polished altar wood beneath. The dead hands flopped back to the headless body's sides.

Afraid of contagion, Rhys daggered through the laces of the leather tunic, yanked it open and used his dagger again to cut a swathe from the tail of the cloth shirt beneath, using it to quickly, nervelessly rub the spatter from his hands and then to clean his blade. Flinging the rag from him, Rhys backed across the small room, then out the door, shutting it behind him.

Just outside, the startled Gwenllian stepped back as he turned, nearly colliding with her. She opened her mouth to speak but he cut her off. "We sleep in the lean-to with Morvran tonight."

As if not liking the look of terror on his face, she asked no questions.

***

Morning sun gleamed dully on jingling steel rings as Morvran plodded down the left turning point of the crossroads. Gwenllian fidgeted behind Rhys. "You can't be thinking of hunting her down. Ellylyw is... You can't stop her."

Rhys did not reply.

Gwenllian pressed, "And what about me? It's not just your life. I have to depend on your untried sword-arm."

"Not as untried as you imagine," he replied, eyes intent on the woods ahead. "Nor is the sword my only weapon."

Morvran whickered.

Rhys reined him to a stop and patted his broad neck, which quieted the aging charger. "We'll camp here."

"Shouldn't we ride 'til dark? Then you can set up camp by firelight while I cook dinner. No offense, but that cold grub you provided last night was...well, believe me. I'll be glad to cook."

"No fire. I am not the only rider using forest paths to avoid Saxon raiders. Here is a stream for water and bathing and a tree whose branches reach the ground. We'll shelter between the branches and the trunk."

"But if I can't cook—"

"There's still bread in my saddle pack. We'll soften it with water and chew salted beef. If you want a salad, you have time enough to forage. Just don't leave my sight."

"And where will you be while I'm working for my supper?"

"Up that tree." Rhys gestured. "Don't let Morvran make another sound. I think he heard a horse on the road ahead, and these are not trusting times."

After slipping from the saddle, Rhys scrambled into the branches. His heavy ringmail and open-faced helmet made him feel clumsy.

As concerned as he was, possibly even more so, Gwenllian stroked the horse and kept him quiet while Rhys scanned the road ahead. Sure enough, in a pleasant little meadow just off the forest path, Rhys saw a great tan charger, twitching its ears and sniffing the air. Nearby browsed a packhorse and a smaller war-horse with a bundle on its back. A single man in the heavy chainmail of a knight, his black hair dripping, was walking back from a nearby bend in the stream. In his hands was his upended helmet filled with water.

The armored man patted his mount's neck, and Rhys fancied he was asking the horse why it had made some sound and whether it had heard another horse on the road ahead. But the charger lost all interest in anything but guzzling from the helmet. The two packhorses crowded near, as well, eager for their turn, both forgetting that they had sensed Morvran's approach. Apparently, the little entourage ahead had just concluded a long, hot ride.

Rhys maintained his concealment, watching the distant knight make a tired and cursory examination of his surroundings, then curry his horses and pitch camp. From the size of his tent and from the bundle of armor the knight unlashed from the third horse, in order to polish it in a barrel full of sand spun between two legs, Rhys concluded that the warrior had set out on his expedition with a man-at-arms of whom there was nothing left but disused armor and a riderless horse. No doubt the lone knight had left the road so early in order to leave himself time for all the chores his man-at-arms would have done. It took some time to care for three horses, erect a tent, polish two sets of arms and dress and cook the coney he had transfixed with an arrow during his day's progress.

Trying, without much success, to stop himself from imagining how good that coney must smell on that cozy little fire, Rhys gauged the manner in which the man moved, and the quality of his gear, and thought carefully. In such circumstances Rhys often found that a long day's plodding actually helped slow his imagination, making it easier for him to take the time to lay step-by-step plans.

He climbed back to earth and joined Gwenllian by Morvran's side.

"Will you fight?" she asked quietly.

"Not tonight." He smiled. "But the morning should prove interesting."

She helped him unsaddle and groom the old war-horse, who was glad enough to be done with the day's journey. Gwenllian stabled Morvran on the far side of a thick tree trunk beneath a broad ring of boughs not far from the tree Rhys had earlier indicated would be his and the maiden's shelter.

The bard pulled a length of rope from his saddle-pack and set out down the path. Finding a spot to his liking, he climbed just high enough to tie one end of the rope ten feet up a stout trunk. Dropping down again, he crossed the path and threw a loop around a high branch on the far side, pulled the line taut above the path, then fastened it with a slipknot.

Returning to the sheltering tree, he found that Gwenllian had gathered a comfortable mound of rushes from the stream to make them two mattresses at opposite ends of the enclosed space. Amused, Rhys noted that she had laid his shield and two crossed spears between the bed mounds. He stuck to his side of her line of demarcation. He was used to traveling alone. The cold would not bother him much.

When Gwenllian launched a long speech to forestall all the tricks she was certain he was about to pull in order to end up in her makeshift bed, Rhys walked down to the stream and took his evening bath.

Returning refreshed, he told his traveling companion, "Tomorrow, I'll need you to play a scene. When I give you the word, act the distressed maiden."

"Why would I do that?" She eyed him suspiciously.

"A rider will come. You must bait the trap."

"A trap? That's not very honorable."

"Do you want to live to see the city of Eboracum? For your own sake, do as I say, and one way or the other, you'll be better off."

"That's...nice and ambiguous." She eyed him askance.

His experience at the hands of Ellylyw and Urre of the Dolorous Mount had robbed Rhys of the pleasure he had once felt in conversation. He sat down to chew his evening bread in silence.

***

Rhys woke in the black of a hooting, rustling night when the shivering girl slipped under his blanket, trying to share his warmth without his noticing. Amused, he carefully turned his thoughts away from his attraction to her—and from what he knew he had to do in the morning—and slowly, gradually, eased himself again down the dark well of unconsciousness.

***

In the gray pre-dawn, he rose to strap on his ringmail and awakened Gwenllian. She clutched the blankets about herself and opened her mouth as if to ask questions. Rhys hushed her. "Dress."

When both were ready to face the day, he climbed his watch-tree and observed the none-too-distant knight packing up his gear. Then the warrior headed toward them along the path.

Scrambling swiftly down to terra firma, Rhys slung his shield across his back, and pulled from his saddle-pack a ball of leather cord he kept for making replacement bootlaces and helmet straps. Cutting a length from it, he took hold of Gwenllian's arm and began to bind her wrists. Gwenllian sent her long hair flying as she tried to wrestle free. "What do you think you're doing?"

Irritated, he frowned. "Setting the stage. You only need to struggle verbally."

She scowled, evading his attempt to set her free wrist by the one he held motionless. "I never do anything that isn't straightforward—"

"Quiet!" His mind was on the rate of speed at which the unseen knight approached. He whispered, "Stop struggling and protest louder."

"I am not about to cooperate in some kind of subterfuge," Gwenllian snapped. "You may have thought what my people did at Castrum Tenebrarum was treachery, but we believed in what we were doing."

Rhys sighed. This was not what the approaching knight needed to overhear. If cooperation was not to be had for the asking, he thought he knew which stones to loosen in order to break the dam. Lashing Gwenllian's wrists to the trunk of a convenient sapling, he abruptly wrapped his hand about the back of her head and pulled her face to his, pressing his lips to hers. She pushed herself free, at last protesting volubly.

He trotted off down the path, followed by an increasingly outraged stream of vituperative analyses of his character and pejorative and entirely unfounded speculations as to his ancestry. He waved cheerily at her, and as he had hoped, the flood of insults grew louder, expanding in scope to include the manifold shortcomings of his entire sex, which the young woman had apparently found occasion to compile at length.

Positioning himself behind his chosen tree by the side of the road, Rhys took hold of the end of the rope dangling from the slip-knot he had tied the evening before and listened to the hoof-falls of the knight's war-horse and the faint ringing of his chainmail.

The knight rode into sight, then, hearing the girl's outraged cries, urged his steed to a canter.

Rhys held his breath, fearing for life and mission should he miss his timing.

A jerk on the line released the slipknot, dropping the rope from the obscurity of the leafy canopy neatly behind the horse's neck, catching slantwise across the oncoming armored chest. Feet braced against the tree roots, Rhys hauled hard. The horse cantered out from under the surprised knight, who clattered metallically into the dust.

Jeffrey T. Heyer

Sliding his shield onto his left arm, Rhys snatched up his spear and raced for the fallen man.

The knight was well skilled. Despite the ambush and fall, he managed to roll up, swinging his shield from his back and unsheathing his sword. He had just time enough to spot Rhys' charge, spin toward him, and raise his shield, just as Rhys hurled the spear.

Ordinarily a spearman would try to slip his weapon past an opponent's guard while a man skilled at shield-work would seek to deflect the missile, sending it harmlessly past him. But Rhys aimed squarely for the lower quarter of the oval shield and gave his best cast, wedging the point into the hardened wood. The long shaft of the spear dragged the shield down, and the knight realized his defensive weapon was now too awkward to wield. He shucked the encumbered shield from his arm as Rhys, who had kept running after his cast, slammed shield-foremost into the knight's chest.

The skilled warrior stumbled backward, but was so stout a man that he kept his feet while swinging his blade through the air but into an instinctive parry where Rhys' sword would have been had Rhys been making a normal attack. But Rhys had not drawn his blade. Instead, he pivoted around the knight's disarmed left side and swung the iron rim of his shield against the back of the knight's helmet with a jarring impact.

Continuing his spin to gain momentum, Rhys ducked low as the knight turned to face him. Rhys' shield rim finished its second arc against the knight's chainmailed calf just below the knee, knocking his leg out from under him. As the knight fell, Rhys threw himself clear, avoiding the sword that scythed grass in his wake.

Rhys slipped off his shield, hurling it against his opponent's sword-arm, bruising the arm and knocking it flat against the earth. Leaping after the cast shield, Rhys planted his boot firmly on it, trapping the arm beneath. Rhys crouched, seized the knight's helmet and twisted, wrenching it out of alignment so that the side of the open-faced helm covered the man's right eye.

Rhys whipped out his sword as the half-blinded knight's free hand groped for his dagger. Rhys hammered his sword pommel against the steel helm again and again until his opponent's one visible eye glazed over. The bard kicked the half-drawn dagger from the limp left hand, tossed aside his shield and pried the man's sword from his clenched fingers. Standing over him, Rhys pressed its point lightly under its owner's jaw.

"Your oath or your life," Rhys shouted. "Swear to accept your fate at my hands with no thought of reprisal."

"Who are you..." the outraged and still slightly stunned knight slurred, "to claim this fate on me? You are no chieftain, nor equite."

"Your rank and mine are immaterial just now." Rhys pressed the man's own sword-point a little more firmly against his soft flesh. "I will have your armor, and I would prefer not to bloody it."

"I am of a house that counseled with Romans when they ruled all these lands," the man yelled, otherwise careful not to move. "I will not yield to one of your station."

"The Romans are long gone, but I can send you to counsel with them, if you wish." Rhys raised the sword over his head, setting himself to swing hard. "Good luck in the next world while your head remains in this."

"Wait," the knight cried. "I will yield, so it do no dishonor to my house."

"Your house need never hear of this. I will make no boasts, having beaten you with rope and bait, not superior swordsmanship." Rhys stepped back and lowered the sword-point. "Take off your armor."

His mouth contorted as by a bitter taste, the knight pulled himself up off the path and began to haul off his armor.

"You have me defenseless, now," the bested warrior said, standing before Rhys clad only in tunic and leggings.

Rhys unlaced his own helmet and tossed it to the man. "If the armor on your spare horse doesn't fit, you can always don this."

To the man's surprise, Rhys stripped off his own worn ringmail tunic and tossed it to his conquered foe. Quick to seize what advantage he could, the knight redressed himself in the inferior third-hand armor while Rhys donned the chieftain's expensive and far-hardier chainmail.

Tightening side-straps, the unhappy knight eyed his captor. "Your accent is not from my district. You are no enemy of my house, and surely you cannot know of my mission. Is it ransom you want?"

"Hardly." Rhys strapped on the knight's scuffed but undented helmet. "I mean to give you something, in fact. As to your mission, let me guess. You recently found yourself in some disgrace and sought to regain your good name by undertaking a hazardous mission for Brathach, Consularis of Eboracum."

Dark Age

The knight's dark-eyed gaze grew cautious.

"I see that I'm right," Rhys noted. "When the Consularis sent you to scout out the ruins of Castrum Tenebrarum, did he tell you the name of the free lance he sent there before you?"

The knight scowled. "Brathach said he had sent a bard but that he was not surprised the man did not return. Did you waylay him, too?"

Rhys buckled on his own sword-belt, then pulled a folded vellum from his pouch and handed it to the increasingly baffled knight.

"I am Rhys of Caer Waroc, the scout whose name the great Consularis apparently forgot. This map details what is left of Tenebrarum's defenses, together with what little I learned of the Saxon force that breached its walls. Treat this as precious. The information on it cost me dear. Tell Brathach his kinsman Madoc Broad Shoulders is dead, along with his entire garrison, but that he hurt the Saxons enough that they must lick their wounds a while. *Remind* the Consularis that unless he sends enough men to shore up the defenses, when the Saxons have spent what they've looted, they will march straight up the old Roman high road past Tenebrarum into Britain's heartland."

The knight shook his head and deepened the small wrinkles at the corners of his troubled eyes. "And you don't want to return to the safety of Eboracum? Or claim your reward for fulfilling a dangerous mission?"

Rhys smiled grimly. He saw no point in sharing his assessment of Brathach's politic character with this stranger. "Something worse than the Saxons was loosed from Castrum Tenebrarum. I must hunt it down."

"*Worse?*" The knight glared at him, openmouthed. "The barbarians have shattered the coastal forts and dug themselves in for good along our whole eastern shore. They raid and they burn our farms in a time of famine, and they take no prisoners, having no way to feed slaves. The barbarians mean to eat the island alive. What could be worse for Britain than Saxons?"

"Ask Gwenllian," Rhys suggested quietly. "See if she'll tell you."

The knight's face set. "The woman I heard in distress?"

Rhys nodded. "Her distress was a show. She is the last survivor of Castrum Tenebrarum. Get her to Brathach. She knows the whole story...though how much of it she will tell is another matter."

"You ambush me..." the defeated knight said, shaking his head, and then he immediately realized that was a mistake after the painful battering his skull had received, "and then you give me everything I need to complete my mission?"

"And thereby complete mine. I am quit with Brathach. Do as I say and you will soon be quit of me without risking the rest of the trip to Castrum Tenebrarum. Even now you do not want to go there."

Rhys drew the broken sword he had taken from Madoc's corpse back at the ruined castrum and handed it hilt-first to the knight, then slid the knight's sword into his own scabbard. After untying his rope from the tree, he coiled it as he jingled briskly up the path to where Gwenllian fretted, chewing at her leather bonds. The young woman was surprised to see both men approaching without signs of damage, and in each other's armor.

"This is Gwenllian the Tall." Rhys untied the knotted leather.

"Caius Senyllt." The knight bowed to her.

"Well met, Equite." Gwenllian smiled with a dip of her brown hair. "I thought I heard..."

"It is common..." Rhys freed her wrists and wound up his slightly chewed leather cordage, "for two warriors to share a little morning's exercise when they meet on the road." He turned toward Caius. "I thank you for trading arms with me. You are far the more skillful fighter, while I will need every advantage I can get where I am going."

Gwenllian's eyes caught Rhys'. "So, you're chasing Ellylyw?" He did not respond, but she saw it was so. She swallowed unhappily. "You're just dumping me off on this strange knight?"

Rhys gazed at her. She looked softer than she had since they had set out from the ruined fortress. Sad to see her go, he shrugged. "You're trading up, aren't you?"

Gwenllian gazed soberly into his eyes. Impulsively, she leaned forward and gave him a little soft, moist-lipped kiss, then pulling back, she smiled and slipped her hand through the crook of the knight's arm.

"Ahh," Caius began, "my...the...horses?"

Rhys smiled again. "A knight needs a young, spry charger to put drive behind his lance, while I promised my old friend Morvran Steel Hooves that I would care for him so long as he lives. Besides, Gwenllian misses a tent more than will I." The scarred bard looked at them both for what he was certain would be the last time. "Who knows? Maybe you will both find places in Brathach's court."

Caius still could not understand his captor. "But you will not?"

Gwenllian's smile disappeared. "He has found his place. At last. Be careful, Rhys of Caer Waroc."

Rhys lightly plucked a verdant leaf from the early morning sparkles in her hair. "Find what you really seek, Gwenllian the Tall."

Then Rhys swung up onto Morvran's back and set the old horse on the track of Ellylyw, Lady of Castrum Tenebrarum, former love, present enemy, threat to the people of besieged Britain and the fate of Rhys of Caer Waroc.

Chapter 8:

The Dead City

His dream world burst, leaving no trace. Feeling his hand close of its own accord on the pommel of the sword beside him, he listened intently, motionless in the darkness, barely breathing. Rhys had slept so little for so long that he could not remember where he lay.

His aging charger Morvran snorted, awkwardly levering his bulk down onto the straw. Rhys heard no other sound but the cry of distant morning birds. At least their clear calls meant the sun would soon rise. He tossed off his blanket and stepped into the morning chill, shocking himself more thoroughly awake. Taut with vague misease, he tented bits of straw over dying embers in the rock-encircled campfire. Tinder followed and caught, providing light and warmth. An empty stable took shape around him, his make-shift hearth in the straw-cleared midst of its earthen floor.

Of course. He remembered his aging mount limping painfully up the slight rise to the great stone wall that guarded the city, its massive rear gate hanging listlessly open on one hinge. Nothing moved within but the carrion crows winging and crying above thatched or tiled roofs...a whole city abandoned.

He recalled glancing anxiously at the red sun hanging dangerously low behind thin shreds of cloud. Rhys had dismounted to lead his four-footed companion-in-arms through the unguarded portal, past gaping household doors and empty shop windows, everything eerily intact. The Saxons had never bothered to sack this outlying suburb, so before night could catch him, Rhys was able to find a stable to hide in and to bar its door behind him and his mount. It was no pleasure sleeping in a place of violence and despair, but since the death of Arthur three generations past, Britain's heritage had been one long slide into chaos. As a hermit had once told Rhys, this was the Aetas Tenebrarum, the Age of Darkness, and more than any other man in the isle, Rhys was aware of just what was moving in that dark.

He shivered himself back into present time. Morvran's snorts and snuffles sounded distressed; maybe that was what had alerted him. Tugging on tunic and breeches, Rhys slipped into his heavy chainmail, ran a hand over his stubbly, claw-scarred face and decided he did not care to shave today. He went outside to make water against the rear of the disused building, then returned to see to Morvran.

The charger looked up for a moment, then dropped his head on the stale straw.

"What's wrong, old friend?" Rhys stroked the sleek black face. Morvran plucked at his sleeve with mobile lips, puffing air in an unnervingly disheartened fashion.

Rhys carefully explored his mount's afflicted leg with practiced fingers, flexing it gently. He found no more amiss than he had the night before. He had probably just pushed Morvran too hard on his single-minded hunt. Like any warrior who survived his prime, the steed had a dozen old injuries that pained him whenever the air cooled. Rhys patted the long, muscular neck, then stopped abruptly, feeling with a shock a crusted wound on the horse's throat. Peering through the faint firelight he saw a clean, shallow cut from a sharp blade. No blood dripped below the puckered edges of the gash.

"You bastards." Rhys seethed.

A fury that surprised him with its viciousness boiled through every artery, wiping away his morning stiffness, priming him to kill. "You revenant bastards, you fed on my horse!"

Blood loss left Morvran too weak to travel. Rhys had no choice but to spend another day and a night in this empty city.

No, not empty. This was proof that the creatures he stalked had, indeed, arrived here before him, Ellylyw, herself, presumably among them.

After belting on his sword and strapping pack and shield across his back, Rhys strode outside, sucked in a deep draft of dark air and bellowed at the ranks of empty windows, "Tired of running, Ellylyw? Want to finish it?" His voice was shaking for all of his attempts to steady it.

He swiveled to shout at a new set of windows. "You should have tried your luck on me last night in my sleep. I know you've made followers in the weeks I've hunted you, but it was *you*, wasn't it, who got inside the stable...stood so close to me...sliced an artery and lapped up my horse's blood? You want me to stay, I'll stay. Dawn is coming. It's my turn, now."

Jogging down the empty street, he searched building

after building in a widening spiral about the stable where Morvran lay. Rhys raved quietly to himself as he tore through empty huts. "You think you're safe because your kind are unknown in Britain, except to me? Well, I may not know much, but I learned a few things before the monster that made you like this was destroyed. You never stir by day. I have until nightfall to run you down before the tables turn again."

He ducked into a large, multi-room house, pausing as something caught his eye. Pale pre-dawn rays seeped through the smoke-hole in the center of the ratty thatched roof, revealing a raised hearth surrounded by chaotically strewn cookware, tossed every which way in the hasty evacuation. In striking contrast, a gaming board had been carefully positioned on the broad stone ring about the hearth. On the board stood a neat ring of carved figures surrounding a lone piece, the set-up for a round of gwyddbwyll, the same woodcraft game Rhys had seen in the mausoleum of the Lady Ellylyw's dark lover Urre of the Dolorous Mount. Rhys felt buffeted by fierce dark wings of hate as he pictured again his terrible struggle with Urre, saw again the destruction of that deadly ruin of a man who had brought this eastern revenant plague from Hungary.

Then Rhys touched the central piece on the game board and smiled. He understood its message.

One player was meant to move the ring of pieces representing hunters trying to corner the king stag. That player was Ellylyw, her hunters whatever unfortunates she had fed upon while fleeing before Rhys on her way to lose herself in the depths of this dead city. Her opponent had only one piece; he was the lone king stag in the center of the board who must try to break out of the ring and escape. That was Rhys.

She was playing with him. A pang lanced through his chest. At least Ellylyw had that much humanity left, that much ability to feel pleasure.

"I'll give you a game," he whispered, hand on hilt.

He moved on.

***

Once tall stone pillars lay shattered in sections before the pocked façade of the local senate house. Beside its gaping doorway luxuriated the smooth-limbed statue so delicately painted he might have taken her for a living woman but for the faceless head, smashed by the Saxons, as pointlessly destructive as their Vandal cousins on the continent. Rhys could not help picturing Ellylyw's breathtaking face on that languorous form, remembering how he had first seen her, confined to her bed at the ruined fortress of Castrum Tenebrarum. Before Urre of Hungary pulled her halfway out of Rhys' world.

Trudging on, he shook off the memory. Carefully tracking the sun's progress as he went, he reached the center of the devastation. Rhys could see well enough what had happened here. When his grandfather was a boy, the Romans had been driven at last from the isle. With them they took the last of Britain's trained soldiers. Invaders poured in, and British shopkeepers stood uncaptained on their city's walls, not knowing how to protect themselves. The hooked spears of Saxon mercenaries had plucked them down like ripe fruit.

Jeffrey T. Heyer

Rhys gazed across the littered square at the distant city wall. From twisted hinges hung fragments of the main gate, shattered by a Saxon ram. Blocking the street to his left lay a clutter of charred timbers where the Saxons had torched a church. They really hated those. The fire had not spread beyond a few neighboring roofs, so there must have been heavy rains during the attack.

The endless emptiness of the buildings surrounding Rhys began to unnerve him. Stalking through the heart of a city so big that it had proved beyond the energy of the vigorous Saxons to lay entirely in ruins, so prosperous that it had yet to have its bones picked clean by all the scavengers in famine-wracked Britain, it struck Rhys viscerally why so many people believed the end of the world was nigh.

Rhys hitched his shoulders, settling his bulky chainmail less uncomfortably upon them. He told himself yet again that he was a bard, trained to preserve and transmit the ancient truths of his people, not to hold a city wall against barbarians. He could do little to save Britain from its slow rape and subjection beneath the savage Saxon heel. Yet he alone knew of the revenants. At least he might keep the likes of Ellylyw from battening on the chaos.

A raven cawed, loud and coarse while landing in the rubble nearby, jarring him from his thoughts. He veered away, knowing the black bird fed on bodies crushed under the fallen buildings. He needed to skirt the ruined area. Even the half-dead could find no shelter where ravens fed.

Forced to veer from his path yet again, he picked his way over holy altars lying at odd angles in the debris, hacked by war-axes. This was taking too long, slowing him with too many detours. Glancing up to track the sun's progress, he spied heavy clouds roiling in from the coast. With a chill he realized their onset would greatly hasten the fall of darkness. Abandoning his fruitless search, he trotted back the way he had come, afraid for his steed.

***

Sharp wind moaned through the narrow alley, and the first big patters of rain bounced off his jingling mail. Rhys sighed, unable to pretend to himself any longer that he could make it back to Morvran's stable in time. He ducked out of the chill wet into a large house and quickly hauled off his chainmail armor. Allowing himself one quick stretch and scratch, he swiftly emptied his backpack while he could still use the waning light to prepare for the night's siege. Breaking the wax seal on a pot of black paint he had scavenged, he fashioned a brush from old rags, thickly coating his armor and even his weapons, aware of the irony that he now bore the color of Ellylyw's former love, Urre, the Black Knight of Hungary, the first revenant to set foot in Britain.

While the paint dried, Rhys rubbed his scarred face and hands with a chunk of dark blue woad found in a dyer's shop. It stank like rank marsh, but Pictish warriors had painted themselves with the stuff for centuries to camouflage the gleam of human skin and to hide their own humanity from themselves before battle. If Picts could stand it, so could Rhys.

The sun had not set, but the storm blotted all light from the sky. Rhys donned his black armor and hung the refilled pack against his back.

Wood creaked behind him. Rhys whipped out his sword, spinning, blade overhead, point forward, left arm sliding into his shield straps.

A dark figure eyed him through a doorless arch, face pale, eyes unblinking, features set. For an instant Rhys felt as if he had been caught burgling the man's house, but he knew what he was really facing, and having set eyes upon each other, what each must try to do.

Rhys sprang, bounding onto a trunk, leaping from its top through the arch where a moment before the figure had stood.

The revenant was already at the central hearth in the room beyond, a thick iron poker in his hand, encumbered by the drapery of his elegantly impractical Roman cloak. Rhys gauged his opponent as he leapt, grasping in a flash that, while he had pursued Ellylyw through waste country, she must have caught this man traveling on business and made him one of her own. The half-Roman must then have accompanied Ellylyw on her long journey north. So, Rhys' foe was no trained combatant, the revenant had instinctively reached for the nearest weapon, trusting in that terrible energy that gave his kind such power.

Rhys swept his sword, and whistling through the air, his blade bit clean through the iron poker and into the side of the revenant's neck. The creature staggered back in surprise, hissing blood as Rhys continued his spin. Before the wounded monster recovered from its surprise, Rhys completed his arc, the whirling blade severing the creature's neck bones. The revenant's body fell, limbs twitching.

In any other battle, Rhys would have plunged on,

seeking his next foe, but a terrible fear of contagion held him in its jaws. Seizing a corner of the Roman cloak, he wiped revenant blood from his blade and his shaking hands.

He ran into the next room and picked his way across a scattering of abandoned toys. Rhys stopped abruptly. Silhouetted in the doorway at the far side of the room was a slim female form, clear and black against a patch of moonlight. His breath caught.

"Ellylyw?" He choked.

The figure withdrew through the door. He raced after it, sword thrust before him. Outside, the full moon had broken through a gap in the storm, giving Rhys a fighting chance against the night vision of the revenants. Silvery light showed a little garden of withered flowers. Dead leaves ghosted across the dry basin of a fountain and into the yawning gulf of an empty bath. Rhys flicked his gaze about the vague, half-lit shapes.

There!

She stood atop a flight of stone steps on a little viewing platform atop the garden wall, her stance casual, unafraid. Rhys, on the other hand, could not stop trembling. None of these monsters could shake him like Ellylyw could, because she alone made him fear himself.

"Gwyddbwyll king," she said, her tones clear and musical, amused and detached.

"It *is* you."

"You have checked one of my huntsmen." She raised a lithe arm. A great owl winged out of the moon to land on her upraised wrist like a hawk on a falconer's gauntlet. Two great wolfhounds bayed from the other side of the wall, then leapt up beside her on the narrow platform. They panted, moonlight mirrored in great round eyes fixed on Rhys.

"A hunt," Ellylyw said, "is better sport with hawks and hounds."

"Why do you toy with me?" Rhys called hoarsely.

"The mouse does not question the cat." The huntress thrust her hand forward, loosing the owl.

Rhys spun on his heel, dashed along the side of the building, skirting the dry bath, heart pounding. He marveled that at the same time he was excruciatingly aware of the delicate beauty of the vine-laced latticework roofing the walkway along which he ran. The swooping owl glided up out of sight, avoiding the confined space beneath the lattice. The hounds bayed again, filling Rhys' blood with spikes. They leapt down the steps after him.

Rounding the far side of the bath, he heard the lead dog's savage growl at his heels. Rhys spun, swinging low with his sword, but the dog sprang to the side, away from the blade. The second wolfhound leapt, slamming into his prey's chest. Feet still under him, Rhys clenched his left hand on the shaggy throat. The hound fastened its powerful jaws on his steel and leather shoulder-guard. Rhys flung himself sideways and rammed the dog's ribs against the pillar beside him. With a yelp the animal let go and slid over the edge of the bath to scrabble down the smooth sides to its bottom.

Catching his elbow hard against the stone pillar, Rhys' hand went numb. He heard his sword clatter to the flagstones beside him. The first dog snarled and leapt, leaving Rhys just time enough to fling his shield before him.

The impact of the shaggy creature bounced Rhys off the pillar. Disoriented in flashes of moonlight and shadow, Rhys fell, mail ringing on the stones, hound pawing madly at his shield, trying to dig through wood and steel to the flesh beneath. The hound in the bath, failing to make its way back up the smooth wall, howled dismally.

Its comrade lunged at Rhys' face, teeth snapping uselessly at his helm as he ducked farther beneath the shield, pressed down by the big dog's weight. Rhys was at an impossible angle, unable to push upward and fling the dog off his left arm, but feeling was jangling again in his right hand, so he used it to draw his dagger and strike blindly. The dog sensed the attack coming, stopped biting at the helm and turned its head to seize the oncoming wrist, but its fangs were too slow to catch in the flashing chainmail sleeve, and the dagger drove to its hilt between two shaggy ribs. Screaming, the dog flailed its way off its intended prey, biting at the pommel protruding from its side.

Rhys already had his legs under him, but as he started to reach for his sword to end the pain of the shrill-whining dog, its flailing paws sent the blade skittering down into the bath.

The bard swore, pulling from its makeshift sheath the broken sword-tip, the butt of which he had, weeks ago, bound with a leather grip. With no better weapon, he swung himself over the side of the bath and landed on the smooth concrete base. The remaining hound flung itself at him, baying furiously. It hit the shield, not quite tumbling Rhys off his feet and seizing the upper rim in great slavering jaws. Hot rank breath struck Rhys in the face. The wolfhound growled in ferocious determination, shaking its head viciously from side to side, wrenching at the shield and the arm strapped to it.

Rhys threw himself, shield-first, on top of the dog, which still refused to let go while scrabbling madly. The bard slipped his arm out of the straps. Even with Rhys' chainmailed weight atop it, the animal managed to paw the shield aside, and thereby bared its belly. Rhys rammed the sword-tip up through tough skin and sinew and stabbed it under the ribs toward the heart.

One howl and a gush of blood issued from the spasming beast, then Rhys swung his shield above his head in time to hear the owl's claws rake its surface.

Moon glints faded from the fallen sword as the clouds closed again, but Rhys snatched up the weapon on the run. He knew that when the Saxons besieged the city they would have been obliged to hold their shields over their heads for long periods to protect themselves from the archers on the walls. But Rhys had never fought in a pitched battle and was none too sure how long he could keep his left arm in the air. Dashing to the steps in the nearest corner of the bath, he made his way out of the exposed trap.

Twice more the winged predator swooped from the night sky to scrape talons across the shield as Rhys sprinted for the garden wall, hearing more dogs howling to each other from all about the metropolis. Thousands of them must have been abandoned in the abrupt evacuation, and it seemed they could refuse Ellylyw nothing, just like every man who met her when she lived.

Claws scored the middle of the shield followed by

Dark Age

another set scraping the left rim even as a third set clicked against the right edge. The aerial predators were increasing in number and daring.

Rhys dashed through an open gateway at the back of the garden and down an alley between two tall wood-walled manors. Attackers from above could not easily angle in under his shield in the narrow space, but his raised arm already felt like lead, and he could easily be overwhelmed should a dog pack come flooding in from either alley end.

He pulled up at a black-shadowed doorway. The door was latched, so he leaned his weight against it, forcing open enough of a crack to slip the sword-tip through and lift the latch.

Claws screeched across the back of his helm, and angry wings buffeted him, then he was inside, re-latching the door behind him. His own loud panting in the dead dark deafened him to any sound of approaching danger. If no moonlight got in, however, he reasoned that no firelight could get out to reveal his location. Crouching on the floor, he pulled a dried rush from his pouch and then flint and steel. Several nerve-racking strikes later, he sparked the rush alight.

Unfortunately, he was now obliged to sling his shield against his back in order to hold forward the little light in his left hand with his sword at the ready in his right. He made his way cautiously amid a maze of toppled trunks and tumbled furniture. Bright wary eyes glinted at him from one corner, a weasel still keeping down the mice after its human employers had fled.

Rush-light shone on a great loom stretching into the

rafters. Before it, a round-bodied woman with wings of gray at her temples moved slowly about the room, oblivious to Rhys and his light. She leaned down, hands moving purposefully through empty air, her face blank, wide eyes devoid of notice that there was no spindle where her hands moved deftly to wind the non-existent thread. Deftly she worked an absent shuttle, integrating remembered thread into a perpetually half-finished skein.

Rhys stared at her slack features, bloodless and wan, and the scars on her throat left by human teeth. She had lost all sense of self. Of all this unknown woman had once been, only this creature of habit survived, endlessly repeating motions that had once given purpose to her life, she was now as mechanical as the barren loom she served. Rhys swallowed, set himself, then struck her head from her shoulders. Her body faltered at the impact, hands and legs twitching spasmodically, as if trying to continue their fruitless tasks, then the teetering body collapsed. The wide-eyed head lay nearby, expressionless as before.

Rhys had to tell her, "I understand."

The wide eyes seemed at last to notice him. Slowly her mouth opened.

Rhys ran from the room. Dogs bayed outside, pawing wildly at closed doors, gnawing at shuttered windows. Soon they would find a way in. Besides, Rhys had to keep moving. Maybe he could no longer hope to corner Ellylyw in this maze, but he had to keep her hunting party busy until he could get back to Morvran.

Lifting an iron holder from a sconce, he lit its candle with his fading rush and trotted on, kicking aside household detritus. The dust in the enclosed space made his sinuses

Dark Age

swell shut and his nose run. Wonderful. More distractions. If he did not soon reach open air, he would start wheezing and coughing. This was not the first occasion he had thought this life-long condition might indirectly prove the death of him.

Rhys rubbed spiderwebs from his face, their tickle irritating. A sudden flow of moonlight spilled through an upper window, lighting a staircase. By its foot reared a dark arch and through it lunged a figure in a forester's rough tunic, face twisted in an animal snarl, wide eyes glinting moonlight, thick-fingered hands snatching at its prey.

Knocked from Rhys' hand, the candle spattered him with hot wax, landed on its side to cast wavering light, sending shadows leaping. The predator threw Rhys to the floor, grappled with him, and wrested the sword from his grasp. The revenant cast the steel across the room, turned ravenous eyes on its supine prey, erratic candlelight gleaming from the narrow bald head, then guttering so only the staring eyes glinted from sudden shadow.

Down toward Rhys the revenant lunged, its teeth clinking against the chain on his armored forearm before they could meet in the sinews of his throat. Rhys stabbed him in the gut with the broken sword-tip and slashed upward, opening a long and bleeding gash.

The revenant threw itself back with a throaty gasp, claw-like hands squeezing the wound shut, trying to hold in its precious blood. Rhys scrambled away through rubbish, losing vital seconds as scattered wooden bowls slid beneath his feet. He hurled a broken chair at his pursuer's face and fled, heard the awkward missile batted aside behind him, and the angry snarl of the blood-drinker close on his heels.

Rhys leaned down, reaching—

Frenzied hands caught the shield on Rhys' back and jerked him upright from the floor, just as his hand closed about the pommel of his fallen sword. A shriek he did not recognize tore from Rhys' throat as he lashed sideways behind him, feeling the blade sheer his attacker's ribs.

The revenant howled, lost its grip on the shield. Rhys whirled full-force, blade taking off its head at a blow. He bolted from the room without pause, gasping, because where one revenant could enter, so could more.

He spied the great front door, threw it open, and dashed into sheeting rain, the main street now a slideway of mud. At least the lane was broad enough that he could freely swing his recovered sword. Shield again on arm, waiting for the strike of hawk or hound, Rhys slipped and slogged through the endless desolation of the night.

Behind him, light flared and he glanced back, skidding. Through the door he had left open, he saw tongues of flame lick across the littered wooden floor, no doubt ignited by the fallen candle. Fire in a close-packed city of thatched roofs could be deadly, but he dared not turn back.

Four big hunting dogs bounded around the corner of the building and launched toward him, rain flying from drenched coats. Claws reached from the sky, tearing his cheek frighteningly close to his right eye, making him cry out.

The stable was just ahead. Rhys put on an extra burst of speed, running harder than he had ever run before. To his surprise, he discovered that he could run a little faster still.

Skidding, windmilling his encumbered arms, Rhys clanged into the stable door, jerked it open, ducked inside, slammed and bolted it as frustrated paws and snapping jaws shook and gouged the sturdy wood. Lungs heaving, sweat lubricated his whole body, stung his eyes. He smelled smoke from the burning manor and hoped there was distance and rainwater enough to save his shelter.

After dropping sword and shield and leaning hands on his thighs, he emptied and refilled his laboring lungs again and again. Then his breath caught. Clear, plaintive notes rang out from the hayloft.

He knew the hand that plucked them from his own familiar traveler's harp. In a panic, he rearmed himself, shield raised as he looked up.

Ellylyw stepped gracefully to the edge of the loft, striking an achingly beautiful chord on the harp and in Rhys' aching chest. A swirl of smoke followed her, drawn in through the open hayloft door behind.

"You destroyed them all," she told him sadly. "All my new companions."

Rhys managed to swallow and to inhale and to lift his sword-point toward her, but could find no words.

"I am alone again," she said, voice high and plaintive. "Except for you."

One corner of Rhys' mouth quirked up, then twisted into a grimace. "You found the perfect city, didn't you," he said, mouth dry. "For the two of us."

A delicate semi-smile wavered about Ellylyw's lips. She leaned tapered fingers against a post.

Rhys opened his mouth twice, then found words. "What now? Do we go on playing cat and mouse in a burning building, just you and I?"

"I have something for you," Ellylyw said tenderly and held out one hand. Rhys stepped beneath the edge of the loft and flung the shield from his left hand, despite the danger. Ellylyw opened her fingers, dropping a small object into Rhys' palm. He moved cautiously back against the far wall, then looked at it. In his hand lay the king from Urre of Hungary's gwyddbwyll board.

Smoke and rain gusted into the loft, and Morvran levered himself to his feet in his stall, shaking his ears in mounting alarm.

Ellylyw dipped her head toward Rhys. "You have bought time while I gather pieces for a new game."

Owl's wings swooped for his face. He ducked, left arm before his eyes, sweeping his blade blindly about him, filling the air with steel. His sword touched nothing. Rhys looked cautiously over his forearm, peering swiftly about him. The owl was gone.

So was Ellylyw.

Saddling the uneasy Morvran, Rhys led him through driving, chilling rain, back the way he had first come, beyond the unguarded suburb gate. The city's dogs had already fled the fire.

Rhys wrapped his cloak about himself, flung his blanket over Morvran's back, then sat, weary back against the city wall, Morvran's warm head drooped beside him. They shivered in the downpour and watched the reflection of the flames flicker in the falling rain.

Chapter 9:

Severance

R hys dropped down from the top of the high stone wall. The clinking of his heavy chainmail as his boots hit the ground sounded impossibly loud in the hush of the dusk-dimmed garden. A dozen paces away, he saw the robed clergyman he sought stiffen, staring at him, hand still stretched toward a perfectly formed rose. The abbot's well-fed face tautened, graying hair bristled, and breath suspended.

A stab of empathy pained Rhys at the naked terror in the older man's wide eyes. The sudden appearance within the guarded enclosure of a young man in black chainmail and helm, claw-scarred face painted blue like one of the fierce, primitive Picts pouring over Hadrian's Wall in the north, would be quite a shock for the cloistered Abbot Severus at the best of times.

Rhys was certain that Severus knew, as well as he did, that fresh bands of wild Gaels were even that moment overrunning the whole west of Britain. More shocking still, a new wave of Saxons from the east were licking their wounds after tearing through Castrum Tenebrarum. Rhys was painfully aware that he had not come at the best of times.

The abbot pulled his shattered aura of authority back

around himself. "You have no right to be here."

"I've heard that all my life." Rhys wheezed, eyes itching a little as he strode toward the cleric through the choking scent of flowering herbs.

Severus snapped, "This is no place for unwashed heathen Picts."

Rhys forced himself to keep marching, surprised and annoyed to hear a distinct tremble in his voice. "I blue my face with woad and paint my armor black in order to move unseen by night. I am no Pict but a Briton like yourself."

"Then show some Christian respect," Severus demanded. "The guards at the town gates should have—"

"I didn't come through the gates, and none but you must know what business binds us."

The clergyman cast a baleful eye over Rhys, noting the crisscrossing tracks clawed through the black paint on Rhys' open-faced helm, matching the scars furrowed under the blue camouflage on his face.

The armored man, well aware he stank of sweat and horse, stepped closer. "My name is Rhys of Caer Waroc, bard by trade. Hard though it is for me to be here, I think you are the only man in the isle besides myself who knows of what I must speak, the-the new...*plague* that took the Lady Ellylyw, wife of Madoc, commander of the fallen fortress above your town. I need your help—"

"Help?" Realization and alarm glinted in his eyes. "There are hard men in my abbey. Men grateful for sanctuary from the law." He turned away, opening his mouth to call them.

"I'm hunting revenants." Rhys hoped to forestall him.

The abbot's eyes, the only sharpness in his round face,

caught and skewered Rhys.

"Those revived from the dead."

"I know the word," the cleric snapped.

"You've seen it happen."

"What makes you think..."

Scabbarded sword jangling against his chainmail, the bard strode up inches from the abbot's face. "Don't waste my time. I've precious little, as have you. You burned all the bodies you found in the ruins of Castrum Tenebrarum. You would never have denied its garrison Christian burial unless you had learned, as I did, that a revenant plague was brought there by Urre of Hungary, the Black Knight of the Dolorous Mount."

The abbot took a step back at that name and straightened. "Only our Lord could come back from the dead. To suggest otherwise is a crime against God and a threat to the souls of men."

"I expected the like from you. That's why I bypassed your guards at the town gate by scaling the palisade. You don't have enough fit townsmen left to patrol the parapets. Reinforce the town guard with some of those hardened criminals you boast of keeping. More importantly, you missed *one* body at Tenebrarum. That *one* will spread the infection. For weeks I've tracked her. Now I'm back here for a clergyman to lay her to rest. Then you can go back to telling yourself it never happened."

Severus snorted. "You say you're a bard—"

"You needn't fear I'll make a ballad of this." Rhys smiled wryly. "I agree there can be no talk of revenants, though not for your reason. Gaelic, Pictish and Saxon invaders are chewing up our island. I won't give Britons

Jeffrey T. Heyer

more cause to panic. Besides, I'll risk my soul fighting revenants, but I won't risk burning at the stake. You're kinder to monsters than to heretics."

"I think you are a crude, worldly man, a free lance, a wandering killer of men and a professional spreader of lewd and frivolous songs. Perhaps even a damned pagan. You've been in the brush too long. Perhaps you don't understand how we do things these days...how I run this town."

Threats always rasped Rhys' nerves. He sucked in breath to quell a sudden rush of rage. "While you hid behind your walls, I've ridden the empty streets of Britain's cities lying abandoned before the invaders. I'm well aware that, with so many cities in ruin, bishops mean nothing now, and abbots like you are the new princes of the Church."

"This is a God-fearing town. With half the isle lawless, these people hunger for order. They often kill for it. And you, a ragged free lance, slip over their palisade to stand within sword's reach of the abbot himself? I think I've heard enough from you." He turned again toward the dark alcove behind him to call his brethren.

Rhys reached out to stop him. "Listen to me."

Severus slapped his hand aside. "You said you needed me, so I know your sword is useless. You have no other power over me."

"*She* will have," Rhys hissed, limbs chilling and stomach sinking from desperation. "Ellylyw, the Lady of Castrum Tenebrarum, was the lover of Urre of Hungary. It was her body you missed. She's like him now. She killed the mercenary you hired to destroy Urre. She'll come for you, soon, and then for me, as I, too, had a hand in destroying the Black Knight of the Dolorous Mount."

The round face twitched. "Even if I believed you, how should I oppose such a creature? I am no warrior."

"You are a spiritual warrior. When it comes time for blade work, I will do what is necessary."

Severus cast a belittling eye over Rhys' black-painted, imperfectly fitting gear. "You?"

"I offer you a chance. Come with me. Use the rituals of the Church to lay a troubled spirit to rest before it hounds you to an ugly death...and worse."

The priest's mouth twitched. "I am abbot here. I cannot simply go."

"You can leave things in your prior's hands for a few weeks. But you can hardly send another on this mission."

"No?" The abbot sniffed, fanning the sweat-scented air from his nose.

Rhys smiled wryly. "Can you trust your secret, and your life, to a subordinate?"

Hatred flared in the abbot's face.

"So..." Rhys nodded. "I was right. No one in town knows you burned the bodies at Castrum Tenebrarum, much less that you did it for a reason you cannot admit even to yourself."

Severus swallowed his hatred and molded his features into an expressionless mask.

"I can find Ellylyw," Rhys said. "You need me to fight this battle for you and to keep it secret after."

The abbot flicked his gaze away. After all Rhys had survived, he hated standing there suffering this pampered man's judgment, but he gritted his teeth, looked the clergyman in the eye, and waited for him to decide.

Severus frowned. "With Saxons everywhere, arms are scarce. Even if you're only a bard, you look brutish enough. You will serve as my armed escort on parish business tomorrow. Prove yourself and I will consider what you say."

Rhys forced himself to grant the cleric a slight bow of his stiff neck.

One corner of the abbot's mouth turned up at that. "For tonight you must stay."

"I appreciate your hospitality."

"It isn't that. I simply won't speak another word to you 'til you've bathed and laundered every item in your possession."

"The road has been hard," Rhys admitted, "and I am always in haste. I would appreciate the opportunity."

***

The woad scrubbed from his face, his frayed and faded clothing fresh, and his arms repainted, Rhys felt considerably more human. Despite the latest famine spreading across Britain, Rhys had supped his fill at the abbey, and on considerably more sophisticated fare than he had managed to glean of late from the forest. Now he rode through eye-achingly bright daylight, his aging charger Morvran keeping pace with the clergyman's overweight little palfrey.

Severus eyed his refurbished but travel-worn escort with little liking, and then turned his head to acknowledge the respectful salutes of four gaunt, dispirited guards in old-fashioned leather armor. The spearmen cringed under

Dark Age

Severus's glare as the two horses jogged through the open town gateway and left the log palisade behind.

Rhys knew he should keep silent, but could not help asking, "Your larder...was it stocked from the garrison supplies stored beneath Castrum Tenebrarum?"

The clergyman's sharp eyes narrowed like archers ducking behind puffy hills.

"I was at Tenebrarum. I saw how much was hidden from the raiders in the cave below...until you came searching the ruins for bodies. Your town goes hungry, yet your abbey dines well."

The cleric cast his eyes over the road ahead. "God provides for His shepherds."

"But not for His flock?"

The abbot rounded on him. "How is it, bard, that you wear arms only a knight could afford? I hear some men follow the armies not to fight but to rob the dead."

Rhys clapped a hand to his hilt. "The knight I took this from was very much alive at the time. I hope he lives still. The isle needs every sword-arm it can get. I take it that you, on the other hand, inherited everything you have. Including this unseemly disdain for those who earn their keep."

"Ah." The prelate sneered. "You favor the current political aberration in this lost isle, this government by commons, a contradiction in terms. Democracy is a straw dog set up by those rebels who betrayed the Romans. It won't last. The great houses will always rule."

The bard replied, "I memorize the histories of the great houses for a living. I know who stabbed whom to make himself great. Your clan badge is Regni, better known as The Haughty Ones of the Isle, the tribe that betrayed Britain to the invading Romans and profited by lands seized from our patriots. Four hundred years later, your clan is still despised by all others. Did that fact influence your decision to hide your wealth in an obscure abbey now that the cities are falling?"

"You are impertinent."

"I'm unimpressed by pretension. My forebears were honest farmers, like most people. My father was chosen judge...spent his whole life struggling to keep alive the law that makes us more than animals."

"Spirit does that, not law."

Rhys patted Morvran's bobbing black neck. "You honestly think this war-horse, half hobbled from too many battles but still in service, has less spirit than you, who live off tithes and stores robbed from a ruined fortress?"

"You *are* a pagan." Severus shot him a dangerous glance, then shook his head as he flicked a fallen leaf from his robe. "You believe animals and plants and stones have spirits. You are blind, deaf and dumb to all that matters in this veil of tears, and I fear for your soul when you pass on."

"I believe nothing whatever," Rhys shot back. "I see the spirit in my horse as plainly as I see yours. There's no more spiritual divide between human and animal, than between races, or sexes, and recognizing our kinship makes the world a better place. Look at the burnt huts we're passing. There are too many factions carving us into hostile camps."

"What makes you think the world is meant to be better?" The prelate smiled bleakly. "I do look at how the wrath of God is made manifest in sinful Britain. This is the domain of evil, the place of testing, an anvil on which to hammer out stronger steel. All true Christians look forward to the apocalypse that will *in our lifetimes* end this hateful world that we may rule justly in the next."

Rhys soaked in the gold and green splendor of the forest they skirted. "You don't feel a part of this world at all, do you?"

The abbot's lips curled subtly. "My place in the world was assured before I was ever born. Right now, I am all the link you have with the society of men."

Rhys looked away, filling his eyes with the bright images of the trail, burning from his mind's eye uglier images of men slain in ghastly ways for beliefs branded unorthodox. The bard clamped shut his mouth, bitten by the irony that in search of help he had put himself in the power of a creature perhaps as dangerous as the revenant he both fled and hunted.

Rhys glanced back at Severus. Was the abbot, too, a victim of corrupted blood, in his case, that of the Regni? No. Rhys had sung once for a chieftain of that clan who had made peace with the Council of Commons. Even the Haughty Ones occasionally bred a decent soul. Rhys was sure that Severus would be as quick to kill those unlike himself had he been born into another tribe and another faith.

Still, Rhys knew enough to say nothing. Why, he demanded pointlessly of himself, did it disturb him so to swallow the man's arrogance? Why did his stomach feel it was boiling up into his chest whenever he had to stop himself from standing up for what felt most important to him?

But Severus was right. Crossing the abbot would break Rhys' last tie to his embattled society.

"My eyes are ever on heaven." Severus spoke with quiet satisfaction.

"Mine tend to follow the ravens. They're circling the clearing ahead. Not a good sign."

"More pagan superstition."

"Ravens eat carrion," Rhys pointed out. "There's death at the farm you're visiting."

In the clearing ahead stood a thin, stooped man in loose-hanging leather vest and patched knee-length breeches stained with soil. There were gaps in his beard, and his tongue worked inside his mouth like a man losing teeth to scurvy.

A bleak sign for Britain when farmers go hungry.

The farmhouse behind the stooped man was in better trim, its circular wattle walls insulated with mortarless stone stacked to the low eaves of the conical thatched roof. Three dogs of no discernable breed came flying over the trampled ground, barking furiously at the interlopers. The smell was no better nor worse than other farms, but the thatch was thick with ravens, their bright, eager eyes a-watch.

Rhys swung easily off his horse, patted Morvran's neck, and lent a hand to dismount the bulky cleric. The farmer made no obeisance to the abbot. He turned faded eyes upon the visitors while leaning on his spade. Another bad sign.

"Well, Gwydn?" the abbot demanded.

The farmer gave him some semblance of a salute.

Rhys sensed not disrespect but bone-grinding weariness and despair. Gwydn did not believe the abbot would help him.

In a flat voice, surprisingly deep, the narrow-chested farmer began without preamble. "Wife's father died. Old Llaesgymyn. Some wasting sickness. No time to spare fetching folk from town. Buried him in south pasture. Old lecher liked the sweet herbs there...the sun. Three nights later, just after sunset, family at supper, door rattles. Someone wants in. I hail. No answer. Door shakes like someone's angry he's locked out. Wife takes cleaver, I take axe. I draw the bolt, door jerks open. There stands old Llaesgymyn. Glowers at me. White as a sheet. Withered. Dirt in his hair, his clothes, his beard."

Rhys caught the abbot's eyes.

Gwydn's scowl stretched his narrow face longer. "Complained he was cold. I took his arm...he was really there. Brought him in. He demanded supper, then stared at the stew but wouldn't eat. Ignored our questions. I thought we'd made a mistake somehow, put him in the ground alive. Waking in dark earth, clawing out of the shroud, the heavy dirt, pushing off the stones we piled to keep off the wolves, would rattle any man. Wife made much of him. Affection only confused him. Old Llaes didn't seem to know his name, just felt we owed him what he needed. Was hungry, cold, lonely, angry, yet wanted nothing we could give. We sat him by the fire with blanket 'round him. Wife kissed him good night. Then rubbed her lips...surprised, like the taste was foul. All took sleep but for him, sitting there in the dark."

The gaunt man watched more ravens darken his roof.

"Old Llaes. First came to us when his wife died and Saxons slew his sons on the road. Live-in father-in-law. Pig mean, too. Still, I took him in for the wife's sake. Twenty year he did no work. Used his weakness to excuse demands from us all. Cursed and bedeviled me. I lived with no peace in my own house because she loved the old tyrant. Llaes' death finally reprieved me, with maybe a good ten year of life left free of his snarls and contempt. Then there he is at the door, demanding to be fed."

The pale eyes stabbed the prelate, squinted, then fixed on Rhys, seeking a readier audience. "I rose before dawn, as always. Llaesgymyn was gone. Wife wouldn't wake. Struck up a light. Found her pale, chilled, sweating. Woman couldn't work all day...first time in three year. Come evening and the door rattles again. There stands old Llaesgymyn. Only now he's pink and filled out a little. Eyes like knives, full of hate."

The farmer shook his lean head. "Knew him for an enemy right down to my bones. But even my own sons wouldn't understand if I turned him away."

Working his tongue about his loosening teeth, Gwydn tore his gaze away, hard-featured face setting harder. Rhys watched him study the uneasy horses twitching their ears and whickering at the now quiet dogs sniffing warily about the strangers. A sudden moistness in the lean man's eyes set him to blinking angrily.

"Again, he sits at table, loathing the food before him. Looking hungrily at his daughter, the woman he'd badgered and worn down, belittled, bullied and whined at for twenty year under her own roof...longer than ever he raised her."

The farmer's pale blue eyes burned into Rhys. "I tell you, warrior, watching him look at her, I hated myself for letting things go so long in the name of kinship. Still, I kept silent. Wrapped him in his blanket by the coals, laid my wife by my side and pulled the covers up to my eyes. Pretended to snore. Saw Llaes in the dim glow from the coals. Saw him rise and crouch next to her. Saw him lift her arm from under the blanket, put her wrist to his mouth. She moaned in her sleep. Then I heard something strange. Like a dog lapping."

The flat voice wavered, and the taut limbs began to shake. "He lapped the blood from her bitten wrist. I threw off the covers, jumped at him, shoved him back. Seventy winters old, older than anyone ever lasted in these parts, old Llaesgymyn bellows like a bullock. He flings me across the room like a sack of flour. Sons are up, yelling, daughters running out in the yard, knives drawn, like they were taught. Something snapped in my head, like a leash that's held a dog back too long. I swore and raved and threw anything I could at the cold devil, battered him like a hailstorm. Hardly mattered to him. He went for his daughter again, and I leapt on his back, fingers in his eyes, screaming, screaming, trying to twist his head off. Slammed me into the wall, broke my back ribs, grabbed my second boy and snapped his arm over his old knee like kindling, bit him in the throat and lapped while the other boys pounded him with brooms, staves, burning logs."

The farmer stopped, breathing hard, face twisting this way and that. "I got me the axe, and Llaes drops my boy, ducks out the door, me on his heels. I ran like I've never run in my life, meaning to cut him down, cut him to kindling, mash the bloody bits into the stinking earth and burn the ground. Never believed your stories of hell, Abbot. Life's harder than eating stones these days, but I never believed a mad God tortures the unwise for all time in ways even Saxons wouldn't stoop to. But I found hell that night, and some part of me will never leave. A hundred lifetimes from now, whatever body my soul's in then, I'll still feel the hate that burned in me that night."

He choked, then spat. "I couldn't get him, you see. Lithe as a wolf, the old bastard dodged me, got to the woods, left me screaming curses in his wake. You claim your Book has all life's answers. Let it answer this one. *How do I find that cold corpse?"*

"Whom have you told?" the abbot whispered.

Gwydn snorted. "Only sent for you to make sure he stays down...or at least to warn the neighbors. Old bastard never tormented them when he lived. Given time, he'll leave the woods, go to them. They'll let him in, to help him. Where would he hide, meantime?"

The cleric looked at Rhys and shook his head slightly.

Rhys understood the signal to mean that he should keep silent. He ignored the order. "Where was he buried?"

A baleful light flashed behind Gwydn's dull, pale eyes. Turning his back on the powerful clergyman, the farmer reached for the axe propped against the stone wall of his violated home. Swinging its haft up onto one narrow shoulder, he put his spade over the other and marched resolutely across his land, broken ribs notwithstanding. Rhys followed at his heels, the abbot trailing behind, deep in thought.

They trooped across a pretty meadow patchily

cropped by a few lean cattle Gwydn had kept alive through waves of disease, famine, and invasion. Ahead, Rhys could see the scattered stones and disturbed earth of the old man's opened grave. He heard Gwydn's breath hiss as they came to a stop by the shallow pit. The husbandman's foot came to rest on a bundle of withering wildflowers no doubt left by Llaesgymyn's daughter and scattered when the revenant had struggled out of the packed dirt.

Rhys knelt by the oblong pit and scraped away the broken brush and loose earth the revenant had pulled over itself.

Gwydn's breath rasped at the sight of the body. He stepped into the pit and jerked open the torn shroud, revealing Llaesgymyn. The corpse's skin had filled out, sanguine and fresh. Late morning sunlight glinted from one dead, half-open eye, glittered on congealed blood in the finger-gouges around it. The other eyelid was dark and swollen shut. The loose lips were full and ruddy, their wrinkled corners turned upward as if the old man dozed, replete.

Gwydn snarled, spittle flying. "That's it, grin at me. Think you've gotten away with something, do you?"

"The smell..." the abbot gagged, arriving behind them.

"Lived with that twenty year," Gwydn said. "That's no scent of rotting flesh. The old man just never cared to clean himself."

"Don't disturb the corpse," the abbot commanded.

Standing in the pit, Rhys looked over his shoulder at him.

"A rite of exorcism should cast the demon from his body."

Jeffrey T. Heyer

"It was *him*," Gwydn insisted, lips curling in fury, "not something else in his body. Lived with old Llaesgymyn too many years not to know. In a way, it was more him than when he was alive."

Crows cawed harshly, settling on dewy grass, boldly encircling the open grave.

"I've warned you heath-dwellers," the cleric said. "Only a priest can lay a spirit securely enough that we can be sure he won't wander. I'm taking charge of this matter. I'll see that he's interred properly with the right words said over him."

"Words?" Gwydn spat, his hatred spilling over onto the aristocratic clergyman. "Words never affected him in his life. You think this thing at my feet cares for words now? My people laid their own under sod for a thousand year and never a one crawled back to steal more life from the living. This leech has taken all he'll get from them I love." He reached for the axe.

The clergyman's voice rang across the meadow. "Stop. Or endure excommunication. You know what that entails."

Rhys watched Gwydn as his mouth twisted like a tourniquet, staring at the priest. Severus turned expectantly toward his armed enforcer. Rhys set his hand on his hilt and met the seething farmer's stare. Slowly, Rhys bent to pick up the axe. Thrusting its handle toward the farmer, Rhys said, "Strike."

Gwydn's eyes flickered acknowledgement. He turned and hewed at the corpse, severing one arm and then the other, cleaving the heart, then striking off the head.

Rhys lowered a hand and tugged the panting man out

of the pit.

Gwydn sank down on the ground, shaking, as a torrent of emotions roared through his narrow limbs.

Death in his eye, the abbot contented himself for the moment with intoning the Office of the Dead while Rhys shoveled earth over the ruined body, and then piled the scattered stones back atop the restored mound.

Passion flowed out of Gwydn, leaving his undernourished body limp.

Rhys got an arm around the thin shoulders and half-carried him back to the farmhouse. The fuming abbot did not deign to enter.

Within the smoky, food-scented homestead, the woman of the house lay curled on her pallet, pale and sunk in deep sleep. Rhys eased the spent Gwydn down beside her, beckoning to the couple's daughters. The sons, including the one with the broken arm, were all out working the fields while the girls looked after their mother.

"Your father is a stout man. He saved you all. Give him some broth, and then liquor. Do the same for your mother. They'll get better."

Rhys stepped to the door, then remembered what he had learned when the Lady Ellylyw had tasted his blood in the vault beneath Castrum Tenebrarum. The bard turned back toward the care-worn young women. "One other thing. However your mother and your youngest brother may eventually die, burn the bodies."

He stepped out into the yard. Ravens cawed in protest. The abbot waited, arms crossed, brows lowered. His voice rang, "Gwydn's disobedience must be dealt with. As for you—"

"As for me," Rhys cut in, sharp as a blade, "I'll complete my mission. Ellylyw has returned to this neighborhood and made Llaesgymyn her victim. She's searching for you. But with Llaesgymyn destroyed, she'll know I'm here searching for her. It's time to finish it. And I won't let you return to town to excommunicate Gwydn and make him a pariah for what's left of his life."

Steely eyes probed at Rhys through the round face. "You will regret giving orders to me."

A fury as murderous as it was abrupt swept away Rhys' restraint, launching him at Severus. Seething, his whole body shaking with the effort, the bard wrestled himself back, rubbed one unsteady hand across his face, tracing the network of scars. Rage trembled at the verge of explosion, while images fell together in his mind as if he were composing a ballad. Half breathless, he let the words spill out of him. "Ellylyw won't confront the two of us together with your 'hard men grateful for sanctuary' to do your fighting for you. She must seek another of Urre's kind to be her protector."

The abbot's eyes blazed, his fury as cold as Rhys' was hot. He pitched his voice low so those indoors could not hear him growl. "There aren't supposed to be any others."

Rhys' eyes shot rapidly back and forth as if he were reading a manuscript. "The tales of the great Arthur, Emperor of All Britons...that's where I first heard of Urre the Black Knight. One of Arthur's chief men was the dreaded war-lord Llancleawc of the Waters. Urre of Hungary fought for Llancleawc and slew the invading chieftain Tiwrnach the Black Gael. The surviving Gaels interred their leader's body in a place called the Giant's

Cave above the River Eamont...yet later, Llancleawc hears that Tiwrnach is abroad, taking Llancleawc's knights whenever they cross to his side of the river. Urre of Hungary must have infected the Gaelic raider just as later he infected Lady Ellylyw. Tiwrnach the Black arose as a revenant. There being few if any others of their kind in Britain, Ellylyw must seek him out. We'll find them both at Tiwrnach's Cave."

Suddenly sickeningly giddy from shortage of breath, Rhys covered his eyes with his still annoyingly shaky hand. "Besides..." He strove in silence a moment to slow his heart from mad gallop to canter. "She cannot bear to be alone." Rhys felt the air between himself and the abbot thin and crackle like lightning in a storm-front.

"How could you possibly know that?" Severus hissed.

Receiving no response, the outraged prelate spat out, "I will go nowhere with you, and I tell you here and now, touch me and you will feel the full weight of the Church drop on your neck. You have one chance left to fall at my feet, kiss my hem, and beg forgiveness, or you break with the society of men forever."

Rhys' pulse pounded painfully in his temples and throat. His ears rang. He let the rising whirlwind spin up out of his gut and sweep his hands about the plump throat, slam the rich-robed spine against the stone cottage wall. Rhys squeezed the soft neck, ignoring the outraged choking cries and the plucking, puffy fingers. Rhys snarled into his face, "If I have to truss you like a pig, I'm taking you away from these people. When we've drawn Ellylyw to a final reckoning at Tiwrnach's Cave, send your heretic-hunters after me if you can. 'Til then you're mine."

"You know..." the prelate gasped as Rhys grudgingly allowed him a little air, "there must be payment for this."

Rhys nodded. "When we're done."

Yanking him from the wall, Rhys shoved the abbot toward his palfrey. Chainmail rattling angrily about him, the bard strode to his own patient mount and swung into his saddle.

Severus glared, unpriestly hate branded deep in his doughy features. With a dignified sweep of his clerical robes, he stepped to his horse, spoke harshly to it, and struggled awkwardly to get a foot in the uneasy mount's stirrup.

Rhys reached down. Instead of offering the customary hand up, the bard seized the palfrey's reins.

Puffing, Severus hauled himself astride the nervous animal.

Without another word, Rhys turned Morvran toward the high road, towing the palfrey and its fuming clerical freight toward a long-sought rendezvous in the north. Rhys' arteries stopped throbbing painfully as the farm fell behind them. He breathed in clean woodland air. A strange ease suddenly buoyed his spirit. His last human tie irrevocably severed, his path set, nothing remained but to walk it, step by step, to Ellylyw and the end.

Chapter 10:

Tiwrnach's Cave

Rhys felt Abbot Severus's eyes trying to pierce his chainmailed back, assessing his growing weakness. An abrupt passionate hatred of the lifelong condition that once again sapped his strength and left him vulnerable burst up through Rhys. Head swimming from lack of air, Rhys realized that the abbot could easily break free now, and that if once he did, Rhys would lose him.

"Flee if you want to, Abbot," Rhys wheezed out, the kerchief imperfectly filtering the travel dust from mouth and nose, muffling his voice. His chainmail jangled as he turned in the saddle to unwind the reins of the horse behind him from his rear saddlebow. He tossed them back to the gimlet-eyed clergyman. "You'll never find your way back through the forest."

Turning his own wearily plodding horse's head from the narrow woodland path, Rhys broke through the trees into open sunlight. Across a grassy field, he spied the old Roman road, its broad square stones, bared of pounded earth by generations of neglect, lancing dead straight across the bright green countryside. Once, Rhys would have expected to see a dozen merchants driving carts in either direction. Now he was surprised to see even one lone

Jeffrey T. Heyer

wayfarer trudging stolidly along the paving, a writhing piglet in his arms.

Urging his stiffening old charger toward the high road, Rhys tossed back over his shoulder, "Take your chances with the Saxon raiders or stick close. Your choice."

Abbot Severus kicked his small palfrey until she pulled alongside Rhys' big over-aged war-horse. The clergyman's round face twitched, eyes dagger sharp. Brushing at the travel stains on his rich vestments, Severus snapped, "Enjoy this now. Your power over me is fleeting."

Their mounts stepped up onto the stone road. Still trying to wheeze sufficient air into his clenching lungs, Rhys jerked the kerchief from his face. Wiping his brow with the inner, least dusty side of the cloth, he then used it to slap clouds from his chainmail. He felt permeated to his soul with dust, dry and desolate and half smothered. Despite the heavy depression further draining his precious energy, Rhys growled back, "I know your power, Severus. I've seen what you do to people in the name of the Church. But I will complete my mission. Whatever the cost."

The cleric snorted. "You think dedication excuses your abducting me?"

"I think..." He stopped. With a little shock of fear, Rhys realized his recurring ailment had so starved him for air that he had completely lost his train of thought. He was further gone than he had realized. Tying the kerchief about his neck like a legionary, he leaned dizzily forward against his saddlebow and managed to gasp in enough air to speak. "I will track Lady Ellylyw down...and end what I failed to end before."

"Talk." The abbot snorted. "This ailment is not your worst weakness. I've looked you in the eye. I know what you are. You can't face Ellylyw. And you know my hour is coming."

Rhys ran a hand over the parallel scars along the side of his face. The smooth, dead feel of the long claw-marks reminded him that, though he had never been handsome, he was now marked for life. Not that romance had bulked large in his few years of maturity.

Still, he mused, there was some good in bearing his past and future cut like a road map into his flesh. Every touch, every reflected glimpse in a pool, reminded him what he must do. And he needed some dark energy to send fire through his nerves, to make up for his inability to breathe. He opened his hand and gazed at the scar across his palm. Most hours of the day or the long, waking nights, he worked hard to avoid remembering what this scar meant, but now he needed to tear open that emotional wound.

Dagger-sharp, dagger-bright the image of Ellyllyw blazed in his mind, her uncannily pale complexion starkly contrasting with her raven-black tresses. His heart seemed to twist away in pain as he felt again every bliss and pain that had shot through his whole being when she had actually touched him—had taken his cut hand—and though she was Commander Madoc's woman, raised his bleeding palm to her lips. He felt her again kiss the gash, and pain, love, fear, lust, shame and inspiration whirled so violently within him that he almost did not feel her tongue, ever so delicately, caress the wound. And gently press it open. And lap the blood.

Looking back, he felt her take something indefinable

from him in the moment that the moistness of her soft but insistent tongue mixed with his flowing blood. Rhys had not felt it then, but he knew now that, just as she had taken his blood, she had just as assuredly left something behind...an infection, a tiny taint of what she had become, and it had grown quietly, nourished in the dark recesses of his struggling soul. Dreading the spread of that shadow in the blood as Rhys did, foreseeing his own eventual utter loss of self, nevertheless, he now tapped into that dark strength...the very inhuman energy that made revenants like Lady Ellylyw so unstoppable.

Pushing himself upright in the saddle again, with renewed concentration and determination, Rhys scrutinized the pedestrian ahead on the road, noting his neat leather apron and tall sleek boots, while reminding the abbot, "There's no sword-arm but mine between you and the monsters I seek. Are you sure it's in your best interest to undermine my confidence?"

The priest's eyes narrowed, noting the change in Rhys' manner and tone. "Perhaps aid is at hand for me," he replied cautiously. "Or do you think you have it in you to kill this stranger before he can summon the authorities?" Severus kicked his protesting palfrey forward. "Peasant," he shouted. "Where is the nearest church or—"

"Townsman," Rhys cut in, "can you direct us to the fortress of Tiwrnach?"

Alert eyes gazed back at him as the wayfarer turned his square, clean-shaven face. "Who would go there?"

"Look at these robes, peasant," the abbot snapped. "You can see what I am."

The townsman's frown deepened. "You're a prince of

the church, I see that, though I'm no peasant." He nodded toward Rhys. "But what are you, then? I've never seen chainmail painted black like that before, and though the paint is half scratched off, that mail's clearly worth a knight's yearly income. The rest of your gear put together isn't worth my boots. Your steed's too old for battle, and begging your pardon, but you're awfully thin and wild-eyed for a man of equite status."

"What do you think he is?" the prelate demanded. "I could buy ten of him for escort."

"Don't worry, Merchant." Rhys grinned. "I'm no brigand in stolen armor. I'm a bard. Or used to be. How I captured these arms is a story for another—"

"By the authority of Mother Church," the abbot shouted. "I demand—"

"Holy Abbot," the traveler interrupted, "there is no fortress nor chieftain to guard these parts, nor any abbey nearby. There is a church in town, a few leagues ahead."

"It seems, Abbot," Rhys said, "we shall enjoy each other's company a while longer." He told the townsman, "This clergyman and I have joined forces against a common enemy."

"For a time," Severus murmured.

The square face regarded the abbot, then Rhys. "You asked after Tiwrnach's hold. I know the place, but it's no fortress. People hereabouts call it the Giant's Cave. It's just above the River Eamont."

Rhys leaned forward eagerly. "Can you tell us which direction?"

The man shrugged. "Why waste words where there's no profit? A ride would suffice."

Looking away, the high-born cleric compressed his lips in distaste.

"Fair enough," Rhys replied. "And I've had enough saddle for one day." Despite his dizziness, he swung down, holding the reins as the merchant mounted in his place, squirming piglet still trapped under one arm. "I am Marl."

"Rhys of Caer Waroc." The bard smiled. "That's Abbot Severus from below the fortress of Castrum Tenebrarum."

"I warn you," Severus put in, "this bard is dangerous and must be brought to justice." He shot a deadly look at Rhys. "You had no right to interfere in affairs below Tenebrarum."

"Nor you," Rhys shot back, surprised by his own explosion of ferocity. "To delay my mission with your local power plays."

"I serve only the Church."

"The Church?" Marl smiled, raising black brows. "I count a dozen sects in Britain, alone. Not to mention worshippers of Mithras, Jove's Pantheon, and a handful of druids in the back woods whom the Romans missed crucifying before they pulled out of the isle."

"Mithras, Jove and their fellow demons," Severus claimed, "are all but abandoned. The very word *druid* will soon be forgotten. As for heretics, you are right, there are many. But fewer every year."

Marl looked at the abbot with such abhorrence that Rhys felt sure the townsman had seen firsthand the horrors Severus's ilk visited on those they dubbed heretical. The merchant chewed his tongue a moment, and then blurted, "The Bishop of Rome may slaughter thousands on the continent, but Britons are an independent breed. That's all I'm saying."

"You speak boldly, Merchant Marl," Severus said, unspoken threat hanging heavy in the air.

Rhys sighed. "Enough quarrels, Abbot. You know what lies before us."

"I do not."

Rhys' strained patience frayed. Knowing he could never return to a normal life in what was left of his embattled society loosened his tongue. With little left to lose, why not give vent to all the years of helpless frustration? "You know full well what plague Urre of Hungary brought to Britain. You've seen its victims crawl back from their graves by night. Meditate on that and ride in silence."

From up on Morvran's broad back, Marl stared down at Rhys, wide-eyed.

"Only our Savior," Severus said, "could come back from the dead. I've warned you of the danger to men's souls, and still you let slip such words? I'm starting to think you pose a greater threat than these *revenants* as you call them."

"Worry about that if we find and stop the Lady Ellylyw. Don't forget she means to avenge on you the destruction of the lover who made her a revenant."

"If not for that threat, I'd have rid myself of you long ago."

"Think I'd give up your company so easily?" Rhys' hands trembled with repressed rage, burning the depressed and oxygen-starved listlessness out of him.

"Now that you profit, Marl..." Rhys led his stolid old

charger Morvran down the clacking pavestones. "Tell me, have there been disappearances near this Giant's Cave?"

Marl licked his lips. "You think one of these *revenants* dwells in the Giant's Cave? You think that's what takes my neighbors in the night?"

"You're shaking, bard," Severus accused Rhys. "Yet you still think *you* can stop these bloodthirsty berserkers?"

Rhys struggled to calm his labored breathing, but every word the clergyman spoke reminded him of the murder of his hermit friend. Rhys swallowed, burying all remembrance of poor *heretical* Caydwr. "Very well. Both of you should know. I found the clue in Arthurian lore."

"You bards..." the abbot mocked him, "can never stop effusing about the great Arthur...as if he were the Messiah."

Trying not to grit his teeth, Rhys replied, "Invaders swallowing our land. Famine. Plague. Is it any wonder people hunger for tales of Arthur, the one man ever to unite our factions?"

Marl nodded solemnly. "Bad as it is, now, Arthur proved we're not destined always to be beaten."

"Now who's preaching?" The abbot smiled.

A howling darkness swirled in Rhys' head, and for a moment he feared he might lose himself in the ferocious uprush of black rage. Memory flashed unbidden this time, sharp as before and more cutting: Ellylyw kissing his wounded hand...the gashed flesh parting under her soft lips, making the blood flow. Rhys shuddered.

This darkness came over him more often with each passing night. And he had no idea how long he might hold out against the revenant infection spreading through his blood.

"Listen to me," he said. "I need your help, both of you." Knowing everything depended on his rusty bardic skills, Rhys began painting word pictures for his companions from his substantial repertoire of Arthurian tales:

***

"Short, thick-thewed Llancleawc rode easily astride the huge war-horse. One of the most famous of Arthur's chieftains, his close-set eyes speared through gathering gloom, intent on the strange procession that marched before his armored company. Eerie notes pierced warm evening air from twin-throated flutes. Wild, disheveled women in black brandished blazing torches, wailing formal dirges in their unknown tongue. Leather-armored men-at-arms trudged behind, bearing a roofed funeral palanquin. On it lay the breathless body of Urre of Hungary, his chainmail tunic riveted over with scores of oblong Sarmatian-style armor plates. The incredibly strong armor, helm, and weapons were all made of black steel.

Llancleawc approved of the funereal imagery. The people of every land he penetrated saw Death heading Llancleawc's host. Raising a gauntlet, the broad-backed chieftain stopped the procession. His followers scurried to make camp in the waning twilight.

A furious shriek as from a hundred-throated beast pierced the gloom. To the shrill of bagpipes, the dreaded Tiwrnach the Gael rode screaming out of the darkness at the head of a vengeful, roaring, warrior host. Tiwrnach's trunk wrapped in thick layers of spotted bull's hide, bull-horned helmet on his dark brows, he crashed through

Llancleawc's guards, hewing down men, driving deep into the half-made camp.

As if alive, from the funeral palanquin sprang Urre of Hungary. In the darkness, Tiwrnach's men could scarcely make out the black-armored Hungarian scything through their ranks. Tiwrnach wheeled his horse about a campfire, glimpsed the black warrior coming for him, gave spur and caught Urre's night-hewed shield with his spear, tearing it from him. Casting the encumbered spear aside, Tiwrnach drew, spurred and struck in one lightning move, dashing Urre's black blade from his hand. The weaponless Hungarian waited for his enemy to circle around for the next pass, then ducked into the charge, throwing his metal-sheathed body against the side of Tiwrnach's careening horse. Seizing the furious Gael, Urre wrenched him from the saddle. Together they crashed to the trampled earth. Choking on flying dust, the mighty Tiwrnach, leader of a hundred raids, died with Urre's teeth in his throat.

One year later, a worried captain entered Llancleawc's great hall to stand before his seat of state and report, "Chieftain, a warrior in black arms captures your knights."

"A bold man, indeed," Llancleawc ground out, his famous temper rising, "to seek ransom from me."

The captain shook his head, drooping moustache aquiver. "The black knight sends for no ransom, but imprisons your men in a stone keep in Tiwrnach's old holdings. Now and then he brings out one or another to beat him, mock him, then return him to the keep, greatly weakened."

"An outrage," Llancleawc roared, eyes burning. "My men. And in territory I thought conquered. Prepare a raiding party.""

***

Rhys ended his recitation with a question. "Tell me, Marl, are there stories in these parts about Tiwrnach's deeds?"

Marl nodded, brows and lips pursed. "They say that after the knight of the palanquin killed him, Tiwrnach's surviving men carried off their leader's body and interred it in the Giant's Cave...until, one night, Tiwrnach threw off the stones they heaped over him and began to capture every knight who tried to ford the River Eamont below the cave. Do you think he is one of these revenants you speak of?"

As they neared town, the trio began to pass little knots of people moving along the road in holiday attire. Severus interrupted the townsman to comment. "Look at these demi-pagans."

"It's Giant's Cave Sunday." Marl sighed. "Used to really be something."

Maidens skipped in low-cut gowns, youths dashed about them in tight breeches and open shirts. Bright ribbons fluttered from sleeves and staves, and people chatted. Yet their voices remained subdued, and Rhys glimpsed darkness behind their eyes.

The abbot shook his head sadly. "This island is full of pagan superstition."

Marl's face twisted. Children trotted alongside the trio, shaking twigs of licorice in leather bottles, then sucking the froth that bubbled up.

Marl gestured toward the shaking bottles. "Our grandmothers say the priestess used to draw water from the

~191~

sacred well and make it boil out of a beautiful copper cauldron, making weather magic and encouraging the Lady of the Waters to return and renew the land. But when Tiwrnach returned from the grave, he seized the cauldron. Now they make do with these little bottles."

Severus turned from a passing monk he had paused to interrogate. "Marl, enough about devil worship."

Rhys said, "I've compared the story of Tiwrnach with what happened to Ellylyw at the ruins of Castrum Tenebrarum. As I described to you, after Llancleawc pulled free the shaft that had pinned Urre for so long to the bed of his funeral palanquin, the Hungarian revenant became Llancleawc's ally. Urre infected Tiwrnach in his battle with Llancleawc, just as later he infected Lady Ellylyw. When Tiwrnach rose as a revenant, the first victims of his night raids would have been the local people. Eventually, instead of trying to fight him whenever he stormed down out of the hill-cave, the people here changed their old Giant's Cave ritual. A little of each person's blood was spilled to fill the ancient copper cauldron you mentioned, Marl. Then they offered it up to the black knight to keep him from their throats. Not content, the vengeful revenant began capturing his enemy Llancleawc's knights, tormenting them and feeding on them between Giant's Well rituals."

With mounting excitement as each detail confirmed his theory, Rhys shared another piece of Tiwrnach's bloody history:

***

"When Llancleawc's forced march reached the Eamont, he found the copper cauldron hanging from a tree by the river...a warning of what the revenant required of any seeking passage.

Llancleawc frowned. Twelve of his knights had fallen before Tiwrnach the Black, but Llancleawc's revenant ally Urre had revealed to him all his enemy's strengths and weaknesses.

Setting the cauldron bubbling over onto the sacred stone beneath and then beating the copper with his sword until it rang like a bell, Llancleawc fulfilled the ancient ritual, summoning a ferocious storm. The din also brought the Black Knight down from the wind-swept heights.

Their battle was terrible. Swords flew and lightning flashed. Steel clanged against steel and thunder rattled the combatant's helms. The undefeated champion Llancleawc shattered lance after lance against Tiwrnach's huge shield. Fiercest skull-splitter of Arthur's age but for the Imperator himself when roused to full war-fury, Llancleawc's shield and armor gave way before the Black Knight's spear-point.

Wounded again and again, Llancleawc cast aside his perforated shield. Convinced that no mortal man could penetrate the mass of iron and oak shielding Tiwrnach, Llancleawc flung his axe into the chest of his opponent's horse, tumbling the black knight violently to the earth. Llancleawc's berserker fit upon him, Arthur's champion leapt and struck and parried 'til, in his flurry of blows, he managed to whip his blade past the unbreakable shield, piercing Tiwrnach through breastplate and bone. Still the Black Knight struck at him, cleaving steel plates on the champion's chest, slicing chainmail rings beneath and creasing flesh.

Winded and faint from blood loss, Llancleawc thrust

through his foe again and again 'til Tiwrnach tottered to his knees. Yet in the space of time it took Llancleawc to tear the black helmet from the tyrant's head, though weakened by half a dozen mortal wounds, Tiwrnach lifted his sword to renew the fight. Llancleawc, quicker, struck off Tiwrnach's head."

***

"The thing that haunts the Giant's Cave therefore cannot be Tiwrnach," Rhys concluded, "and any of the captive knights he bled into his basin might finish out their days with nothing worse than nightmares, once Llancleawc freed them. But one of the knights must have been bitten. He returned as a revenant to Tiwrnach's stronghold. There being few if any others of their kind in the isle, Ellylyw must seek out that knight."

"You can't know that," Severus exclaimed.

"Look around you, cleric," the bard replied. "We're in the Aetas Tenebrarum, the Age of Darkness. Cities burn. Barbarian hordes cut down the living and mutilate the dead. Even a creature like Ellylyw must find a protector. She doesn't understand what's happened to her. She must seek others of Urre's kind to learn what she's become. Besides..." He strode a few paces in silence. "She cannot bear to be alone."

"How could you possibly know that?" Severus asked.

"She told me as much."

The abbot gasped. "You...*spoke* with her?"

"Dawn was close. It was too late to fight."

Rhys caught Marl eyeing him. The merchant licked his lips. "Perhaps...if the holy cauldron is returned to the sacred well, our prosperity would return."

"You think this metal vessel and not God's Grace somehow holds your luck?"

Marl gazed steadily at the clergyman, then shrugged. Leaving the semi-festive, semi-furtive crowd behind, he led his companions off the road and across a shallow ford. Gesturing toward a high cliff-face, he slid from the horse. "The Giant's Cave."

Rhys studied the cliff. "Where?"

Marl sighed. "You can't see it from below."

"Without a guide, I'll lose daylight searching."

"Mmm." Marl looked at the squealing piglet in his arms. "It's one thing to recount old ballads on a well-lit road. It's something else, come the latter end of afternoon, to approach the Giant's Cave. Where's the profit?"

"Where's the profit," Rhys asked, "in watching your customers disappear?"

"There is that, of course." Marl sighed and looked sorrowfully at his squealing burden. "Little pig, you just won a day's reprieve."

***

Puffing from the climb to the cliff-top, Marl pointed out a rough stairway cut into the sandstone and curving down across the steep ridge. "The Perilous Way." Marl brushed sweat from his brow. "As it is, it'll be dark before I reach town."

"You'd better hurry." Rhys nodded. "Thank you."

Marl mustered a half-smile. "Come by Marl's Shop on your way back through town. If you don't, I'll know you... Blessings of the God and Goddess upon you. Go with

God, Abbot, though I scarcely like you. Come on, piglet. If I get home safe, you might end up a breeder. I don't think I'll have the heart to eat anyone who makes it through this night with me."

As Marl retraced his steps, Rhys tucked his reins about Morvran's saddle-bow, knowing he would not wander. The abbot's palfrey he tied to a bush, which she began to lip. After slipping his shield strap from his back, Rhys hung it on his saddle. It would be an encumbrance in the cramped cave. He made his way carefully down the carven path. The clergyman, grumbling a prayer, huffed after.

The way was, indeed, perilous, narrow and difficult even with the aid of the steps. The sun had slid down to the horizon by the time Rhys got the bulky priest to the hollow in the hill. Ignoring a second cave a few paces beyond, Rhys focused on the heavy iron gates, black with age, blocking the first entrance. Two of the thick bars were bent enough to let a large man slip through.

An odd red glow in the cave beyond unnerved Rhys. Was it firelight reflected from deeper within the cavern? No. The glow was steady, and other patches shone vivid green, an unearthly wash of colors to glimpse within the earth.

Gathering his nerve, Rhys slipped between the bent bars. Eyes adjusting, he saw to his relief that it was the sunset that brightened the native red of the rock walls where they were free of the dull earth. The emerald patches felt slick like algae. Rhys mused nervously that, like himself, this blind, living substance strove to drink in all it could of the failing light.

He fortified himself with a look back through the bars at the beauty of the world he was leaving behind. Forty feet below, glittering in the last red rays, the Eamont rushed about its endless business, the ford Marl had led them across still muddied from their passage.

"Look," Severus spoke softly, pointing directly across the river. In a field of waving green, Rhys spotted a tiny, wattled church.

"St. Ninian's," the abbot whispered, comforted by the sight. "A hundred years before Arthur's knights came here, the first apostle in the north tried to make this place holy."

"Blessed be his memory," Rhys breathed.

"You pretend to be Christian, now?"

"May Ninian aid us tonight, and the Lady of the Waters, too."

"You fill me with confidence," the cleric said dryly. He looked about. "You really think someone could live in this hole?"

Rhys gestured at the darkening panorama before them. "It's certainly a strategic vantage point. As for the accommodations, a hard place for long-term prisoners, but I've spent the night in worse. I don't think revenants require many creature comforts."

Rhys helped Severus squeeze his bulk between the bars and then delved deeper. The abbot looked back at the deepening darkness. "No time for searching," he murmured. "Wasn't there a second cave?"

Rhys picked a spot and set down his pack. "The revenant might be in either, in some covered pit. We're out of time."

He unstoppered a ceramic jar from his pack, then

doffed his chainmail.

"What are you doing?" Severus asked.

"Re-painting armor and weapons black." Rhys pulled out a brush. "Steel catches any glint. Revenants dwell in darkness. They have eyes like owls. They're stronger, less vulnerable, less frightened of consequences. He must not see me before I strike."

The uneasy churchman snorted. "For all my questions, you never made clear my part in all this."

Rhys did not look up from his brushwork. "Just stand there."

"Here? Where will you be?"

"Behind this boulder, where the shadow's deepest. Pray, so the revenant will hear you."

The round face went blank in the last light. "I'm bait."

"Ellylyw will come for you, killer of Urre."

"You sinful wretch, accursed in the eyes of the Lord."

Rhys met his gaze. "Remember the hermit Caydwr?"

"A damned heretic."

"A healer. More wildman than priest. Wonderful with animals. I liked him. You had him killed."

"That alone would earn my place in heaven."

"You may soon know."

"You want the revenant to slay me?"

"Don't you tell your flock to develop *a thirst for martyrdom*?"

The abbot thrust an accusing finger at him. "You're under the revenant's thrall. You show all the symptoms...lassitude and despair, then sudden fanatical drive. Hatred of society...and of God. You procurer for the Devil's spawn."

"Oh, I mean to take the revenant's head," Rhys assured him. "Ellylyw's, too. My symptoms are an accident of birth. I suffocate when I'm exposed to certain plants and furs. Men like you always read something more disturbing into my condition. But the wheel of the world is off its axle, and I must help set it right, so I came to you, Abbot. After all, who brings about the Aetas Tenebrarum if not men like you?"

Shocked, Severus protested, "I've always served the Light of God."

"If you shine brighter than your Pagan rivals, why torture and kill them? Your light, Abbot, is a bonfire burning all who see the world as you cannot."

"Yet you condemn me for seeing the world as you cannot."

"I condemn your murder of Caydwr."

"He was an animal."

"He was more alive than you'll ever be." Rhys rubbed a powdery ball of dark blue woad over his face for further camouflage. "You are paid in your own coin. Or will you swear never again to encompass the death of one of another faith?"

"I'd rather die. You will be damned for this."

Rhys shrugged. "According to you, I'm damned regardless."

"Sooner than you think." The abbot smirked. "While you were telling tales to your mouthy merchant, I slipped a note to a passing monk. By now he'll have fetched the town watchmen. Try to leave this cave without me and they'll cut you down. Once Ellylyw has been dealt with, they'll take you for trial as a heretic. I told you your power over me was fleeting."

Rhys donned his painted armor, then prodded the priest with his black sword. "Try to run and I'll spill your blood as a lure. I will complete my mission. Whatever the cost." He settled himself a sword's length away behind the boulder.

Swallowing hard, Severus began mumbling prayers.

A faint click of stone stopped him.

Silence followed.

Rhys heard a whisper as of cloth against stone. Severus stared at the cave mouth.

A tall silhouette stepped before the iron gate from the direction of the neighboring cave. Slipping lithely between the bent bars, the figure dashed down the dark cave, cloak and loose sleeves flapping, chainmail jingling, and seized the howling abbot, yanked him out of range of Rhys' blade. Bending the priest's back over a boulder, it sank its teeth into the man's throat. Severus shrieked, "Rhys! God! God!"

The bard sprang, swinging, but the revenant stopped lapping and ducked sideways into shadow, nearly dodging Rhys' strike. Instead of severing the revenant's neck, the black blade barely slashed it. Borrowed blood sprayed, enough to stagger a man, make him faint within seconds, die in minutes.

Yowling like a cat, the revenant clapped a hand to the pulsing wound as the substance of its strength pumped from it.

Rhys sprang forward, his pulse pounding in his ears, and swung down two-handed. In one swift move, the revenant drew its sword and parried, losing a notch from its hundred-year-old steel. It lashed out a metal-toed boot, taking Rhys' feet from under him. He hit the stone floor, scrabbled painfully into darkness while the revenant bellowed its frustration and pain.

Severus burbled, and the dark thing struck him senseless with its left fist, ripped a swathe from his rich robe, and wadded the cloth against its pulsing throat. Sword in its other hand, the injured revenant stepped into blackness, probing for Rhys. The bard tried not to breathe, unable to see the black-clad knight.

Its blade clacked against stone a few feet to Rhys' left. Dizzy from lack of breath, Rhys knew he had only seconds, but feared to make a move he would not survive, should he stumble in the dark or miss-guess his timing.

The knight's sword struck sparks from a man-sized rock, revealing for an instant the revenant's position. Rhys leapt upright, still breathless, hurling his all into a two-handed swing. The impact half numbed his hands, striking sparks as steel sheered steel. Rhys' heart lurched sickeningly. Again the creature had sensed his attack and parried swifter than he could strike, but the revenant's aged and damaged sword snapped loudly, the blade clattering to the floor. Rhys felt his own weapon sheer through, glancing from an armored shoulder, his point snagging the makeshift bandage, tearing it from the creature's wound.

Rhys cut again, fast, but aimed low, assuming the revenant would expect another neck blow and duck. Again the bard's blade connected, biting through armor, clipping the knee joint. The creature howled and clanged to the rocky floor.

Unable to breathe properly in the musty cave, half stifled from having to silence his breath and then fight for his life, Rhys' head swam. Elated, nonetheless, Rhys caught the sound of the unseen thing scrabbling three-limbed toward the cave mouth. Still, Rhys feared to hack blindly, strike stone and break his own blade.

Severus moaned. The bleeding revenant crawled atop him. Bared fangs glinting, it hissed at its pursuer. "Back, or I tear out your holy man's throat."

Rhys charged, war cry ringing uncertainly off the weird red and green cave walls. The revenant threw itself backward, but one hand caught in the chain suspending a cross from the abbot's neck. The knight fell, howling into shadow, unable to jerk its hand free in time to avoid the whistling blow that half severed its spine. Both legs now useless, it raised its chest from the floor on its arms, shrieking, pulling itself forward into silhouette against the cave mouth.

Rhys swept off its head.

The bard wavered, panting to the priest, "I'm not in the revenant's thrall. But Ellylyw tasted my blood in what I thought an innocent kiss. I feel the darkness growing inside me. Can you?"

"Save me," Severus begged, both shaking hands clapping another length of torn cloth against his still bleeding neck. "Call the watchmen the monk summoned. They should be close by now."

"And let you return to the town you tyrannized in life, to terrorize your flock after death?" Rhys lifted his sword.

"No," Severus whispered, his wide glittering eyes fixed on the rising blade.

"For Caydwr," Rhys said, swinging down hard, laying Severus' head in the dust beside the revenant's.

Before the shakes could claim him, Rhys squeezed out through the bars and made a quick survey of the smaller neighboring cave. The copper cauldron of the old tales sat on a raised stone in the revenant's lair. Tucking it into his pack, Rhys returned to the first cave. Sword in one hand, with the other, he lifted the two heads by their hair.

Under the dim light of a half moon, the burdened and shaky Rhys struggled laboriously up the Perilous Way.

Five town watchmen in leather armor waited at the top, spear-points leveled. The monk whom Severus had sent had done his duty. Rhys tossed the heads at their feet, letting moonlight flash along the blood on his blade.

"He killed the abbot," a heavy-bearded man growled.

A younger watchman with quick, nervous eyes gestured in amazement at the second head. "He killed the *knight*. Marl told us the truth, it was some kind of revenant...and he killed it."

The watchmen all stared in amazement at the sweat-soaked, scar-faced young man wheezing badly and shaking in his boots before them. The blue woad dripped from his features onto his black armor.

"The second cave..." Rhys puffed, "is decorated...with heads on stakes. None of the revenant's victims...will take his place."

The watchmen stared blankly.

Rhys shrugged. Perhaps they understood. Perhaps they simply could not absorb this many strange things at once and could not decide, therefore, what to do with him. He unslung his pack and tossed it before them.

The younger guardsman tugged out the dully gleaming copper vessel. He gasped. "The Cauldron of

Renewal."

Rhys heard in that simple exclamation hope so fierce it choked the man's voice with anguish.

Hugging it to his chest, like an abducted child recovered safely, the young watchman dashed down the path toward town.

Heavy-beard hefted his spear, repeating pointedly to his remaining comrades. "He killed the abbot."

A broad-beamed man spat in the knight's dead face. "If *that's* not God's work, what is?"

The man turned homeward, two lean companions following without a glance at the bearded guard. Alone now, Heavy-beard looked from the abbot's severed head to the now motionless swordsman leaning on his dripping blade. Scowling, Heavy-beard turned to follow his fellows down the hill.

Rhys looked out over the quiet moon-dim valley. Morvran clopped close to nudge him. Rhys patted the long face, then sagged against him, spent. He whispered, bereft, "Ellylyw didn't come."

The dark energy on which he had depended for too long evaporated, and he dropped onto his backside in the dirt, his back against Morvran's leg. The charger did not care for this and stepped aside, craning his maned neck down to pluck his friend's cloak with nimble lips as if he might pull him up out of the well of despair that blinded him. Rhys flopped onto his back and blinked at pin-prick stars. He nearly floated out of his exhausted body in his effort to use all the breath he could muster to feed his whirling mind.

How could he find her?

She had not known the woodland paths or roads, yet she had acquired a horse and done quite well at staying ahead of him. He could not track her indefinitely. How long could he survive if he located her only when and where she wished to toy with him? He had to determine where she was headed and get there first.

Unwillingly, Rhys suffered a pang of compassion for Ellylyw, something agonizingly close to the love he had smothered away. Ellylyw had been locked away from life for so many bleak years...then freed at last, but with no place of rest, not knowing even what she was...he could appreciate that kind of pain. But it was his mistake that had loosed her from the chains in which Madoc had restrained her, and who but Rhys knew what these revenants were or how to stop them?

A little breeze chilled him as he was haunted once again by the image of Ellylyw standing in the loft in the abandoned city, smoke from burning homes billowing like great wings about her. Once more he heard Ellylyw, her voice high and plaintive. *"I am alone again. Except for you."*

He should have been right to come to Tiwrnach's Cave. He knew for a fact that her lover Urre the Hungarian was the first revenant to bring this blood-drinking plague to the isle. That meant the only way Ellylyw could find an armor-clad revenant protector with the resources of a chieftain was to track down one of Urre's victims infected back in Arthur's day.

Suddenly he felt ten kinds of a fool. As he had told his companions, the tales of Arthur's court recorded plainly that Tiwrnach the Black was beheaded by Llancleawc.

Ellylyw was too cautious to gamble on his having left a successor. Of course she had not come. *Fool. Fool. Fool!*

Clear as a bell he heard it: *the Tale of Peredur Pierce-Vale*—Peredur the Divine *Fool*—Peredur, who had once battled the Knight of the Tomb.

Yes. The spiritual warrior Peredur had been sent to a place called the Pictish Rock. There he made challenge to the image of a black knight carved into a slab that closed off the entrance to some forgotten chieftain's tomb. The knight depicted on the stone then arrived, unheard behind the challenger, and engaged Peredur in mortal combat.

The black knight, silent, faceless behind his black visor, proved frighteningly strong. But Peredur's unearthly spiritual aura protected him; he flew into an altered state when the heat of battle came upon him, not a berserk rage such as made Llancleawc so unstoppable, but an unearthly grace and economy of movement. The holy warrior pierced the Knight of the Image through with a death blow.

Yet the black knight, streaked with his own scarlet and despite the champion's almost preternatural strength, threw Peredur from his horse and drove him into the opened tomb, then escaped on the man's terrified charger. All in all, an extremely odd tale. Unless one knew about revenants.

Peredur had not slain the Knight of the Rock.

Rhys shivered at the cold touch of destiny, realizing that Ellylyw, knowing these stories as well as he, would seek out her protector, not at Tiwrnach's Cave, but in the tomb known as the Pictish Rock, also called the Rock Gladoens. If Rhys had his geography right, the Rock lay in Estrake. Urre's old conquest.

His breath coming more easily now, despair receding swiftly, Rhys told the light barely leaking through the pinprick stars, "I may be a bigger and less divinely inspired fool than was Peredur, but I will find the Rock Gladoens. Let come what may. *And when she rests by day at his side, I will have my chance to strike.*"

Chapter 11:

The Rock Gladoens

Tugging his worn cloak tighter about his cold chainmail, Rhys squinted against the wind. On all sides, the broad, flat sweep of wild heath rippled like the sea at every gust.

"Too many days without sleep," Rhys muttered, as the heather seemed to convulse around him like a dying thing. Its fluttering, shaking shadows seemed to harbor restless predatory shapes. He jerked his glance from side to side, struggling to convince himself the endless movement in his peripheral vision was no half-seen enemy keeping pace with him. The rapid, numbing air streamed past, making him feel he was hurtling at great speed toward an inevitable collision. He felt poor Morvran slow beneath him, joints stiffening. Rhys patted the thick-muscled neck. "I know your old wounds ache, but we must go on, friend. We must go on."

A low mound rose from the plain, gray in waning evening light. For all the wind's tugging, a few last patches of withered heather clung tenaciously to the top of the rise. Scrub trees hunched about the circumference, stunted and twisted. The air felt dead for all its chill rushing. Rhys knew this was the place, the revenant he sought had lain in this tomb so long that its presence had leeched the vitality from the vegetation covering it, even the very air passing over it.

Boulders ringed the round barrow tightly to keep in the mounded earth and to mark the boundary between the land of the living and that of the dead. Rhys reined up before a great gray slab blocking the rude stone lintel set in the hillock's side. Incised in the slab was an intricate and beautiful Pictish symbol. It meant nothing to the chilled bard. Picts had built raiding outposts in the isle for three hundred years, and still no Briton knew their signs.

The carving was old, but Rhys stood in his stirrups, systematically scanning the whole circle of horizon for any hint that Picts might still be present. The Painted People were busily reclaiming this province of Estrake from its last British holdouts, and Rhys knew that, if he was spotted, they would kill him and Morvran on sight.

Morvran's head drooped into the scraggly heather. Swinging down from his spent steed, Rhys smiled grimly. It amused him that even with so much at stake, he felt excited to set eyes on the image cut beneath the unreadable symbol—a crude portrait of the Knight of the Tomb from a tale he loved—that of Peredur, the Divine Fool.

Rhys frowned. The ground before the carved slab was undisturbed. Blinking blearily through the dying light, Rhys mumbled to himself, "I can't be wrong. Not after all this. Yet the tomb is still sealed."

Morvran twitched a despondent ear. Rhys slapped his leather-clad thigh. "Wake up, Rhys. This just means the Knight of the Rock has some concealed exit. Underground, perhaps. Unless these night-walkers have mystical powers beyond what I've seen."

Rhys looked about, mouth dry. Having reached his goal, he found he had lost all confidence in the plan he had developed over the last few sleepless nights. Drawing a deep breath, he clutched a handful of dead soil and addressed the cloud-streaked, deep-purple sky. "I may be a less inspired fool than was Peredur in his day, but I *will* do this. Let come what may."

From his saddle-pack he drew the board for his gwyddbwyll game and, hands shaking, placed it on a flat-topped boulder jutting from the side of the mound. His hunger for dreams brought back jarringly bright, sharp images and emotions from the beginning of his long hunt. The dead city bulked again about him, the reek of corpses trapped under torn-down pillars made him gag again as when he had hunted Lady Ellylyw through deserted streets.

He glanced up at the purpling sky apprehensively, picturing, as if the image overlapped the current leaden clouds, the sudden roil of black thunderheads that had brought premature nightfall to the empty city. Not empty. Revenant-like shapes lurched at him from the edges of his vision, dissolving to nothing when fear whipped his eyes toward them. He tried not to remember how Ellylyw's victims had hunted him through that night, concentrating instead on painstakingly forcing his hands to steady.

The familiar feel of the gaming pieces he had carved himself—all but one—calmed him. The huntsmen...he set them carefully in their starting places spread about the edges of the board. Then the fear and dread he had felt that night in the dead city tugged him down into another dream-like flash of memory.

He spun to the side, groping for his sword, nearly

knocking down the gwyddbwyll board, thinking he saw again in his peripheral vision the terrible image of the armored revenant of Tiwrnach's Cave, its spine severed by Rhys' wild, blinded blow, chest propped up from the earth by its arms, hands hauling its limp, nerveless body behind it, scrabbling frantically for the cave mouth. He thought he heard again its armor scraping over the jagged stones.

"Not there," he insisted to himself, shuddering uncontrollably. "You laid that one in the earth. You survived. This plan may be crazy, but if you stop to think it through again, you're lost for sure."

Striving to shake the images from his eyes, he glared up at the last red rays of sunset and shouted defiantly, "Why not risk everything upon a rumor?"

The shakes stopped. He set the carved gwyddbwyll king on the center square. Would he play the huntsman's part this time, he wondered, and trap his kingly prey? Or would the revenant take the outer pieces and close a trap of his own on Rhys' king before the sleep-starved bard could take all the foes that encircled and bedeviled him?

Rhys pulled a small bow from his gear, strung it and thrust three arrows into the earth at his feet for quick retrieval, though he doubted he would have time to draw and loose even twice. Tugging out his sword, still unevenly blotched with black paint, as much of it had been lost, he thrust its point into the earth behind the arrows the more speedily to access his final line of defense. If his arrows did not stop the revenant, he doubted his sword could prolong his life, but he could more easily face ugly death with his hand clutching the familiar pommel.

The orange glow faded behind the wind-rippled

Jeffrey T. Heyer

horizon. Ragged strips of cloud raced across a three-quarters moon. Rhys stood before the Pictish Rock and shouted the challenge from the Tale of Peredur. "Knight of the Rock Gladoens, face me or I carry from here your honor."

His dry, cracked voice sounded childish in his ears. Biting wind whipped the heather and the loose locks of Rhys' hair protruding from under his helmet's edge. Again he howled into the night. "Gladoens, come forth, or I carry away your name."

Morvran shook his ears, dispirited by so long a march and so dismal a destination. Rhys felt like an idiot, standing in the cold night air and yelling at a picture on a stone. The corner of his eye caught a massive bear-like hulk hunching toward him. He whirled to face it, bow leveled, string taut...found just another boulder.

Lowering the bow, easing the tension on the string, Rhys shook his head in chagrin, the wild energy that had driven him so far, flagging abruptly. Slumping, exhausted, he felt the whole scheme that had led him here had been imbecility brought on by dearth of sleep. He turned from the graven knight to gaze out across the flat landscape in search of some distant shelter.

Black armor glinted moonlight. A visored knight stood thirty feet away. Rhys stifled an outcry. Morvran gave a horrified whinny and galloped away, hating the strange predator but pulling up and nervously holding his ground a dozen yards distant, too well trained to abandon his war-leader entirely.

The dark figure drew a long sword made of black steel such as the Scots used for night raids.

"I challenge..." Rhys croaked out. He coughed and drew his bow taut. He shouted clearly this time toward the figure now striding unhurriedly toward him. "I challenge you to a game of gwyddbwyll."

The figure loomed close, raising the black blade above its black helm.

Forcing down rising panic, Rhys cried, "I make an honorable challenge."

The faceless figure continued its even pace. A few more steps and Rhys would have to loose his shaft and try to snatch up one of the arrows at his feet.

"See..." The bard quavered. "The board is ready, and I've made the first move. It's your play."

The black knight stopped, so near that despite his heavy armor, he might close the distance before Rhys could put an arrow in him. The Knight of the Tomb hesitated, heavy sword effortlessly upraised. "You know something of us, southern man." His deep voice with its peculiar northern accent rang metallically through the eye-slit in the black visor. "You gamble your life. And more."

"Always. The game has begun. Can you leave it unfinished?"

Breath hissed from black metal.

Rhys spoke slowly, wrestling the quaver from his voice, testing his theory. "A merchant below Tiwrnach's Cave told me of revenants stopped when the grain or gold they had hoarded in life was spilled before them. I think you have no sense of time. I know what that's like...to feel devastated, unable to think freely. You're a predator, focused entirely on the task before you with no thought of consequences. That's why a revenant breaks off its attack to pick up every scattered coin or dropped grain of wheat before turning again on its prey."

"You spill no gold nor grain before me, southern man."

"All your life you hoarded fame."

A short, harsh cry came from the dark helm, a sound like metal arms clashing, the dry wreckage of laughter. "What fame have I now?"

"The bardic college where I studied is ash in the wake of the Saxon invasion." Rhys was acutely aware he was giving the performance of his life. "But I remember the tale of Peredur's battle with the Knight of the Tomb. Emperor Arthur himself, commander-in-chief of all British forces, dispatched Peredur to a place called the Rock Gladoens to challenge the image of a knight painted on a slab. The challenged knight arrived unheard and engaged Peredur in mortal combat."

The black sword hung motionless above the helmet.

Rhys pressed on, afraid that only his words hung between him and the sweep of the black blade. "The knight Gladoens' first stroke clove Peredur's shield, then he shattered plate-after-plate of Peredur's armor, slicing through the steel rings of his chainmail and the thick leather beneath. But Peredur's unearthly grace let him sense where his foe was about to strike, and Peredur slipped smoothly inside his enemy's defenses, turning his attacks back against their author. Again-and-again, Peredur's falcon-swift blade bit through black steel 'til dozens of wounds sapped the monstrous strength of the Knight of the Tomb. Knowing that a single direct blow from the black knight would cleave him to the bone, Peredur dodged and leapt, forward and back, 'til he found his opening and at last drove his point through the black breastplate. The Knight of the Tomb staggered, but did not go down, sending Peredur scrambling back with a swing of his shield-edge. The black knight, now streaked with scarlet, drove the champion into the opened tomb and sealed him in, then escaped on Peredur's charger. But before dawn, the knight was obliged to return to the tomb, and Peredur escaped after a second ferocious combat. I knew from this that you were a revenant."

"Is that what you call us?" the hollow voice asked, abstracted, perhaps half lost in memories unvisited for a generation. "What means any of that now?"

Rhys' right arm shook as he struggled to keep the drawn bowstring taut. "Decades ago, you came forth to battle Peredur, though he could never have moved the stone to reach you. You came because he challenged your image. As do I. Knight of the Rock Gladoens, the grains of your honor lie scattered before you. The gold of your fame rests in these carved figures. Can you abandon it, even to feed?"

Gladoens looked at the bow in the bard's hand. His metal-sheathed head swiveled reluctantly, his hidden eyes taking in the gaming board where Rhys' opening move demanded a response.

"I want to kill you, now," the knight spoke, tonelessly.

"And I you," Rhys replied, his whole body now shaking with the strain of keeping the bow bent.

Gladoens' armor clinked as he stepped to one side of the boulder to survey the board. "Eight challenges in a row have I won at the conflict you've chosen. Nine is a number of completion and end of cycle. Nine victories it should be.

Then I can feed." His black gauntlet moved a huntsman.

Rhys stepped cautiously to the other side of the boulder while slipping the bow over his shoulder. He noted Gladoens' gambit and blearily revolved his gaming strategy while moving the central king. Rhys had grown up with his lungs often filled with liquid, leaving him unable to work or practice arms for many days at a time. Books being scarce, he had honed his skill at gwyddbwyll beyond that of the average player. Now his whole life had become one prolonged figurative game of hunted hunters with Lady Ellylyw. Rhys tried not to shiver as a chill surged up his spine at the rapidity and effectiveness of his opponent's response. He raised the king and set him down on a safer square.

The two players thrust and parried about the board, each feeling out his opponent's style and strength. The black knight paused to eye the board, and Rhys risked probing the distracted revenant for information. "Urre of the Mount made you what you are?"

Gladoens' black gauntlet glinted, catching a stray moonbeam as he picked up an intricately carved black horseman from among the huntsmen on the board. He lifted it slowly before eyes invisible in the darkness behind his visor. "Urre," he replied, voice expressionless.

Hope leapt in Rhys' heart. The piece in the revenant's grip was the one Ellylyw had dropped into Rhys' hand while the dead city burned. Rhys had seen it days before on Urre's own gaming board in his mausoleum on the Dolorous Mount. Some artist of Emperor Arthur's day had carved it into the likeness of Ellylyw's dark lover, and she had taken it in token of her loss. The Knight Gladoens had recognized the likeness of the foe who had infected him. That wakened a fervent hope in the sleep-starved bard that the revenant's obsessive focus would lead Gladoens to respond to any question asked, so long as he remained preoccupied by the game...and so long as he had no reason not to answer.

"Why didn't Urre behead you like his other victims?"

Setting the carved knight upon a square that cut off the direction of retreat for Rhys' king, Gladoens aimed his black visor squarely at the board. "When Urre of Hungary first brought the curse to Britain," his metallic voice replied. "He was a maimed knight, carried about by his servitors in a funeral litter."

"Yes," Rhys said. "I encountered Urre at Castrum Tenebrarum far below the great Roman Wall. It is an old tale that in Emperor Arthur's day, the Armorican chieftain Llancleawc at last drew the seven lance fragments from Urre's perpetually bleeding wounds. Because Llancleawc freed Urre of his weakness and pain, Urre became the shadow warrior who fought for him by night."

Rhys held his breath. The memories he had stirred in Gladoens seemed to slow the knight's moves on the board. The revenant's focus remained fixed on gwyddbwyll, while he spoke without thinking, perhaps scarcely noticing that he spoke at all. "When I lived, I resisted Llancleawc's reconquest of his father's lost northern realm."

The desolate lifelessness of his responses tugged at Rhys, to drain his already limited energy.

"Urre would not have made me this thing if I had not so savagely slain Llancleawc's people...if I had not hated the Hungarian with so violent a flame that it finally warmed even his cold heart to vengeance. It was Urre who had me interred in this ancient tumulus, had the Picts put my image on the rock, binding me forever to my ancestor's tomb. It is strange to remember these things again, unthought of for so long. The movement of the men across the board reminds me of the dark game we played. Though not with wooden men on a board. I can almost feel the passions that once burned in me."

He moved a piece.

Rhys reconsidered his strategy, then stalled. "Why would Urre give an enemy such power as this condition gave you?"

"Ten years he kept me in thrall to hold Estrake for him, answering all challenges, leaving Urre free to further Llancleawc's mad ambitions. Do not delay beyond the time allotted for your move."

The bard slid his king over a space, unable to resist asking this man from an earlier time, "You saw the great Arthur, Head Dragon of the Isle?"

"Never."

"Oh." A window on the brightest day in Britain's long, darkening history closed in Rhys' face. "It might be worth dying here to get a glimpse through eyes that once beheld Arthur."

"Urre," the voice said as dead as ever, "like Llancleawc, served the Pendragon. The Hungarian told me once that Arthur could make even him see the sun. You have not moved wisely. You see I am cutting off your king."

"Not if I move here."

Gladoens studied the board, then: "Who comes,

bard?"

Startled, Rhys barely managed to avoid catching the eyes glinting behind the visor slit. "Pardon?"

"There is one on the road who follows in your wake."

Rhys gaped at him, rapt with mounting excitement and a dark, irrational rush of jealousy that made the half-formed things slithering about the edges of his dream-starved vision writhe and leap. The revenant's words distracted him. Suddenly dizzy, Rhys felt a cold stab of fear. He knew he needed all his over-strained faculties to stave off the assaults of Gladoens' carved men. Redoubling his concentration, Rhys focused on the board and swallowed. "The one who comes, the one on my trail is Ellylyw, Urre's lady." Her name hurt his tongue.

"He made her like us, then." Gladoens shifted a man nearer Rhys' king. "Terrible."

Rhys wrestled against an overwhelming pang of compassion for Ellylyw.

With a jolt of fear, he realized he was slumped against the side of the mound. Rhys straightened. He had been asleep, but for how long a moment? Cold eyes pierced him. Sweat trickled down Rhys' sides in the cool night air. The growing dread he had been holding at bay for so long squeezed his chest. He strove to fight it back with another question. "How did you know someone was coming?"

"She is here in your blood. She has infected you." Gladoens shifted a piece, further narrowing the scope of movement of Rhys' king. "If Urre's woman comes, the Hungarian must have met his end."

"On the Dolorous Mount."

A piece on Rhys' right slid abruptly to a new square

as by some dark magic, and he grabbed for it, stopping himself just before touching his opponent's piece and thereby forfeiting the game. Urre's gaunt, dead-pale face seemed to grimace in miniature from the carved man, mocking him. Rhys realized it had not moved. It was the dreamworld again, infiltrating his vision. He slid his king away from Gladoens' trap.

Once again the revenant upset his opponent's balance. "You destroyed Urre for the Lady Ellylyw? Yet she must already have been what you must one night become."

Rhys flinched, staring at the blank visor, forcing himself to reply, "Yes."

"Now you hunt her, one who cannot have her."

Rhys suddenly hated him. "Yes."

"Why?"

Slipping his king back another square, Rhys racked his brain for some scheme to keep uncornered. "I didn't know what she'd become. I loosed Ellylyw from the chains in which her husband bound her and thereby cost him his life."

The revenant raised visor-framed eyes from the board to transfix Rhys. "And in all Britain, none but you know what revenants are, or how to stop us?"

Rhys felt his throat constrict. "Yes."

The visor turned toward the board, and Rhys could breathe again, though he felt marked by a new blackness behind his eyes.

Gladoens asked, "Has this Ellylyw made others of our kind?"

Shivering, Rhys saw her again—Ellylyw, still elegant and graceful, smoke from burning homes billowing about her. He cleared his throat. "I beheaded them all."

His insides knotted with guilt and grief, as for the thousandth time his memory rebelled against his will, and her last words before she fled the dawn that day came back to haunt him—plaintive, lost: *"I am alone again. Except for you."*

Rhys dug his nails into his palms to drive the picture from his mind and help him concentrate on the game that kept him alive. Not daring to lose the initiative, he ventured, "Have you raised other revenants?"

"Urre taught me to feed on those I slew in the wars, beheading them. Two of us was enough. How can you hope to corner one like Ellylyw, southern man? You cannot challenge her to a duel by gwyddbwyll."

"I see myself in her shoes...at the end of life." Rhys felt himself opening up to his opponent against his will, spilling his truths with his waning energy. "I see myself sliding out of my body, looking down on my ruined corpse, only to be pulled back into cold flesh, revived and enslaved to terrible drives. When Ellylyw makes you her protector, and when she rests by day by your side, I will strike."

The Knight of the Rock nodded in appreciation of Rhys' rationale.

When all the world goes mad, order becomes a thing of ineffable beauty.

Rhys felt a twinge of pity for this walking ruin, this monument to bleakness. He could not help but continue. "Before I encountered the horror that's consumed my life, I made my living, such as it was, singing of Emperor Arthur. I know only two tales of Arthur's court that resembled Urre's enough to suggest that the knights involved were infected by the revenant warrior. One was the tale of Tiwrnach the Black Gael. I reached his cave before the lady could seek him. He is no more. The other was Peredur's battle with the Knight of the Tomb."

"Your Ellylyw would know my tale, too?"

"When first I saw her," the bard said, as if to a friend and confidant, "I thought her to be half her husband Madoc's age. But in all the legends I learned, there was only one British lady Ellylyw, the daughter of Neil the Gael, at Arthur's court. She would have heard Peredur's deeds from his own lips as he reported to the Emperor."

"We stay as we are," the desolate voice rang from the metal headpiece, "until we are stopped."

"Yes. But Ellylyw must search her way toward you along unfrequented back roads, avoiding Saxon invaders, seeking a new place of the dead in which to lie each dawn. Of course, death is everywhere in the Age of Darkness.

The black gauntlet reached for Rhys. Realizing he was out of time, he hastily made his move. The gauntlet paused. Gladoens reviewed the board, then lowered his hand. "Urre's lady approaches. Will she taste different, I wonder, for being his?"

Rhys shook with rage. "You'd prey upon her?"

"Are you her hunter or her protector?"

Rhys glared at the armored creature. "Both, perhaps."

"Or neither. I will take strength from her in several ways. Vengeance, too, though she may find some sweetness in the bitter draught."

"Are you mad?"

"Your word means nothing. Your king's in peril."

"I'm not cornered yet." Rhys regarded the blank steel

across the board. "Remove your helmet. Let me see my enemy."

The toneless voice replied, "I was buried in this steel."

Rhys rubbed some feeling back into his face, blinking away a growing menagerie of illusory crawling things writhing their way deeper into his visual field. Cocking his head, he tried a new tack. "You actually fought the great Llancleawc. What was he like?"

The moon sailed slowly across the dark sky while Rhys kept the revenant playing the game and talking of vanished days.

***

Far off across the sea of heather, a cock crowed. Rhys' king still danced about a swiftly narrowing wedge of board. He was out of options. One more move would trap him and the revenant would be free to slay his defeated foe.

Rhys sprang upright, flipping the board into the air, and sprinted away.

Gladoens knelt and methodically picked up the pieces one-by-one. Out of sight halfway around the mound, Rhys scrambled to its top, then crept on his belly until he could see the knight below.

Gladoens placed the last piece back where it had stood on the board. "You can only move here." His hollow voice rattled metallically.

The black gauntlet shifted Rhys' king into the trap. "And I move here."

Gladoens cornered the king, then laid it on its side. "The king is dead."

Freed from the challenge, image intact, Gladoens

looked for his opponent and found that he had vanished.

Rhys held his breath. The air smelled of dawn, the sky was lightening in the east.

Gladoens strode swiftly three quarters of the way around the mound and rolled a boulder from its base. Slipping into a narrow tunnel, he allowed the rock to slide back in place behind him.

Atop the barrow, Rhys lowered his bow. Gladoens had his ninth victory at gwyddbwyll, but Rhys had won the game. A wild elation spilling frequently into paralyzing terror racked Rhys in opposite directions. Marl, the merchant in the town below Tiwrnach's Cave, had given him the crucial weapon—no enchanted sword like Arthur's Caledvwlch or Peredur's reforged Grail Sword, but an exploitable quirk of these creatures' damaged minds. Now Rhys had learned even more of their shadowy psyches from the lips of Gladoens himself—and in the process stretched out the game until dawn's approach drove the revenant to ground.

Clambering down, Rhys whistled the uneasy Morvran to him, pulled his two spears from the gear on the horse's back and trotted to Gladoens' concealed entrance. Jamming the spear-shafts under the boulder, and using a rock as a fulcrum, Rhys put his back into it, puffing and wheezing, levering for all he was worth despite the liquid clogging his lungs, until the boulder fell away from the tunnel mouth. Flint struck steel, sparking alight a rush from Rhys' belt pouch. Then, sword in one sweaty palm and rush-light in the other, the bard crawled awkwardly down the cramped hole into stale, choking, earthy air. The passage was crude. Tomb robbers must have dug it long ago.

Sweat stung his eyes as he reached a framework of logs, dry with antiquity. Looters had laboriously sawn through them, carrying away a three-foot-square section. Rhys imagined the desecrators finally cutting through to the chamber within to find the revenant waiting.

Dead air set him coughing as he wormed his legs in front of him to drop through the gap in the log wall and into a low-ceilinged chamber. His rush-light burnt low and blue. Wheezing painfully, he fumbled a second rush from his pouch to light with the first.

The rotted remains of a wagon lay in a heap in one corner, rush-light flickering along the smooth sides of bowls, platters and butcher's implements of gold and bronze scattered among the crumbling boards.

In the opposite corner, a great bronze cauldron stood on intricately molded legs, its rim encircled by grinning gold lions. A boar-embroidered banner lying across it was centuries newer. Gladoens' war-colors, no doubt.

The rest of the wall beside the cauldron was taken up by a low bronze couch or bier resting on eagle talons. On it lay Gladoens himself, sword pommel clutched in both hands against his black metal carapace. War-axes, spears, bow and quiver hung along the raised back of the bronze couch, caked in dust.

Rhys tucked his rush-light in a gold candleholder, reached down toward the revenant and, clenching his jaw, unbuckled Gladoens' chinstrap, then pulled free the visored helm. Shoulder-length black hair with white wings at the temples fell out of the black steel. Gladoens' bloodless features were blunt, squarish, hard-chiseled, ebony beard short and confined to the chin, mustache thick, long and drooping, brows bushy.

Dark eyes stared half-open, dull, unmoving. Rhys knew that outside the sun was up at last. Gladoens lay like the dead.

"Ellylyw will never reach you," Rhys muttered, his voice sounding in his own ears ridiculously young and shaky in this dead, ancient place.

He hesitated to say more. Could this breathless shape hold some awareness? If Rhys' own infection one day brought him to this, would he dream in this state? Thinking he saw movement, startled, he spun toward the wagon. Nothing lurked there but the meaningless grotesques darting everywhere, which he could no longer blink away. Even the revenant's blunt features seemed to shift, but Rhys knew it was undreamt dreams spilling into his dry, tired eyes.

A grislier task than removing the helm awaited him, but if Rhys was to achieve a final reckoning with Ellylyw, he must not only survive this encounter but profit by it. Carefully searching out the black armor's many hidden straps, he unbuckled each piece from the warrior's corpse.

Black spots burst frenetically before his eyes, and he stumbled, starving for breath.

With a start, Rhys realized that his eyes were open and that it was utterly dark. Time must have passed. He was lying at an uncomfortable angle, a pile of armor digging into his back. His swirling wits coalesced enough for him to realize his muscles were stiff, so he must have lain there for some time. Terrified, he gasped. "How long?"

Scrabbling flint and steel from his pouch with painfully tingling fingers, he clumsily sparked up another rush-light, thrusting it shakily toward the bier. Gladoens lay still in his dark leather tunic and breeches, but the freshly lit rush was already blue and sputtering. Rhys' head pounded and he could not think. The air was almost gone. Rhys picked up his sword, but found the ceiling too low for him to swing the long blade. Sheathing it, he shuffled to the disintegrating wagon.

Gleaming grave goods swam among teeming moats. Rhys stumbled to his knees in rotting wood. The pain of impact clearing his head a bit, he seized a bronze cleaver. Time and consciousness fleeting, Rhys pulled out his whetstone and honed the ancient blade.

Losing time lighting yet another barely glowing rush, Rhys crouched his way under the low ceiling to the bronze bier.

Gladoens looked at him, groped at his chest where he had left his sword.

"Sundown." Rhys gasped.

The revenant, finding himself unarmed, sat up and reached for a hanging war-axe. Rhys swung the short heavy cleaver.

The blow toppled the revenant back, neck bleeding profusely. Aghast that he had only mangled the knight, Rhys lifted the gory cleaver as best he could and swung again, desperate, this time severing the head, snapping the age-eaten eagle-taloned feet beneath the bier. The room spun. Rhys felt a violent whirlwind tug him half out through the top of his head, the vortex bursting up beyond him through wood and stone and earth, shooting into the sky as whatever was left of Gladoens escaped his shell.

Pulling himself halfway back into his wheeze-racked

frame, bumbling half-conscious with prickling digits, Rhys bundled his foe's arms and a few small gold artifacts into Gladoens' war-banner. He dragged them behind him, in a long, awkward struggle up the constricting passage toward faint light and increasingly breathable air. Weak, worn, drenched in sweat, head spinning and throbbing, parched lungs sucking endless draughts of life-giving night—which seemed almost blindingly bright after the dark of the tomb—Rhys heaved the bundle to the earth. He struggled to lever the boulder back over the hole, then sank to the earth to pant beside it.

When he could walk and almost think, he dragged the heavy bundle around to the front of the mound, his back aching from being bent so long.

Morvran whickered to him, low and miserable.

Beside the trembling, drooping horse stood Ellylyw, pale and still in her white silks, one slim hand by the shallow knife cut on Morvran's neck where she had been lapping. The lady's eyes mirrored moonlight like an owl's.

"This is all you've left me," she said. "You've taken Gladoens, too. How do you keep going, Rhys of Caer Waroc? How do you survive everything I throw at you? What do you have to live for?"

Rhys shook his head, drawing his sword unsteadily.

Ellylyw stepped lightly toward him. "You begin to intrigue me, Rhys. I think I have scarcely tasted you at all."

He thrust the sword toward her, two-handed, preparing to lunge, as single-mindedly intent as any revenant.

She sidestepped out of range. "I cannot enjoy you like this, half alive, stinking with sweat and the staleness of the crypt in your hair."

She swept out an arm, long sleeve fluttering over the long sweeps of barren, wind-wracked heathlands. "Look where you've left me. No grave of my own. I must find some other place of death for a day's refuge. I've traveled so far. How much farther must I go tonight?"

Her white horse, former property of the mercenary white knight, trotted up to her.

Morvran shied weakly away.

Ellylyw raised a slim shoe to her stirrup and flowed lithely up into her saddle. "I think I could kill you now, Rhys. But who would share my victory?"

Setting her steed trotting away across the desolation, she called back over her shoulder, "You have one foot in my world already. Clean yourself up, Rhys. I'll come for you soon."

Rhys fell to his haunches, wheezing. He was the gwyddbwyll king spent by breaking out of the circle of deadly huntsmen. Daybreak would soon make him the hunter. The final round of the game was about to begin. He collapsed on his side in the dirt, watching Ellylyw dwindle in the moonlight.

Chapter 12:

Souterrain

The tracks disappeared on a patch of rough shale. The green grass beyond yielded no clue.

He could not lose her.

Rhys stepped forward, hand on his sword-hilt, Gladoens' black chainmail covered with plates clinking about him in the quiet morning as he led his horse by the reins. The aging charger set all four hooves and snorted, refusing to go farther.

Rhys regarded Morvran sharply, then raised a black gauntleted hand to his own claw-scarred face while scanning the verdant plain. He could spy no trace of his quarry's passage. This flat land bothered Rhys. He enjoyed the open expanse of it, but its essential featurelessness oppressed his spirits. The low slope rising before him was as grassy as the rest of the plain stretching away to a distant ridge of low trees. Everything sparkled with dew, bright green, teeming with life and promise. And yet... Was not this one low mound on which Morvran refused to set foot a little less lush than the rest? The blades of grass grayish and drooping as if the soil beneath was less rich, or as if something yet farther down drew the life out of them...

Leaving his horse to graze on greener grass, Rhys circumnavigated the wide base of the low rise. Did it form, perhaps, too neat a circle, as if someone long ago had shaped this bit of earth? Rhys had seen the barrows the bronze-users had raised in ancient times over their leaders, but such mounds were heaped high. The shape before him was neither clearly natural nor plainly artificial. If someone had created it, the unknown makers must have meant to hide their work.

Just as what Rhys hunted meant to hide itself.

His heart beating a little quicker, Rhys cast his mind back across the legends he had so painstakingly memorized in the bardic college a few long-long years ago. It struck him that his was not the first century in which Britain had been plagued by ruthless raiders. Perhaps this was no gentle hill, but an earthen chamber camouflaged with turf. The bard could not recall any old tale describing such a thing, but then people did not put their secret defenses into song. He continued his circuit, scanning the slightly withered grass for sign of an opening.

Fog crept behind him over the distant treetops. It had not caught him yet, but soon it would obscure his search. Bad weather often seemed to aid the creature he tracked, as if the hunted one wielded dark magics. Perhaps she did. Animals wild and domestic acted as if she had trained them to do her bidding.

A single bush varied the featureless grass slope. If Rhys had not been hunting so sly a quarry, he would never have glanced twice at it. Now he thrust the butt of his spear into the bush and rattled it. The whole thing rose on the end of the shaft, rootless, a cover broken free back in the woods and set here to hide an opening in the earth.

Rhys tossed it aside. Years of erosion had clogged the

hole with dirt, but Rhys crouched and poked his head into the dark. A narrow passage stretched into utter darkness within the low mound. Its walls were dry-stone, meticulously fitted by hands that must have long since melted back into this earth. Whatever the ancients had meant to safeguard here, they had spared no expense of labor to do it. Now, he was sure, something else had come to make use of their forgotten arts. He rose.

No room for a shield in that little space. He eased his arm from the strap and slid the shield from his back to the grass, feeling terribly exposed without it. Spears were equally impractical. His throwing spear long lost, he thrust his jabbing spear into the ground for quick retrieval upon his exit. At the impact, the ash-wood shaft, cracked in its last combat, snapped in two. Groaning in irritation at this further betrayal, Rhys tossed the broken haft to the withered grass and glanced briefly at the late morning sun sinking deeper in the waves of fog pouring toward him. Drawing flint and steel from his belt pouch, Rhys struck alight one of his recently harvested rushes.

***

To keep his wits sharp, Rhys estimated how much ground he had covered as he crouched uncomfortably along, his left arm aching from holding the rush light before him. He must have shuffled at least a hundred feet in a slow curve down and about the low mound. Sweat dripped into his eyes and his lungs labored, as if the stale air they heaved lacked some vital property necessary to keep him fully alive.

Something growled ahead.

Rhys went rigid. How could he fight a large predator in this crouched position? His leaden left hand had to keep up the slowly burning rush. He could not stand erect or swing his sword. Quickly, he thrust the butt-end of the rush between two stones on the wall, glancing into the snarling darkness ahead, burning his fingers, but managing not to drop the precious light onto the packed earth floor.

Claws clicked against stone.

Rhys dropped to one knee, bracing the pommel of his sword like a boar-spear against his boot. The very darkness of the tunnel mouth seemed to hurtle toward him, somehow clearing the sword despite the low ceiling, slamming into him, dislodging the rush from the wall. Rhys' back was driven against the earth, and claws raked across the chainmail on his shoulders and chest as the fallen rush snuffed out and blackness closed about him.

Gasping, choking on his own fear, Rhys shoved his sword hand upward, his left feeling fur over hard muscles. His attacker scrabbled, yowling in his ear, its own weight against the edge of the blade Rhys pressed upward. Hot breath hit Rhys in the face as fangs clicked together, just missing his throat.

Angry now, Rhys snorted the predator's stinking breath from him as his gauntleted left hand found the point of his blade and seized it. Now holding the sword by both ends, Rhys heaved himself to the side and felt a satisfying impact as he caught the unseen attacker between blade-edge and stone wall.

The thing yowled louder, sharper, a feline cry of fury and pain, claws raking Rhys' abdomen, armor saving him from disembowelment. Hot, foul breath beat against his face, warning him where the jaws would snap shut. Both gauntleted hands clenched on his blade, forcing it tight against the squirming creature, Rhys kneed the unseen beast. Flailing hind legs protected its soft underbelly, and it twisted from under the sword to dart toward the exit.

Rhys swept the sword about swiftly, clacking it against stones on either side and floor and ceiling, moving forward and forcing the creature to back farther along the tunnel. Rhys' spine and shoulders ached, his lungs felt bruised from breathing so hard, his head swam and his arms already felt loose-muscled from weariness, yet he forced himself to keep his blade sweeping blindly about. Afraid he would soon be exhausted, he pressed on as fast as he could, forcing the creature back and back until dim light seeped around the tunnel curve, showing him a scrambling black shape.

Desperate, it sprang back toward him, got a claw past his swing, and clawed his thrust-forward head.

Rhys screamed in fury as fire seared his face. His left eye flared into unreal blazes of light, seared by excruciating waves of pain.

The great cat fell backward, landing on three feet, the fourth leg curled against its chest.

Rhys screamed at the creature, charging, bouncing his dulled blade against all sides of the tunnel, one eye blind, the other half-blind with pain and flashes of after-image-like light.

The great black feline darted away into the pale gray light, then turned again, having caught its breath.

Slapping his sword pommel into his left hand, Rhys drew his dagger and flung it, but cramped and without depth perception, the cast merely obliged the beast to leap lightly back toward the now visible exit. Sword again in his right hand, Rhys roared, scrambling toward the feline. Despite the creature's urgent need to stay and protect this place, the stung bard's ferocity drove the cat back before him to the threshold. Fearing the light outside and half-blinded by it, the feline turned at bay, matching Rhys' ferocity with its own, lashing with swift claws and lunging to snap long teeth.

Rhys felt his blade clip flesh, and the great cat shrieked. Knocked to its side on the floor, flailing, the cat clamped its jaws around Rhys' boot, fangs punching through the thick leather, breaking skin and mashing muscle. With a shriek of his own, Rhys thrust, driving his blade into the injured creature's side. The jaws unclenched from his ankle as the black body convulsed, stretching out its limbs with a choked cry like a hurt child, then a spirit shot up and out of the furred meat.

Rhys stumbled out into dim, foggy daylight, dropped to his knees in the soft grass beside the pack he had left outside the tunnel. Fumbling free his canteen, he laved his wounded face and sucked down comforting water. He would have given much for a strong jolt of whiskey, but he had been far from people for too long and had no such amenities left.

Moaning, he delicately explored his damaged eye with shuddering fingertips. Drawing the broken sword-tip he had long ago fashioned into a crude dagger, he pulled open the pack, yanked out his one remaining spare shirt and daggered the sleeve from it. Rhys wet the sleeve with his rapidly diminishing water supply and wadded it against his throbbing face. There he lay in the sweet grass, the world spinning about him, his slack muscles shivering as he listened to the birds twitter and the distant boughs creak, feeling the outrage in his flesh and the awful loss.

***

The fog had grown thick and the day dark when Rhys again had the energy to raise his head. The throbbing had slowed and the ceaseless pain dulled enough to let him think again, and he was so bored with lying there in pain and misery that he was desperate for distraction. Unwadding his crude bandage, he rubbed the worst of the blood off onto the grass, then wrapped the cloth about his head, cutting a few more strips from the ruined shirt to bind everything in place.

"What were you?" he snarled at the dead feline, then ducked into the tunnel and dragged the black-furred corpse out into misty daylight. Though far larger, of course, the beast was shaped pretty much like the ordinary house cats the Romans had brought to the isle as more personable replacements for the household weasels that kept down vermin. Rhys recalled a few stories from the northern hills of Faery Cats of great size like this. Their origin remained unknown. The stories simply described them as one of the dangerous monstrosities apt to prey on luckless travelers who strayed from the high roads.

Then again, the Romans had rebuilt some of the isle's ancient monuments into arenas and imported exotic predators from Asia to fight there. Perhaps a few panthers had gotten loose and adapted to the cool clime. Rhys smiled crookedly at the thought that a descendant of such feline fugitives might well make its lair in an abandoned tunnel, and protect it savagely. There might even be young down there...or worse, a mate.

Rhys stretched his aching back. He had lost blood. He lacked the strength for another such fight in close quarters. He had dulled his blade, diminished his supply of rush lights, not to mention water and bandages, and the day was waning. Once the sun set, the revenant he hunted would be free and strong. Rhys told himself he should find shelter while he could and rest until he knew how much of his sight he would get back...

His wound twinged. He knew if he turned aside now, Ellylyw would find him first. And this time he would not survive.

His dagger lost, Rhys jerked the broken spear from the ground. Crouching his way back into the tunnel, he used the jagged-ended two-foot spear-haft as a cane to hobble into the dark.

Reaching the point at which the great cat had attacked him, Rhys raised his rush light. Just ahead, above eye level, was a small platform. The tunnel continued beyond it at the same cramped height as before, but in this one spot the ceiling rose an extra six feet to accommodate the platform, a perfect vantage from which a single guard could ambush anyone daring enough to creep down the long tunnel. The great black cat must have leapt from this niche, clearing Rhys' couched sword-point.

Cautiously, he moved on, now scanning the ceiling for other raised areas while keeping his one good eye on the dark passage ahead. Against the left wall ahead yawned a narrow opening. Reaching it, Rhys thrust his light into its dark mouth.

A *cul de sac*, empty. No doubt a storage space. He crouched onward.

Abruptly, the cramped tunnel ended, much of the wall ahead blocked by a single large flat stone. Was there nothing here? Was all this for nothing? To the left wound another dark passage. Sighing, sick of being underground, Rhys yearned for open sky. His wounds pained him all the more at the sight of the second shaft. Still, there was nothing for it but to expend more of the dying day crouching along this new branch.

His sword arm ached from using the spear-end as a cane, and his back felt like it would never straighten again, but at last he reached a small beehive-shaped chamber at the tunnel's end. The bluish remnant of his light revealed little enough there to reward his determination and sacrifice. Wrinkling his nose at the rank smell, he was at least able to stand up. He lit one of the last rushes in his belt pouch and examined the dirt floor. Claws had scooped out a small pit against one wall. In it lay tufts of fur. A bed whose owner would not return.

Rhys swore, bent his back to his unpleasant task and hunched his way as quickly as he could back to the main passage. There he sat for a moment, slumped against the wall, panting in the dead air. The scent of cat irritated his sinuses, and his nose had swollen shut. Wheezing and miserable, he cast his one eye around the oppressively close dry-stone walls.

The large flat slab blocking the end of the main passage caught his attention. It did not match the small surrounding stones. In fact, it looked a bit like a door. Half willing to end his pain and weariness in an abrupt cave-in, Rhys thrust the point of his spear between the slab and one of the smaller stones and levered at it. The slab shifted.

It had been jammed firmly into place, but was not bearing any weight. Neither was it terribly heavy. Excited, Rhys carefully repositioned his lever. It would not do to snap the steel.

Rhys heaved and the slab groaned free, falling backward into open space. Rhys crouched through, rush-light before him. Stubbing his toes and then shins agonizingly, he tumbled onto his face, losing his light. Instinctively, he flailed his weapon about him, clinking it off stone. He froze, listening intently. No sound. No hint of life. No suggestion at all of immediate threat, yet Rhys' heart hammered noisily at his ribs. His labored wheezing sounded dangerously loud in the confined space.

Carefully setting the spear where he was certain he could blindly seize it again, he struggled to his bruised knees, toes throbbing, shins aching as if broken, and pulled flint and steel from his pouch. A few strikes lit another precious rush. Light fluttered about a more substantial beehive chamber, the hidden terminus of the subterranean structure. Yet it, too, was empty.

Casting a quick glance behind him, Rhys saw that a long, triangular-shaped stone had been set on the earthen floor just inside the concealed entrance as a toe-catcher and the floor of the chamber beyond it dropped a good foot down from the approaching tunnel—a final defense. This whole structure was probably a camouflaged temporary refuge from raiders.

Spinning back toward the open space before him,

Rhys gulped air hungrily, starved for breath in the closeness. Looking more carefully, his wavering light revealed to him in the center of the circular space another pit scratched into the earth, this one wider and longer and deep enough to mask its contents in shadow.

Rhys rose shakily to his feet, tucked the truncated spear-shaft through the back of his belt and wrapped clumsy, oxygen-starved fingers about the pommel of his sword. The blade scraped too noisily from its scabbard as he stepped cautiously toward the pit he was certain would prove an open grave. The shadows within it withered before his approaching light, revealing a pale woman on her back in the dirt.

Ellylyw, her hair disordered, her gown rent and stained with travel and hunting, dusty from the earth in which she lay in this dead place from an unknown time. Yet still his breath caught. Still, he found her beautiful, her delicate features calm, even beatific as in sleep.

Afraid of losing himself, Rhys forced his gaze from her unconscious, striking face. High up on one wall he spied a black shaft. An air vent, no doubt. No light seeped through it. Perhaps it had collapsed somewhere above. Or perhaps night had fallen outside. With a thrill of fear, Rhys realized he had lost all sense of time laboring through the tunnels. He had to strike fast and hard. He turned back to face her.

The black steel blade he had taken from the burial chamber of the dreadful Gladoens of the Rock hung heavy in his hand. How could he mar her beauty? The livid complexion made her ebony tresses the more striking. The full curve of her ruddy lips bespoke a sensuous richness

Rhys had never known. She had not asked for this fate. She did not deserve to be mangled in a pit beneath the living earth.

Her image rippled, warning Rhys that the dust and stale air and scent of cat were exacerbating the life-long condition that frequently caused his lungs to fail. Weakened, not only by constricted lungs but by pain and blood-loss, he was rapidly losing his ability to strike. Yet this was what he had fought so long to achieve.

Ellylyw...

Feeling guilty at the thought of harming her, panged as well with the certain knowledge that he should strike while he could, Rhys sheathed his sword and stepped to the wall to thrust the rush light between two stones. Distracted by the noise of his own wheezing, he tugged the shortened spear from his belt. A few clumsy steps brought him back to the oblong pit. He tried to pray, but no words would come. Too many emotions collided in the narrow space of his steel-banded chest for any one of them to take the fore, but he could not waste more time. He had not gone through so much for nothing.

He stepped awkwardly down into the trench, straddled the corpse, and raised the spear above his head with both hands wrapped firmly about the remaining haft. Face dripping with sweat, the raw wound where his eye had been burning from the salt, his remaining eye stinging, too, he paused to catch as full a breath as his congested lungs could still take. The trembling of his frame spattered little drops from his writhing features.

With a yell half-strangled in his throat, he drove the spear downward until its point caught between her ribs.

Surprisingly little blood welled up about the weapon. Not sure what the creature's vulnerabilities might be, Rhys wrenched a stone from the floor, held it two-handed and hammered the butt of the broken spear, blunting the jagged wood. Hearing her ribs crack, he winced, but continued hammering, driving the spear-point clean through her sternum, out her back and into dry earth beneath.

Flinging the stone aside, Rhys pulled himself jerkily out of the grave. His joints suddenly gave way beneath him, dropping him face-first into choking dust. Pushing himself into a sitting position, he hacked and coughed, moaning at what he had done, unable to pull a breath down into his swollen, liquid-filled lungs. The light flickering across Ellylyw's still face burned blue. He would have to light another rush soon.

Her eyes opened. She looked at him, bleak, reproachful. He heard his own voice babble something, then clenched his jaw shut, seizing control of himself, though aware that his whole body trembled like a plucked harp string.

"What have you done to me?" Ellylyw's hands fluttered weakly to the wooden stump protruding from her ribs, but could get no grip on it. Those delicate fingers fell limp at her sides. "Why, Rhys?"

He felt as if his own chest were pierced. "I couldn't let you go on, Lady."

"But I will go on. Don't leave me like this, Rhys. I couldn't bear it."

"I thought you would die...be free—"

"You've trapped me, pinned me like a butterfly. I loved you, Rhys."

His throat clenched, distorting his voice. "You never loved me."

"I chose you. I still choose you, despite everything you've done to me. You've hounded me, hunted me, stalked me, staked me. It's still not too late. I can take you into my world. You're halfway there already. There's nothing left for you without me. You know that. You have no place. Your gifts as a bard will never be appreciated. The Saxons have torn Britain open to feast on her heart. You are marked by us. Your only place is with us."

His teeth ground together as he forced out a dry, choked reply. "You have lost yourself, Ellylyw. Your world is more barren than burning Britain. You prey on the innocent."

"Am I not innocent?" she asked, her voice high and child-like. "I follow my instincts, feed as I must. I draw life from any wellspring that presents itself. Who are you to say the wolf has no soft feelings for the fawn in its jaws?"

"You're worse than a wolf, my lady," Rhys said, dismayed to hear his voice catch and break. "You spread the plague that claimed you."

"We, too, are part of the natural order, however unnatural it feels to you or to me. The two of us are joined, Rhys. Remember when I kissed the wound in your hand before you freed me from the vault below Castrum Tenebrarum? I tasted your blood. I am in your blood. You have been true to me, in your way, ever since."

"And this is best for you."

"To lie alone in the dark? For how many years? A dozen? Motionless. Deprived of sight or sound in this tomb. Nothing to feel but my flesh desiccating. Awareness tethered to dry flesh until...when? A hundred years from now, when some wanderer ventures near, finally dares to obey the whispers I seep into his mind, makes his way down the old tunnel to find me, pull the spear from my leathery flesh and sacrifice in surprise his blood to redeem me from the tyranny of the grave?"

"No..."

"Will your life be any better? Maimed, despised, rootless, every day another struggle to feed on something weaker than yourself...something that will not live again when darkness falls, unlike my prey. To feel yourself weakening, rotting alive, choking on the dust of the earth, hungering for life your deficient lungs will never allow you, until one day you meet a quicker blade, a subtler schemer, a hungrier wolf. Unless you, yourself, are the one I draw back here to lift me from the paralyzing bed. You can never be free of me, Rhys. I cannot let you go. Don't leave me."

"I'm sorry that your lover Urre of Hungary was destroyed before he could tell you what you are. I know what it's like to be adrift. No one ever explained this condition I was born with that's choking the life out of me. I don't know why it has maimed me."

"You've barely one foot in the world of the living. Step down here with me. Bend down, let me kiss you. Just once. After all we've been through."

"I've sacrificed what little I had to pursue you. There's not much left to lose."

"I know. I meant to strip you, bit-by-bit, abrase you 'til the true steel shone."

"But I won't sacrifice the ability to choose...the thing

that makes me human."

"Is being human such a prize?"

"Don't you miss it?"

She sighed. A little blood bubbled about the spear.

Rhys closed his remaining eye, winced against the pain. "You do. I thought so. I know I do."

"Then you know you're changing."

He rubbed the side of his face that did not sting. "Of course. I feel it all slipping away. I swing from dark to light in wild sweeps. A tiny thing sets my emotions raging. Except when I'm too starved for air to feel anything but emptiness."

"You will be like me, some night, Rhys. And what will you do then if you're alone? You beheaded all those I brought up from darkness, and all that Urre raised before me. No one left on this island even knows what you're becoming. You would be alone. Alone for so long—"

"If it comes to that, I'll kill myself."

"It will come, and killing yourself will only hasten the process."

"I won't spread this plague," he shouted, his voice hurting his ears in the small space, shocking him with his own ferocity. His brows clenched so hard the muscles in his forehead ached. His fury toward his long-time enemy burgeoned toward hatred. "I will find a way."

"I am the way," she crooned.

"Do you think I wanted to love you? Do you think I ever had any illusion that you cared at all for me? Love got into my blood, and I cannot get free of it. It won't let me destroy you."

He paced about the small chamber, raving at the stone

ceiling. "I gave up everything. I tracked her down. My face is a crosshatch of scars mapping out the long chase. I stopped her. What more do you want from me?"

"I never meant to make you love me," she said softly. "And once you destroyed everyone else to whom I might turn, I had no choice but to turn on you. Our kind are fixed of mind. You know that, Rhys. I can never let you go. But you...you can release me. What must I pay you to buy back freedom? Must I lie for you? I can do that. Truth is not one of our fixations."

Her unblinking stare captured his gaze. Breath caught in his choked lungs, left him suspended between death and life. Her smooth, delicate face twisted into a smile. "I love you, Rhys."

He flinched. "Don't. Love is real to me, whether you deserve it, whether I've earned it, whether either of us wanted it. Don't mock my pain."

"I love you."

"Stop."

"Better than Madoc, better than Urre, I love you, Rhys of Caer Waroc."

"You don't!"

"I'm all there is," she told him, her voice no longer seductive or powerful or confident, but that of a lost child alone in the dark, telling herself she is not afraid.

The hatred that buffeted Rhys as fiercely as dark wings, flew off without trace. His love for Ellylyw flared up so intensely he felt waves of heat and light coruscate from him, soothing his lacerated flesh, bathing her still form. He ached to make some last gift to her, leave her something from him that she could value. Yet he had only one thing left to give.

"In a time not long ago," he began, his throat relaxing, his bard's voice again rich with subtle shades of expression, "a widow, devastated by the loss of her family in the wars, raised her remaining son deep in a dark wood, far from the brilliance of the Imperator Arthur's court..."

There, in the beehive chamber in the heart of a man-made hill, Rhys told Ellylyw the Story of Peredur. The wounded bard put his whole heart into the telling until his audience and he himself lost all grasp on time or place and rode together the exhilarating waves of emotion and revelation that made up Peredur's mysterious and meaningful history.

Until at last, Rhys described the legendary hero's darkest encounter. "And Peredur drew, and despite all prophecy, stood upon the wall guarding the Perilous Cemetery."

As he continued, the bard whisked his own blade from its sheath and brandished it as Peredur had, challenging all the hostility of the unknowable world with Peredur's words: "'Shock me with your ferocity and hate if you will, all you hostile spirits, yet I will endure.' And Peredur sprang from the cemetery wall down among the black shapes that seethed and wove among the monuments." Rhys leapt down astride the pinned lady. "And Peredur looked into the face of his own dark Fate and embraced the Fay Morgana, and told her, 'Though you have proved a thousand times that you will never love me, still I will always love you.'"

And as Peredur struck, so Rhys swung downward, and the black blade of Gladoens severed the neck of the Lady

Ellylyw, spattering the bard's boots with her blood and wrenching the heart out of him on a fishhook.

Rhys wept while rubbing the blood from the blade in the dry earth for fear of more rapid infection, rubbing his boots dry with folds of Ellylyw's ruined skirt, then clawing his way out of the grave, crawling back through the long tunnel, the dying blue light winking out behind him, leaving him to scrabble slowly in choking blindness, a maimed and mindless animal, toward fresh air somewhere far above.

Epilogue:

The last bitter-sweet notes of Rhys' harp reverberated through the cool night air and dissipated in the infinite darkness. Even the mice were silent in the thatch atop the pock-walled old Roman tax-office, which now served as an inn. The flames on one of several torches about the courtyard popped, but the sudden sound did not break the spell. The crowd was one animal made of separate parts united briefly to experience the same terrible topography of struggle and passion.

Rhys felt painfully alive, all the emotions he had poured out in the Lay of Ellylyw swirling inside him. He bowed his head and let his hands fall from the harp-strings.

The great animal before him breathed and broke apart into individuals once more, each applauding or speaking or sighing. People began to come forward to leave something at the bard's feet as reward for what he had given them. One or two donated a coin, but most these days gave more certain recompense: food or drink, a brooch, a cloak, a lovingly hand-stitched blanket. Rhys nodded in appreciation to each of them as they laid down the offering or paused to speak a word or two about what the tale he had sung had meant to them.

Once they had done so, they scattered, each to his or her own journey, most back into the inn for the night.

But there was one man, a knight in undamaged

chainmail, its polished links gleaming with reflected torchlight. The professional warrior stared intently at the bard and did not move a muscle.

Well-trained. Wastes no motion until he is ready to make his move—waiting for the crowd to clear. Some vengeful kinsman of Madoc's, maybe?

Then an achingly familiar silhouette entered the periphery of his vision, across the last few departing members of the audience, she caught and held his eyes. The form he could not miss stole the breath from his lungs. His heart lurched, his blood ran cold, then a hot flush flooded up into his suddenly burning face.

The shining cascade of raven-black hair down to the narrow waist, the exquisite curve of the small of her back, the grace with which she turned slowly toward him...

"Ellylyw..."

Then the woman faced him, blinking in surprise at his rapt stare. Of course, it was not Ellylyw, but for a fleeting instant she had been with him, just out of reach. The shock of sheer hunger and need welled up forcefully and rattled Rhys to the core.

She smiled slightly, as if moved by his tale and the passion of the performance that had painted his pain in her imagination so vividly. She gave him a little nod and turned shyly away—a not unfamiliar moment for any performer. Except...

He felt his arms lift without his volition, and he almost stepped forward to draw her in, press her against him, enfold her in his arms and kiss her softly pulsing throat.

Rhys spun away, every muscle in his body trembling

with horror. And raw desire. He flipped the hood of his cloak over his head to hide his ravaged face in its shadow.

A man tugged at his elbow.

Rhys restrained an abrupt urge to lash out at him, to make the man feel in his flesh the bard's rage and grief and horror.

"It was your face," the man said in a strange, rapt tone. "The black band over the missing eye. The deep scars."

Rhys turned toward him, lest his eyes be caught again by the woman with Ellylyw's hair and shape...but a stranger's face. It was the knight who held his sleeve. Up close, the torchlight revealed him to be a young man, his face as unmarked by battle as his glinting armor. There was a subtle design inscribed on the brow of his helmet: something like a rose, though Rhys could not see it clearly. It smacked of piety of some form, and that made Rhys deeply uneasy. He wanted to move away from the symbol, but the knight held him firmly.

"There, said I," the knight continued in a strong, quiet, intense voice, "there is a man whose story was earned with blood and sweat. That is why I joined the crowd."

The hairs of the fur about the collar of the warrior's cloak stood straight up as if they were the man's own hairs proclaiming alarm and anxiety. A bard must listen to his audience, but the spiritual aura of the knight seemed to push Rhys away even as the man's powerful grip held him to the spot.

"What is it that you want?" Rhys asked, keeping his voice calm and polite, though the passions of the Lay still roiled his depths.

The knight's wide eyes looked a little mad in the torchlight. Rhys watched him struggle to find words, reject them, consider some others, and yet remain silent.

Abandoning the direct approach, the knight veered off on an oblique course. "Why, with the Three Isles of Britain falling in ruins around us, do you tell such tales when you could wield your sword against the Saxon invaders?"

"The raiders are brutal bastards and their settlers cut down forests and mar the land with their crude kind of farming. They have brought a dark age upon us, to be sure. But in the end, they are just primitive people seeking a better life. There are far worse things in the darkness within every one of us. Spread the story you have heard. People must remember what others suffered to get us where we are. Someone must remember what it takes to face the darkness and keep it from rising."

Nearby, the woman who was not Ellylyw lingered, perhaps intrigued by the bard's interest in her. Even at that distance Rhys could smell the woman's flesh—a subtle note amid the myriad scents of all the other bodies that had come and gone, each unique. He breathed in her scent.

It called to him.

Rhys tugged free his sleeve to stride instead to the hitching post where old Morvran waited, head down, too sleepy to crop the grass that sprouted in a desultory fashion about the water trough.

But the knight caught Rhys' shoulder with a grip that stirred sharp, fearful memories of the iron clutch of the black knight from Hungary. The bard spun toward him, right hand on the verge of reaching for his sword and left hand ready to draw his dagger. Rhys was suddenly struck by the glowing aura of strength and vitality radiating out from the knight. A sudden fierce urge welled up from the bard's hidden depths to rob his interrogator of this power—to absorb it—to warm his cold flesh by theft and feel as vibrantly, desperately, painfully alive as he had felt a moment ago when he had sung the Lay of Ellylyw, joining every heart in the courtyard to his.

Yet the tense knight's aura was subtly soured, troubled by strange energies from another source, outside the man. It felt as if the warrior had been touched by something not quite human and some of its baleful essence had remained.

"Listen," the knight said, "I have a story I think you alone could understand."

"I've had enough stories," Rhys snapped, hand on his sword pommel, though he knew it would be suicide to draw on a knight. Suddenly he did not care. "Let me guess: you think some poor woman is a witch and she put a curse on you and you think I'll kill her for you, like the White Knight who murdered Caydwr. I have seen enough for a dozen lifetimes. Think harder about what you heard tonight and do not leap to easy conclusions."

Rhys reached Morvran's side and stroked his long, sleek neck. The old charger whickered quietly, wanting to sleep where he stood, but still game after all these years to carry his rider wherever the spirit moved him. That bond calmed Rhys a little.

"I *have* thought." The strange knight persisted. "And my tale is not for these people's ears. Forgo a soft rented bed for the night and camp a quarter league north of town in the first stand of trees on the plain. You will have a grassy hollow and a pleasing stream to wash in, fallen branches for a bright fire and leafy boughs to stave off the wind so well you will need no tent. I shall follow your firelight and tell you something of Emperor Arthur's deeds that few men know."

The magic of Arthur's name piqued Rhys' interest. Before he could form a response, the knight flung his dark cloak about himself and plunged away through the last lingerers to blend with the night.

Working hard not to look at the woman whose scent aroused him, Rhys mounted Morvran and rode away.

***

Rhys' campfire leapt and danced. No one on the road could have missed the light. Morvran, more comfortable now that he was free of saddle and bridle, tossed his head and whinnied. An answering whinny came back from the darkness. Hooves beat upon the road.

Rhys slipped into a stretch of high brush he had selected for his ambush, naked sword in hand. The black steel would betray no glint of firelight.

The hoof-beats thudded to a halt, and a man's voice came from just beyond the wavering circle of illumination. "It is I, as I promised."

A great war-horse clopped heavy-hooved into the flickering light, and the unnamed knight swung athletically down, leather creaking, chainmail clinking.

"Are you up a tree," the man asked, holding his hands out to the flames both to warm them and to show that they were well away from his pommel. "Are you behind a trunk or in that brush over there? I am as desperate to talk as you are to sing your truth. But I have no wish to pour out my heart to the darkness."

Too fit for me to fight, the bard judged, *but he is not seeking blood. He wants something else... Belief. He wants me to believe.*

After sweeping aside the leafy branches that had screened him from sight, Rhys walked casually into the fluttering light. "Say what you came to say."

The young knight frowned, struggling again to find the words that could convey the huge urgency of his need. "Have you heard the tale of Arthur and Gorlagon, the king who is sometimes a wolf? After what you sang of the piper who called the wolves about Castrum Tenebrarum, I knew you would have some understanding of the things of which I must speak."

Rhys shook his head, his one good eye squinting through the light that burned too brightly for his comfort these nights. "I do not know the story."

"You should. You must. But I am forbidden by oath to reveal such secrets to one who is not an initiate."

Rhys shrugged.

"But what you went through was a kind of initiation."

"To say the least."

"There is someone on my trail. I can feel him drawing near. For all Britain's sake, my mission must not fail, but I am out of time to find my people and the place."

"What mission?" Rhys strongly suspected that he did not want to know.

The knight barely breathed a word that sounded to Rhys' quick ears like Graal. *Does this knight believe in the Holy Grail?*

An eerie moan rose low and quiet from the trees nearby, and Rhys turned to see moonlight glancing from owl eyes staring down at him from a branch above. A strange tingle ran up from the base of his spine to the crown of his hooded head and seemed to spray up out the top like liquid lightning. Strangely energized, he sensed that something critical was about to happen. He waited to hear what the knight would say next.

"You must know..." the knight hissed, his smooth features distorted with distress, "that Emperor Arthur and his knights learned of the hidden court only the destined can find. All this devastation..." He swung out his thick, chainmail-clad arms as if to take in all Britain—perhaps the world. "All this is because the hidden king lies maimed and sick. I haven't time to explain much, but I am kin to the lame king. And kin, too, to Gorlagon, more wolf than man, who maimed the secret ruler. You must help me piece out the clues and find the hidden court before Gorlagon or his pack find me. I can cure the maimed king and end his suffering, but I cannot do it alone."

The thrum of a spear cutting the air was so faint even Rhys' painfully sensitive hearing barely caught it. In the next instant, he saw the point punch out through the knight's chest. The man wobbled. Eyes wide with surprise, he opened his mouth to speak, but only blood and froth sprayed out. His knees buckled, and he sank to his haunches on the spattered grass, clutching uselessly at the spear-point protruding from his ribcage.

His eyes burned into Rhys', and his lips moved in an agony of choked off words. He toppled forward on his face.

Rhys dashed out of the firelight at an angle to the

Dark Age

direction of the spear's flight. He blinked rapidly, eyes adjusting with startling speed to the comparative darkness of the bough-shadowed moonlight. He searched back and forth across the area, catching no glimpse of any enemy.

He stopped stock still. No sound of running feet. No crackle of leaves. No swish of brush.

He quieted his breathing and stretched out with other senses...but there was nothing...no one. He returned to the knight's side, set a foot against the corpse's back and wrapped his hands about the shaft protruding from his back. With a great tug, he wrenched the spear from between the rib bones. The sleek ash-wood shaft was painted black, and the bloody blade was black steel, like his sword. It was a bolt from the darkness impossible to see coming. The style was British, not Saxon. This was no blundering raider's butcher tool but the weapon of a skilled assassin with an amazing arm.

He cast it into the fire and turned the body over. Tiny flames flashed from sightless eyes.

"Who were you?" Rhys whispered. "What was the point of all this?"

Then he felt it: the icy trickle of terror and the hot flush that came when he felt destiny tap him on the shoulder. He stripped off his own weapons and Gladoens' armor and packed them away to trade someday for supplies or to use again if needed. Then he unlimbered the chainmail from the limp corpse. He tore a scrap of cloth from the dead man's tunic to rub the blood off the gleaming links. He donned the chainmail, strapped on the helmet, despite his distrust of the unreadable symbol on its brow, then he belted on the dead man's sword.

Rhys pulled the small spade from the bundle of kit Morvran carried by day behind the saddle. Rhys customarily used it to bury his waste and garbage; tonight, he drove it into root-thick earth and dug a shallow grave—the best he could do in such soil. After laying the nameless knight in the pit, Rhys covered him up with the devouring dirt that would turn his cast-off shell into food for the trees and shrubs about them. He set an unmarked stone at the head of the low mound, stood, and walked back by the fire. It had burned low and did little more than snap and spark.

The bard looked away from it in the direction from which the invisible hand had flung the spear.

"I am not like the knight you just murdered," he called out. "He was shaken at catching a glimpse of the darkness spreading about the world outside himself. I know the horrors that live in me. Maybe one day my mind will weaken, and the rage will consume me until someone has to make an end of me. But not if I can help it. Meantime, I'll use my shadow to beat back yours, Gorlagon. If I live to tell that story, too, that will be enough to keep me going. If I fall at your hands, like this man, maybe I will die with my teeth in your throat."

An owl shrieked, and all small furry beasts lay low.

Rhys grinned. "I'll take the dead man's quest. I'll look for the maimed king's hidden court and try to heal him. Maybe he can even cure me, but I will not rest until I slay you, Gorlagon. And if you kill me, man-wolf, you better not leave enough of me to rise as a revenant. Because, if you do, nothing will stop me from tearing out your throat and reveling in your hot blood."

About the Author

Jeffrey T. Heyer has made his living as an actor and director for 40 years, with 88 entertainment employers. He has had scripts produced at the GroveMont Theatre (Monterey), Actors Collective (Monterey County), B3 Theater (Phoenix, AZ) and elsewhere. His theatrical career began when he played Dracula. Feeling asthma suck the life out of him, leaving Jeff more dead than alive made him empathize with vampire victims. The consequent limited ability to defend himself against violent aggressors made him empathize with those who, ruined by a vampire, lose their higher selves and descend into the shadow. Much of his fiction has followed suit.

Jeffrey T. Heyer

Enjoy more short stories and novels by many talented authors at

https://www.twbpress.com

Science Fiction, Supernatural, Horror, Thrillers, Romance, and more

www.ingramcontent.com/pod-product-compliance
Lightning Source LLC
Chambersburg PA
CBHW071132260626
47162CB00003B/766